ALWAYS SAY GOODBYE

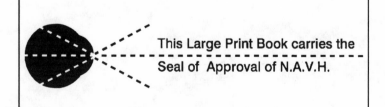

This Large Print Book carries the
Seal of Approval of N.A.V.H.

A LEW FONESCA MYSTERY

ALWAYS SAY GOODBYE

STUART M. KAMINSKY

WHEELER PUBLISHING
An imprint of Thomson Gale, a part of The Thomson Corporation

THOMSON

GALE

Detroit • New York • San Francisco • New Haven, Conn. • Waterville, Maine • London

THOMSON

GALE

Copyright © 2006 by Double Tiger Productions, Inc.

Thomson Gale is part of The Thomson Corporation.

Thomson and Star Logo and Wheeler are trademarks and Gale is a registered trademark used herein under license.

Wheeler Publishing Large Print Hardcover.

The text of this Large Print edition is unabridged.

Other aspects of the book may vary from the original edition.

Set in 16 pt. Plantin.

LIBRARY OF CONGRESS CATALOGING-IN-PUBLICATION DATA

Kaminsky, Stuart M.
   Always say goodbye : a Lew Fonesca mystery / by Stuart M. Kaminsky.
     p. cm.
   ISBN-13: 978-1-59722-460-4 (hardcover : alk. paper)
   ISBN-10: 1-59722-460-X (hardcover : alk. paper)
   1. Fonesca, Lew (Fictitious character) — Fiction. 2. Married women — Crimes against — Fiction. 3. Widowers — Fiction. 4. Chicago (Ill.) — Fiction. 5. Large type books. I. Title.
   PS3561.A43A79 2007
   813'.54—dc22   2006101079

Published in 2007 by arrangement with Tom Doherty Associates, LLC.

Printed in the United States of America on permanent paper
10 9 8 7 6 5 4 3 2 1

To John Neuenfeldt, who has
patiently put up with us
these many years

Promise me you'll never forget me because if I thought you would, I'd never leave.

— Winnie the Pooh

Don't let yesterday take up too much of today.

— Will Rogers

Only in the agony of parting do we look into the depths of love.

— George Eliot (Mary Ann Evans)

When I was fourteen, Death came to my bedside and I said, "Please wait till after my recital on Sunday." When I was twenty-four, Death came behind me at my desk and I said, "Please wait till I finish the book I have been writing." When I was forty-four, Death came again and I said, "Please

wait till I finish this chapter." When I was fifty-four, Death returned and I said, "Please let me finish this paragraph." When I was sixty-four, I said to Death, "Please let me finish this sentence." When Death returns, I'll say, "Please, one more word."
— Rebecca Strum, *Mountains of the Moon*

Everything has a moral, if only you can find it.
— Lewis Carroll

Prologue

The pit bull, standing on his rear legs, strained against the thick leash around his neck. The lean young man in a cowboy hat, well-worn jeans and a black T-shirt, muscles tight, held back the dog whose legs were now clawing rapidly against the dirt floor.

Inside the knee-high wooden wall that circled a dirt-floor ring, stood a 300-pound wild hog, tusks removed with a bolt cutter, scars along its back. The reluctant hog was prodded from behind with a metal rod by a man in a red T-shirt and cowboy hat. He was the twin of the one holding back the pit bull.

Behind the wooden wall were four rows of paint-chipped metal folding chairs on which sat about one hundred men, women and children.

Adults paid six dollars to see what was about to happen. Children were admitted free.

Men, women and children waited impatiently, eyes moving from dog to hog.

Lew Fonesca stood behind the back row of folding chairs where he could see Earl Borg seated in the front row on the other side of the ring. Borg had made the three-hour drive from Sarasota up I-75 and across I-19, and then onto an unpaved road at the end of which was the barn, the ring and the people swaying and bobbing in their seats. Lew had made the same trip from Sarasota to the town of Kane, stopping at a small gas station and general store that advertised in peeling letters on the dusty window, THE BEST BOILED PEANUTS IN THE SOUTH. He had asked the overweight woman sitting on a stool behind the counter where he could find the hog-dog fight. The woman wore a loose-fitting orange sweatshirt over a faded blue dress. She pulled back a sleeve of the sweatshirt and pointed to the plywood wall behind Lew.

Three posters were thumbtacked on the stained plaster wall. One of the posters was for the HAWG DOG FIGHT. The poster promised the appearance of Santana, "the fiercest pit bull in the South," and "the man killer hog." There were directions to the mayhem in red letters. Lew thanked the fat woman, who nodded and rolled her sleeve back up.

He had no trouble finding the barn.

The summer day was Florida hot and humid. The smell of animal and human sweat was almost overpowering inside the barn, which was even hotter and more humid than outside. The crowd didn't seem to notice. They were focused on something else.

The crowd was loud, some people clapping and smiling at each other. Their clothes, hair and sun-pink look made it clear that for many of them this was the best they could afford for a Saturday afternoon's live entertainment.

The only outward difference between Borg and the others around him was that they looked lean and hungry and he looked healthy and sleek in slacks, a black T-shirt and a dark sports jacket. People, particularly the twins when they weren't wrestling the animals, paid homage to Borg by somberly nodding when he spoke. Earl Borg was the only multimillionaire in the sweatbox heat of the barn and the others all knew it. The closest person to Borg in income was Sully Wright, the citrus farmer, who could count on a net annual profit of about thirty thousand dollars if there were no blight, freezes, hurricanes or further government restrictions.

The tugging pit bull looked at the hog and made a throat-clearing sound that brought applause and hoots. The hog responded with a snort. The crowd seemed to think, wanted to think, that the hog was like a bull snorting, eager to paw the ground and attack. To Lew the snort pulsed with fear.

There was no doubt about what was about to happen in the ring. The only question was how quickly it would take place. Borg was taking last-minute bets, all cash, and pocketing it. He didn't have to write the names of the people handing him dollars, fives, tens and even a few twenties. He was known here. He knew them.

Earl Borg's wife's lawyer had sent Lew here to serve divorce papers. That was what Lew did. He was a process server, working just enough to keep himself in food and pay the rent with a little leftover for videotape rentals, resale shop clothes, YMCA membership, soap, toothpaste and disposable razors.

The job was easy. Mrs. Borg had known exactly where her husband would be and when he would be there. The only problem now for Lew was placing the papers in Borg's hand and getting out of the barn alive and, hopefully, untouched.

Lew wore his usual jeans and a clean drip-dry short-sleeved blue shirt with no buttons missing, a Cubs baseball cap on his nearly bald head. He fit in, almost invisible, a lean man with a sad Italian face, a lapsed Episcopalian in Baptist country. Lew had once been an investigator in the office of the Cook County States Attorney's office. Lew had once had a wife he loved and an apartment on Lake Shore Drive. Now he was serving papers for Sarasota lawyers and living alone at the rear of a Dairy Queen parking lot in a small two-room office in a building that merited condemnation. It was the way he wanted it.

The twin holding back the pit bull cried out, "Go" and freed the dog, who shot across the ring and sunk its jaws into the hog's snout. The hog squealed in agony, swayed slightly but didn't move. The dog moved to the animal's side. The crowd went silent to hear the clamping of the dog's teeth as it made its deep, quick gash. The crowd went wild, many of them standing, shouting out "Santana" and "Get him"!

Borg watched emotionless, checking his watch, lips pursed.

The hog teetered and fell on its side but Santana didn't let go. Both twins ran into the ring. The one in the black T-shirt shouted, "It's over."

The man in the red T-shirt moved in with a wooden pole the length of a baseball bat, put a foot on the fallen hog's back, and wedged the pole between the jaws of the dog.

"Are they finished?" asked a girl about nine in the row in front of where Lew stood.

"Don't know, baby," said the mother, who could have been any age from fourteen to thirty.

The crowd was silent again. Lew made his way slowly around the wall of the barn. Borg was handing out cash to a grinning wrinkle-necked old man in slacks, a yellow shirt and a green bow tie.

It took about a minute to pry the dog loose. Red T-shirt lost his cowboy hat in the process. Santana was muzzled the instant his jaws opened. The dog was led out of the ring by the man in the red T-shirt, who paused to pick up his hat, to cheering from the crowd.

The man in the black T-shirt went to the fallen hog and said gently, "Get up, boy. You did just fine."

"Get up," urged a woman's voice from the crowd. Others took up the chant. "Get up."

The twin in the black T-shirt pulled a bottle of apple cider vinegar from his pocket, opened it and poured it on the panting hog's wounds.

Lew was now in the rear of the barn, looking down at Borg's back.

The crowd cheered as the hog wobbled to its feet. The man in the red T-shirt was back now, a muzzle in his hand. He put it over the mouth and head of the dazed hog.

"Children ten and under," the man in black shouted.

Children rushed out of the stands, about twenty of them. Some had come armed with sticks. Others used their hands and feet. They pummeled the bloodied hog, who unsteadily tried to get away but had no place to go.

"Okay" shouted the man in the black shirt after about a minute. "We want to save him for another day. Let's all give the hog a big hand."

The audience, including Borg, applauded the animal.

"This little lady here," said the man in the black T-shirt, singling out a pretty, smiling blonde who appeared to be about nine.

The audience applauded again.

"You all know Lilla, right? She's our guest of honor and she gets to name our hog," the young man said, placing his hand gently on the girl's shoulder.

The girl looked up at a smiling woman seated in the stands in front of Lew.

Borg looked at his watch. His gambling high had been over the moment he handed the cash to the old man. The look on his face changed from one of self-satisfaction to respectful attention as the girl spoke.

"Fred," she said. "That's my big brother's name. He was killed in Iraq by a bomb."

The man in the black shirt removed his hand from the girl's shoulder, began applauding and announced, "Then Fred it'll be."

The crowd stood and joined in with applause and a few whoops and hollers. Borg began making his way up the aisle. He paused when he saw the man in front of him looking at him. Lew was thin, short, balding, his face perpetually sad.

Borg was tall, broad with thick arms and wary. His fists were clenched.

The hog was led out of the ring with people shouting, "Take care now, Fred!" and "Good job, Fred!"

Lew reached into his back pocket, pulled out the trifolded papers with their blue cover sheet and handed them to Borg.

"She told you where I was," Borg said.

Lew was silent.

"I didn't think she knew," Borg said, look-

16

ing at the trifolded sheets in his hand.

The crowd buzzed past them, people looking at the big and little man whose faces were no more than a foot apart.

"How much do you get for giving me this?" he asked.

"Fifty an hour plus expenses," Lew said, meeting his eyes.

"I'll give you three thousand dollars to take this back and say you couldn't find me."

Lew shook his head no.

"Five thousand," he said, holding the papers in front of Lew's face. "Cash. Now."

Lew couldn't explain it to him. He didn't need money. He made enough to keep living in the room behind his office in Sarasota. He had his memories, his depression, his integrity. None of them were for sale.

"What do you want?"

Lew had walked into this place somewhere in Dante's *Inferno*. He wanted to get out. He wanted his dead wife back. He didn't want to face his nightmares. And now he had a new nightmare of pit bulls, helpless hogs, the smell of blood, the stifling heat of the barn and the faces of the people. There was a sadness to what he had seen, but then Lew sensed some level of sadness, loneliness, loss in almost every face he saw.

"I said, 'What do you want?' " Borg shouted.

"To go back to Sarasota."

Borg punched him in the stomach. Lew winced as little as possible and didn't double over. This had happened to him before. It was part of the risk of being a process server.

Almost everyone had left the barn, except for the twins, who were now standing behind Borg.

"Trouble?" asked one of them.

Borg grabbed Lew's shoulders and slammed the back of his head against the wall. Lew didn't react. Borg's hands were shaking.

"No trouble," said Borg, standing back.

He turned Lew around and shoved him over a row of chairs. One of the chairs magically folded, spun over and landed on Lew's legs.

"You want us to — ?" asked the twin in black.

"No," said Borg, looking down at Lew.

Something changed. For an instant Borg looked exhausted. He was breathing hard.

"Help him up," said Borg with a sigh, putting the papers in his pocket.

The twins moved forward, shoved the folding chair away and helped Lew up. Both twins smelled of tobacco and frightened animals. Lew threw up, not much. They had to back away to keep from getting it on them. Lew wiped his mouth with the back of his hand, managed to walk back to Borg and said, "You've been served. Two witnesses. I'll need their names."

"You're not gettin' our names," the one in the black T-shirt said.

Lew smelled more strongly of vomit than the one in black did of animal blood and cigarettes. The twin backed away half a step.

One dog and wild boar wrangler was on Lew's left, the other on his right. Borg was in front of him now, looking down.

"You weren't here," he said calmly. "And you're never going to be here."

Lew tilted his head to the right and spoke into his shirt pocket, "That's enough Ames. You can take off."

Borg grabbed and ripped the pocket, pushing Lew back. A thin small black metal box spun to the ground.

"What is it?" asked Red.

"A transmitter," Lew said.

Borg leaned over and picked up the black metal box. Then he laughed.

"What's funny?" asked the man in the black T-shirt.

Borg held up the box and looked at Lew.

"It's an old transistor radio," said Borg. "Hasn't even got batteries."

He handed the radio back to Lew and smiled.

"Hold onto that thing," he said. "It'll probably be worth fifty bucks when the *Antiques Road Show* comes back to Tampa. Now get out of here. I've got things to do."

Lew turned to leave, crossing the ring, stepping on popcorn and into wet red patches of mud and blood.

"Wait," Borg said behind him. "She's put me through hell. Now she wants everything and . . . forget it."

Lew started toward the exit again.

"Hold it."

Lew stopped and turned around, sweat lined his baseball cap, trickled down his forehead, spotted his shirt. He was swaying slightly now, his stomach warning of more treachery.

Borg, a cowboy on each side of him, reached into his pocket and came out with a thick wallet. The twins stood, arms folded, watching. Borg pulled out a handful of bills and handed them to Lew. There was a hundred-dollar bill on top of the pile.

"No strings," Borg said. "An apology and to cover damages."

Lew, swaying like Fred the hog, looked

into the man's eyes, and handed the money back. Borg took it and said, "Some other time maybe."

Lew nodded. Borg held out his hand. Lew took it. Borg's hand had a slight tremor. The twins were confused.

"Fred the hog is a female," said Lew.

"We tell the crowd our killer's been castrated," whispered Borg. "They don't want to see Santana tear a female apart. At least most of them don't."

"Some do," said the twin in the red T-shirt.

"Some do," Borg agreed. "And more than some know Fred is a female and they either lie to themselves or with a wink share that truth with others who are doing the same thing. It's part of the game."

Lew nodded again and headed for the exit.

He had a bottle of water in the car he had rented for the day. The car had air-conditioning. Not all the cars he rented did. He wanted to get to the car and the air-conditioning before he passed out.

The next time he saw Earl Borg was more than three years later when Lew discovered . . . but that's three years later.

1

Three Years and Two Months Later

Lew had come to Sarasota more than four years ago wanting no place to go, nothing to do, no people to be responsible for or to be responsible for him.

It didn't happen. He wanted the dark cell of his existence behind the Dairy Queen on 301. Two small rooms overlooking the parking lot, hard to find. Almost none of his business came through the door. He had a Florida process server's license and an arrangement with four law firms to serve papers. Not much money. But more than enough for him.

He wanted each day to be a dark blanket that no one pulled back to let in the light. That seldom happened. And today he was neatly and reluctantly putting aside his search for solitude.

Lew's first stop that morning was the EZ Economy automobile rental down the street.

Once there had been two men there. For a couple of years Lew thought they were father and son or two brothers. They weren't.

They were a comedy team whose only appreciative audience was each other. Lew was one of their favorite targets as they drank coffee out of Styrofoam cups or stood with arms folded and negotiated.

The older of the two, Fred, had died a few months ago. Bad heart. Lew had never told him that he shared his name with a hog. Lew thought the company, which had never been a thriving business, would close. But it didn't.

"Lewis Fonesca," Alan, the bulky survivor of the duo, said from behind the desk, feet up, rubbing the sides of the cup. Coffee steamed between his hands. He watched it. "What can I do for you?"

"A car," Lew said.

"Going?"

"Tampa airport. Be gone I don't know how long."

"Business?"

"I'm going to find the person who killed my wife," Lew said.

"Good luck," Alan said. "Take whatever car you want. The Saturn's still in good shape. A few scratches. I think you put a few of them there."

"How much?"

He shrugged and looked for secrets or the face of his dead partner in the coffee cup.

"I don't know," he said. "Twenty-five."

"A day?"

"No, for whatever time you have it. Hell, you can own the damned thing for fifty bucks. I'm having a going-out-of-business sale."

"Since when?"

"Now."

He reached into the desk drawer, came up with two keys on a small metal hoop and tossed them to Lew.

Lew expected a joke, a jibe, a half-witty insult, but without Fred, Alan couldn't find one.

"Any jokes for me?" asked Lew, who had been assigned by his therapist, Ann Horowitz, to come up with a joke for each of their sessions. Usually Alan and Fred could be relied on for at least a backup.

"No. Not anymore. Papers are in the glove compartment. Bon voyage," Alan said, sitting slumped behind the desk, not looking at Lew.

"I liked Fred," Lew said.

"Who didn't? Wait. I take that back. A lot

of people didn't," said Alan. "It's this business."

Alan tightened his lips and looked around.

Lew wanted to tell him that he didn't want to own a car, fill it with gas, have it repaired, have to report it if it were stolen, which was highly unlikely unless the thief couldn't see. Simply put, Lew Fonesca didn't want the responsibility. He didn't want any responsibility. He had spent four years trying to avoid owning or caring for anything. He had succeeded in avoiding everything but people.

He wanted to say something hopeful, helpful to the man behind the desk, who avoided meeting Lew's eyes, but he could think of nothing to say, nothing he was capable of saying that wouldn't be a lie.

Lew would either return the car when he was finished using it or he would give it away. He would probably return it. He didn't want the responsibility of finding a new owner.

Lew stopped at the DQ lot to get his already packed carry-on duffel bag and drop it on the passenger seat.

Dave, the owner of the DQ, was out on his boat in the water. His arms and face were tanned, lined and leathered from years on the deck. Lew tried going with him once.

Once was fine. He handed the girl behind the window a folded note and asked her to give it to Dave. The girl was new, couldn't have been more than sixteen. Her face was freckle-covered, her eyes sleepy, her mouth partly open and her hair struggling to escape the rubber band that held it back.

"There are almost six thousand DQs in the world," said Lew.

The girl, note in hand, looked at him and crinkled her nose.

"Twenty-two countries," Lew went on. "Company started in an ice cream shop in Kankakee, Illinois, in 1938. First franchise was in Joliet, Illinois, in 1940."

The girl's mouth opened a little wider, showing not-quite-even teeth.

"The original DQ motto was 'We treat you right.' Now it's . . . ?"

"I don' know," said the girl.

" 'DQ something different,' " said Lew. "I prefer 'We treat you right,' and I try to have at least two chocolate cherry Blizzards every week. You do good work."

"Thank you," the girl said. "Almost six thousand around the world you say? Maybe some day I could work at a DQ in England or Japan or some place like that."

"It could happen," said Lew.

The girl was smiling to herself as he left.

He got to the Texas Bar & Grille where the morning crowd was dwindling after plates of barbecue breakfast burritos and Texas fries. No lights were on but the sun spread through the tinted windows. Ames McKinney — seventy-four, tall, lean, white hair, and wearing a flannel shirt — came around the tables and looked down at the seated Lew. Ames was his friend, his protector, but not this time.

"Goin'?" he asked.

"Yes."

He understood. Ames wanted to go with Lew, but he understood.

"Thought anymore 'bout what you're gonna do when you find him?"

"No," Lew said.

"That's one way to go about it," he said.

Lew shook his hand. His grip was hard, tight, sincere.

"You take care," he said. "I'll look in on your goods."

"Thanks," Lew said and then, "Goodbye."

Ames nodded his goodbye and turned back toward the bar and the small room down the narrow corridor next to the kitchen where his room was. Ames had once been rich. Now he was the cleanup man in a bar and he liked it just fine.

Lew's Uncle Tonio once said, "Always say

27

goodbye."

Short absences, long absences. Forever. "Goodbye." God be with you. Any absence might become forever. Lew didn't remember whether he said goodbye to Catherine on the morning of the last day of her life.

He had said his goodbyes to Sally Porovsky last night. Sally, an overworked social worker with two kids, had touched his cheek and said, "Look in your pocket when you get outside. Goodbye."

The Long Goodbye, Goodbye, Mr. Chips, "Goodbye Mama, I'm Off to Yokohama. Goodbye dear and amen, here's hoping we meet now and then," "Every time we say goodbye." They all applied but lately the word *goodbye* had begun to sound odd to Lew, to look odd on paper. He wanted to make it mean something to him again.

He said, "Goodbye," and Sally closed the door.

In the moonlit parking lot next to her apartment, he took out the sheet of paper she had placed in his pocket. It read, Find him, take care of yourself, come back. Sally.

Lew had said his goodbyes to Flo Zink, the bangle-clad, frizzy-haired, feisty little seventy-one-year-old woman who favored Western clothes and music. Her choices of both were badly out-of-date.

Flo was from New York. Her husband had died, leaving her lots of money and a drinking problem. She had worked out her drinking problem motivated by the prospect of being allowed to take in Adele, a sixteen-year-old girl Lew and Ames had rescued from a daddy-sanctioned life of prostitution. Adele had an infant baby named Catherine. The baby had been named for Lew's dead wife. When he said goodbye at twilight, Flo was holding the baby. Jimmy Wakely and the Rough Riders were singing "When You and I Were Young Maggie Blues" through speakers placed throughout the house. Adele was out but would be back in an hour. Lew couldn't wait.

Flo held Catherine out for Lew. He was afraid to touch her. He didn't have bird flu or the plague but he knew his depression could be infectious.

Finally, Lew stopped back at his office and called Ann Horowitz, his eighty-two-year-old therapist whose main, but not only, virtue was that she charged him only ten dollars a visit. He was, she said, an interesting case.

"Lewis," she said. "You're leaving in the morning?"

"Yes."

"Good. Call me if you need me. You have a joke?"

Getting a joke from a chronic depressive is not that hard. Getting the depressive to appreciate the joke, to smile, to laugh, is almost impossible.

"Yesterday I called the makers of Procrit, Ambien, Lipitor and Cialis and asked them if my doctor was right for me. They all said no."

"Lewis, you make that up?"

"Yes."

"I told you there was hope," she said. "Now go find the man who killed your Catherine."

Thirty-four thousand feet above the Gulf of Mexico, Lew sat in an aisle seat at the very back of the Southwest Airlines plane out of Tampa. The back seats didn't recline, but they were the closest ones to the restroom. There is no real silence on an airplane. The flying machine is constantly roaring, whistling, grinding and changing its mind about the thrust of the engines. Inside the plane, children whine, adults lie to just-met seatmates, a couple hugs, their eyes shut. Flight attendants up and down the aisle pass out cholesterol chips in little bags you can't open.

Ames had given Lew a book to read, *A Confederacy of Dunces.* It lay in his lap unopened.

The young man next to Lew scratched his cheek as he looked at the screen of his laptop computer and tapped in something. He was wearing headphones and humming a song Lew didn't recognize. The image on his screen was the Warner Brothers black-and-white shield. Then came the words, Joan Crawford in *Mildred Pierce.* Lew closed his eyes, trying not to watch, trying not to say the words as the characters spoke.

He didn't concentrate. He drifted through a dark sky. Lew was floating, tumbling in nothingness. Then sudden panic. He tried to open his eyes. Couldn't.

"You okay?" the young man with the laptop said with concern.

Lew's eyes opened. He was panting. The man was about thirty, with dark curly hair. He was looking at Lew with concern. His left eye was green. His right eye was too, but a darker, lifeless green. The right eye, he could see now, was definitely glass.

"Yes," Lew said, sitting up. "Bad dream."

"Sure?"

"I'm sure," he said, but he wasn't.

When Catherine was alive, he had dreaded flying, had held her hand tightly when they took off and landed, had silently cursed the madness of the other passengers who didn't realize that the odds of their dying were higher than they thought, that they were in a machine, a very heavy machine, that could lose an engine, a single bolt, a stretch of wire, and they would all be dead.

When Catherine died, that had all changed. Flying presented no problems, no fears. The worst that could happen was that the plane would crash. He could live with that. He could die with that.

He must have slept, because the captain was announcing the beginning of the plane's descent into Chicago's Midway Airport. The young man closed his laptop, looked at Lew with his bad and good eye, and smiled. Lew nodded.

When the plane landed, Lew went to the exit, duffel-shaped carry-on in hand, between baggage claim 3 and 4. Outside Lew saw his sister's husband, Franco, in his white Ford tow truck at the curb, looking across at Lew and holding up his hand.

Lew knew why he had panicked on the plane. He was going back to Chicago. Now that he was here, the panic threatened to return.

He climbed up into the passenger seat and put his bag on the floor. The interior of the truck smelled of grease and oil.

"Lewie," Franco said, reaching over to hug him. "Lewie."

"Franco," Lew responded.

Lew had known Franco Massaccio since childhood. A barrel of a man with an easy grin. Genius didn't run in Franco's family, but hard work and loyalty did. Franco was loyal and a good husband to Lew's sister Angela. He liked talking religion. He was a reasonably good Catholic. Lew considered himself a reasonably bad Episcopalian.

"You never get used to the smell, huh?" asked Franco. " 'I like the smell of the streets. It clears my lungs.' You know who said that?"

"No."

"Bobby De Niro in *Once Upon a Time in America*," said Franco. "An Italian playing a Jew. Well, listen, what are you gonna do? Right?"

"Right."

"You have it?" Lew asked as Franco looked over his left shoulder and eased into the traffic.

"It's at home," Franco said.

Lew nodded and looked out the window. Standing at the curb was the one-eyed young man with the laptop. He was looking back at Lew.

"Friend or something?" asked Franco. "That guy back there?"

"Something, maybe," Lew said, looking back.

The young man with one eye focused on the back of the tow truck. He was looking at the license plate number.

"Want to know about what's going on in the family, Lewie?"

"Later," Lew said, looking over his shoulder at the one-eyed man who got into a green Buick that pulled up to the curb.

"Want the radio?"

"No," Lew said.

"Want to go into outer space in a Russian shuttle?"

He was looking ahead and grinning. Franco had a strange sense of humor, but at least he had one.

"Would I be alone?" Lew asked, looking at the familiar brick bungalows on Cicero Avenue.

"No, you'd have to go up with the national baton-twirling champion and an abusive long-retired astronaut."

"I think I'll pass."

"Suit yourself," Franco said with a shrug. "Like a miniature Snickers bar left over from Halloween?"

"Yes."

"Glove compartment," he said.

Lew opened the glove compartment and small wrapped bars of Twix, Snickers, Milky Ways, and Twizzlers tumbled out. He leaned over to scoop them up and put them back.

"I'll take a Twix," Franco said.

Lew handed him one and took a Snickers for himself.

"Two things I gotta tell you," Franco said, opening the candy wrapper and popping the mini-Twix bar in his mouth while Lew carefully tore the Snickers bag and took a bite.

"First," he said. "Terri, Teresa, is a freshman at Northern Illinois. Doing great. You know that?"

"No."

Teresa was Angela and Franco's daughter.

"Political science," he said.

The entrance to the Dan Ryan Expressway was right in front of the truck.

"Second, a car is following us," Franco said calmly.

Lew didn't turn around to look.

"Driver's young, big, buzz cut," said Franco. "Passenger is the one who was looking at you at the curb."

Southwest had open seating. The one-eyed man had chosen to sit next to Lew.

They were on the expressway now.

"Want me to push them to the rail?"

Franco said. "I'll get out, yank 'em out of the car and find out what the hell they're doing."

"No," Lew said. "But if you can get behind them I'll get their license plate number."

"This have something to do with Catherine?"

"I don't know."

Franco slowed and when the other car was no more than fifteen feet behind them, Franco pulled suddenly into the next lane cutting off an SUV. The driver of the Buick didn't have Franco's skill or experience. Franco cut across lanes, dropped back and then scooted right behind the Buick. Lew wrote the license plate number in his notebook.

"Okay," said Lew.

Franco was grinning and shaking his head.

"I can't believe this, Lewie. You've been here what, five, ten minutes and people are following you. Beneath that beat-down exterior, you are one piece of cake."

"Thanks," said Lew.

Franco picked up the cell phone from the charger on his dashboard and punched in two numbers.

"Rick," Franco said into the phone. "How's with you? Me too. Say, listen, can you run a plate for me and the driver's license? Great."

Franco looked at Lew who read the plate numbers. Franco repeated them to Rick.

"Got that?" Franco said. "Great. What you say we go for beef sandwiches at Fiocca's for lunch next week? Name the day . . . okay. Wednesday at one. Make it fast on those numbers."

He pushed a button on the phone and put it back on the dashboard.

"Now do we stop 'em?" asked Franco.

"Yes," said Lew.

Franco grinned.

"Great to have you back, Lewie."

Franco moved into the lane next to the Buick. Lew could see both the driver and the one-eyed man. They didn't look back at Lew.

Franco checked the traffic behind him and moved the tow truck to within inches of the other car. The driver tried to move forward, but there was another slow-moving car in front of him. Franco gently eased the truck against the Buick at forty miles an hour. The other car started to lose control, regained it, and came to a stop against the rail. Franco parked ahead of the car, looked at Lew and said, "What do you want to know besides why they're following us?"

"They're following me, Franco."

"Same difference. You, me. I'm fuckin' offended."

Franco was staring at the rearview mirror. The car parked behind him didn't move. No doors opened.

"They might have guns, Franco," Lew said.

Franco opened his tow-truck jacket revealing a holstered weapon.

"Legal," he said. "Glock Twenty-eight . . . 380 caliber. Six inches long, a little over an inch wide. Weighs less than twenty ounces. I've got a permit. I'm a tow-truck driver in Chicago."

"You ever shoot anybody?" Lew asked.

"No, you?"

"Once," Lew said, looking at the car which Franco had pinned to the steel divider.

Franco looked at him, waiting. Lew offered no more.

Franco turned on the radio, which was tuned to the police band. He kicked up the volume and got out of the truck, checking traffic.

"Leave your door open," he said, starting toward the other car.

Lew got out. He had almost forgotten the noise of expressway traffic, the clanging, coughing, squealing, braking, screeching agony of bouncing trucks and addicted horn pushers. And then there were the highway fumes. The memory became a reality again.

As Franco approached the Buick, the driver was looking over his shoulder, trying to find room to back up and then get back into traffic. He didn't have time and there were no breaks in the traffic.

Lew's eyes were on the one-eyed young man, who didn't look the least bit concerned that the barrel of a man was lumbering toward him.

Franco reached for the handle of the driver's door. It was locked.

"Open it," he commanded over the noise.

The driver showed no sign of opening the door. Franco reached into the lower pocket of his jeans and came up with a small silver metal hammer. He showed it to the driver who knew what it was, a compact powerful hammer made to go through automobile windows in an emergency.

The driver looked at his passenger, who nodded to indicate that the driver should open the window. The window rolled down.

"We're not —" the driver said.

Franco reached through the window, grabbed the man's jacket and pulled him out. The man was big, not as big as Franco, but a certain two hundred pounds.

"The police are going to be here," the driver panted as Franco pushed him back against the car.

"Take them ten, maybe fifteen minutes," said Franco. "You could both be hurting a lot by then. I'll know when they're coming."

He glanced at the tow truck. The voice on the police band was clear in spite of the traffic that zipped by.

Cars began to slow. There would be a gapers' block in a few seconds. The possibility of seeing death or destruction or someone being beaten because of road rage was too much for most people to resist. They had to slow down, catch a glimpse and drive on, comforted by the fact that it was someone else who was at the side of the road.

The one-eyed man sat calmly, looking forward. Then he made a decision, opened his door, got out and faced Lew.

"Talk to me," Franco said to the driver.

The driver said, "No."

The one-eyed man turned and fixed his only eye on the driver. There was a distinct family resemblance. Brothers, cousins?

Franco looked at Lew who nodded, and he let the driver slump against the door. Lew walked toward the one-eyed man.

"Why are you following me?" Lew asked.

"To keep you alive," he said.

"Men in blue are coming, Lew," said Franco.

In the distance, weaving toward them, a police siren shrieked. Traffic was at a very slow gawker's walk.

"Who wants me dead?" Lew asked.

"Let's just say a very bad person who knew your wife," the one-eyed man said.

"A very bad person," Lew repeated.

The young man pointed to his glass eye, giving a hint of how bad this person could be.

"Here they come," said Franco, standing by the driver who was still shaking.

The police car inched its way through the traffic, flashing its lights. Cars and trucks made room.

"This bad person kill my wife?"

"I don't know," the young man said. "Probably."

The police car pulled in and parked in front of the tow truck.

"Why does he want me dead?"

"You have something he wants," he said, turning his head toward the police car from which two uniformed officers emerged, both black and with weapons in their hands.

"What do I have and why did he wait so

41

long to kill me?"

"He didn't know where you were. He found your name somewhere, an article perhaps on the Internet," said the young man. "Then you bought an airline ticket. If we could find out about that, he can find it. I flew to Tampa and stayed with you from the second you got to the Southwest counter."

"Why do you want to help me?" Lew asked, but before the young man could answer the police were too close to continue.

"Everybody just hold it where you are," said the older of the two cops.

He was lean, homely, dark and serious.

"What's going on?" he asked.

He and his partner, who had television star good looks, moved toward them.

"Roadside assistance," said Franco. "That's my tow truck. He called me."

"That's right," said the driver.

"We got a call saying someone was being pulled out of the window by a man who looked like Mike Ditka."

"Hear that, Lew? Not the first time someone thought I looked like Iron Mike," said Franco with a smile.

"Hey," the older cop called impatiently over the madness of the cars and trucks rushing by in both directions.

"Right," said Franco. "Driver here was in a panic. Froze. Thought his car was about to blow up or something. I pulled him out."

Franco looked at the driver.

"Right," the driver said.

"What's wrong with the car?" the older cop asked, suspiciously looking at Lew and then at the one-eyed man.

"Short," said Franco. "He smelled burning wire. It's fixed now."

"I owe this man," said the driver, glaring at Franco.

The cops looked at each of the four men in front of them. The older cop decided that the group looked a little strange maybe, but not formidable. Both cops holstered their weapons but kept a hand on them.

"Move out," said the cop. "You're tying up traffic."

"One second," Franco said. "He hasn't paid me yet."

Turning to the driver, Franco said, "That'll be fifty dollars. Cash."

The driver looked at the one-eyed man who reached into his pocket and came up with two twenties and a ten. He handed them to Franco. Lew had a lot to ask the one-eyed man but he had moved into the car along with the driver. Franco tapped Lew on the shoulder and Lew followed him to the tow truck.

"Now that was fun, huh, Lewie?" he asked, hitting his horn, easing into traffic.

"One couldn't wish for more," Lew said, reaching into his duffel bag and pulling out his Cubs cap.

"Still got that?"

"Still got it," said Lew who put the cap on his head.

Ann Horowitz had said that Lew wore the cap for many reasons. She said that one obvious reason was to cover Lew's balding head. "That," she had said, "is good. It shows that you still care about how you look to the world and how you look to yourself. It's a sign of ego. It's a very small tear in your precious depression. If it is, I want to find the tear and sew it up. Don't worry. We'll apply a very local anesthetic."

Lew felt that his depression was too important to him to lose. Ann knew this and knew about what he might have to deal with if it were gone.

Ann also believed that the cap was an attempt to hold onto something positive from the past, memories of Banks, Williams, Santo, Dawson, Sosa, Cey, Sandberg. Lew liked that interpretation. Whatever the cap might mean, he always felt a little better, a little more protected, when he wore it.

Franco's cell phone, now back in the dashboard charger, buzzed. Franco asked Lew to get it as he worked his way toward the outer lane.

"Hello," Lew said.

"Hey, where's Franco?"

The caller, who had a raspy voice like Lew's Uncle Tonio, was chewing on something.

"Driving. Traffic on the Dan Ryan's backed up. I'm Franco's brother-in-law."

"Hey, Lewie? Is that Lewie?"

"Yes."

"I'm Rick. Heard you went nuts."

"Yes."

"You better now?"

"No," Lew said.

"Hey, it happens. Think you're nuts, you should see my sister-in-law. She's like fruitcakes all the time, you know?"

The outer lane was moving and they were on their way. Lew could no longer see the one-eyed man's car.

"Got a pencil, something?" asked the voice.

"Yes," Lew said, taking out his notebook.

"Car belongs to a John Pappas."

Rick gave him the owner's address and said he was faxing a copy of Pappas's driver's license to Franco's house.

"I'm looking at it now," said Rick.

"What's he look like?" Lew asked.

"Fifty, maybe a little more, maybe closer to sixty," said Rick. "Hair white. Looks a little like that guy on *Law and Order,* Dennis whatever. Guy that used to be a Chicago cop."

Pappas was definitely not the driver Franco had pulled out of the window.

Franco reached for the phone. Lew handed it to him.

"Hey way, Rick," he said. "That lunch's gonna be on me."

He paused, listening, nodding his head, smiling and then said, "Ditkaland forever. See ya."

He handed the phone back to Lew. Lew hung it up.

"Rick's not a cop," Lew said.

"No, but his daughter Maria, thirteen, smart, knows how to use the Internet like you wouldn't believe," said Franco.

"It's not legal," Lew said.

"So's jaywalking. You care?"

"No."

"We'll find him," Franco said. "The son of a bitch who killed Catherine. We make a good team, huh?"

"Yes," Lew said.

"In the compartment between us, in the

armrest, I've got packages of that spicy beef jerky."

Lew opened the compartment and found about twenty wrapped thin ropes of dark red jerky. He took one and handed one to Franco.

"Love those things," he said, opening the wrapping of his jerky with his teeth. "Hey, give Angie a call. Tell her where we are."

Talking to his sister would be another step into the past. He had only been in Chicago for about an hour and had had already taken dizzying steps.

"Just hit forty-seven," Franco said, pointing at the phone.

Lew picked up the phone and hit the numbers. One ring and Lew's sister was on the phone.

"Franco, you got him?"

"Angela, I'm back."

John Pappas stood at the window on the second floor of his house in suburban River Grove, "the Village of Friendly Neighbors." In one hand he held a white porcelain cup and saucer. Next to the cup was a still warm, honey-covered slice of baklava. His mother had finished baking the treat less than an hour ago. Her phyllo was almost see-through thin, the nuts and raisins it held touched the right edge of sweetness and memory.

Pappas, hair white and full, his face a sun-etched almost-almond, slightly pocked, reminded most people of someone they had met, although they couldn't recall who.

Pappas looked across the lawn to the tree-lined street with fall leaves falling and little traffic. He sipped the thick coffee and took a comforting bite of pastry, careful to avoid any honey that might drip off and stain his white shirt. He wore a fresh white long- or short-sleeved dress shirt every day.

He stood thinking of Andrej Posnitki, known as Posno. Posno was never far from his mind. Posno was the reason Pappas was nearly imprisoned in this house. Posno was the reason his son Stavros had lost an eye. John Pappas took the last morsel of his delicacy, licked his honey-dappled fingers and imagined what Posno might be doing at this moment.

Andrej Posnitki, in his own apartment on Lake Shore Drive in Chicago, looked out his window at a sailboat on Lake Michigan, driven by a gust of wind.

Short, broad, head shaved, skin almost white, he could be described as either a barrel or a crate. He weighed almost three hundred pounds and every ounce could and had been delivered many times through his fists. He preferred his hands to a blade or a gun, but he had been known to use whatever was available to threaten, maim or slay his enemies.

He had no family. He had no friends.

"The devil always provides," he said.

Posno worked alone. His fees were fixed and no one who hired him questioned or failed to promptly pay.

His appearance was calculatingly menacing, but his voice was calm and he had a passion for poetry. He read it, listened to it on CDs, even gave occasional open microphone readings of his own work at a small bookstore and coffeehouse within walking distance on Broadway.

One of Posno's enemies, his primary enemy, was John Pappas. Not long ago the two had been inseparable, partners.

Pappas had been in the kitchen at the back of the Korean restaurant on Clark Street when Posno had picked up a butcher knife, its blade still carrying globules of animal fat. He had brought the blade down at the weeping man kneeling in front of him. The man had tried to cover his head. Two severed fingers spun past Posno's face. Blood gushed from the Korean's split head,

49

turning the man's apron from dirty white to a moist splotch of red.

Pappas stayed in the corner, watching. No blood touched him.

Pappas had been in the hallway behind Posno who rang the bell. The tones inside played the first nine notes of "Anything Goes." This was followed by footsteps and a woman's voice behind the door saying, "Who is it?" Pappas had answered, "Your neighbor upstairs."

"Mr. Sweeney?" she had asked.

"Yes, I need some wine, any kind, for a dish my wife has just started cooking."

She opened the door. The man who stood in front of her was definitely not Mr. Sweeney. It was Posno, who stepped forward quickly, and put his thick hands around her neck before she could scream. Pappas had stayed outside.

And there was Jacobi, right on Maxwell Street, among the crowd in front of a shop that sold shoes, seconds. Shoes, paired and tied together by their shoestrings, were piled high on a cart in front of the store. Posno had a thin, sharply pointed steel rod up his sleeve. Jacobi was rearranging shoes to keep the stack from falling. When Posno struck, deep under the man's ribs, the shoes came tumbling as Jacobi grabbed the side of the cart. Posno had jumped out of the way. The heel of a shoe hit him above his right eye. He knew the thin rod was leaving a wet trail inside his sleeve that he would have to clean himself. Pappas had watched. He had no jacket to clean, no blood on his hands.

Yes, they had been partners. Pappas had the connections, could get the clients, but Pappas couldn't kill. It had been a good partnership.

Pappas came from a large, extended Greek family, a tradition, a culture. Posno had arrived from nowhere, alone, throbbing with anger balanced by poetry.

Pappas had distanced himself, came close to ending his very existence. They both knew that if the Fonesca woman had left her evidence file and it was found, it would be Posno who went down. He would take Pappas with him. He would be better off if there were no Pappas and he knew Pappas would be better off without him. The two men had much that separated them but much more in common than either liked.

Posno turned from the window, reached into his pocket, took out his mini tape recorder, pressed a button and slowly spoke, not knowing whether the words were his own or something that had fixed to his memory, something waiting for this moment.

> Speak not of tomorrow
> or how long a man
> may be happy.
> Change, like the
> shifting flight
> of the hummingbird
> or the dragonfly,
> is swift and sudden.

He hit the pause button and, still watching the sailboat heading toward the horizon, pushed it again and said, "Catherine Fonesca."

2

Franco got off the Dan Ryan at Jackson Boulevard, went east to Racine and then south on Racine to Cabrini Street in the heart of Little Italy. A block away was Taylor Street, both sides of which were crowded with Italian restaurants brought back to life when Lew was a kid by the University of Illinois Chicago campus. The university had embraced the neighborhood, threatened to engulf it, and eventually came to a mutually advantageous understanding.

Lew had grown up in this neighborhood of stubborn, proud, often brilliant and sometimes crazy, first, second and a third generation of primarily Sicilian immigrants. He knew the streets, the parks and many of the families that had not been pressured out from the west by the constant expansion of the University of Illinois Medical Center, and from the east by the university's ever-growing Chicago campus.

Some thought the university had saved the neighborhood with dollars. Some thought the university had ended the neighborhood. Some lost their homes and had to move out, mostly to Bridgeport near the White Sox's Cellular Field and an enclave of Italian-speaking residents within the mayor's Irish home turf.

Franco and Angela had stayed in Little Italy in a three-bedroom, eighty-year-old frame house on Cabrini Street across from Arrigo Park. There was a newer model Ford Pinto in the driveway, but not enough room for the tow truck.

"So, remember Toro's Garage?" Franco asked, pulling into a parking space on the street. "Still there. I throw business his way. He lets me park my cars. Got five now. Toro, he fixes 'em up, sells 'em. We split the profits. You need a car, you got your pick. I usually park at Toro's and walk home, but today . . ."

He parked between a Lexus and a dingy gray Saturn.

They got out. Lew's sister was in the doorway, hands at her sides, examining her brother as he crossed the street. Angela and Lew were born a year apart. He was the older. The family resemblance was clear, but there was something strong, almost pretty about her. She was wearing jeans and an orange long-sleeved pullover. Her dark hair was pulled back and tied with an old-fashioned orange ribbon Lew had given her for her twelfth birthday.

She came forward to meet them.

"Lewis," she said. "All right if I —"

"Yes," he said, putting down his bag.

She took five quick steps and hugged him. He felt her breasts, large like his mother's, press warmly against him. He tried to hug her back, wanted to hug her, couldn't. He didn't want too many doors open, not now, not yet.

Franco stood quietly a dozen feet away.

"Welcome home," she said, finally stepping back. "Hey, I'm crying. I was always the crier, right? Me and Pop. Let's eat."

"Wait," said Franco. "I picked up fifty bucks on the way home from a guy who was having car trouble. Let's celebrate. Il Vicinato. *Pollo Vesuvio.*"

Angela looked at Lew and knew what to do.

"Tomorrow, maybe," she said.

As they moved into the house, Angela said, "I've got that envelope. Thick. Guy brought it here a few days ago. Well-dressed, little pudgy, you know?"

Lew knew who he was.

"It's on your bed, Teresa's bed," she said, taking his duffel and handing it to Franco who walked off with it.

Nothing had changed except for the large screen television in the living room. Sicilian memories pre-1950s. Nothing modern. Everything comfortable, musky dark woods. Chairs and a sofa with muted dark-colored pillows that showed the indentation of three generations of Fonescas who had lived here.

"Drink?" she asked, touching his shoulder as Lew sat in the chair Catherine always sat in when they came here. "Sangria? Just made a batch from Uncle Tonio's wine."

"Sure," Lew said.

"Coming up," she said with a smile.

When she left, Franco came back in the room and moved to the window.

"I figure they know how to find us," he said. "They got my license plate number. They're doing the same thing to us we're doing to them."

"I know."

"What do we do now?" Franco asked, moving from the window with a smile and a clap of thick hands.

"Drink sangria, close our eyes, hope the wheels slow down, have something to eat," Lew said as his sister came back with a tall green and blue ceramic pitcher on a tray surrounded by three tumblers. The pitcher, which Lew had forgotten, had been made by his great-grandfather when he was a boy in Palermo. Seeing it, Lew remembered.

He wanted to go back to Sarasota. Now.

"So, after dinner?" Franco asked, holding his beaded glass of sangria.

"I've got some reading to do. And then I need a nap."

"Okay," Franco said.

"A toast," Angie said.

The glass felt moist and cold in Lew's hand and the almost transparent slice of lemon floating on the wine looked like the reflection of the moon.

"Great to have you back, Lew," said Franco, holding up his glass.

"Find peace," said Angie.

They waited for Lew.

"Cu a fissa sta a so casa," he said.

It was one of no more than a dozen things Lew could say in Italian. They drank.

Franco looked puzzled.

" 'The fool should just stay home,' " Angie translated. "When do you want to eat?"

"If I sleep more than three hours, wake me up," Lew said, putting his empty glass on the tray, picking up and chewing on the lemon moon.

They nodded and Lew went to Teresa's

room, closing the door behind him. He hadn't remembered his niece's room, hadn't remembered how small and neat it was, bed against the wall now covered by a sky-blue blanket covered with soap-bubble circles, her grandmother's rocking chair in the corner near the only window, an old walnut teacher's desk complete with inkwell. A computer keyboard and mouse sat in front of a darkened monitor. Next to the desk stood a floor-to-ceiling bookcase, its shelves shared by books, CDs, DVDs and colorful three-ring notebooks.

If it weren't for his search for Catherine's killer, he would have darkened the room, taken off his shoes, gotten into bed, curled into a ball and slept for a day, a week, forever.

On the bed was the thick envelope. He was reaching for it when there was a knock at the door.

"You sleepin'?" asked Franco.

"Not yet."

Franco opened the door. In his left hand was a bag of potato chips. He popped a handful into his mouth. A single orange-red crumb floated to the floor.

"Lewie, we're worried about you. Life moves pretty fast. If you don't stop and look around once in a while you could miss it.

You missing it, Lewie?"

"You got that from *Ferris Bueller's Day Off.*"

"Doesn't make it wrong. There's a lot of truth in movies if you really listen."

He held out the bag.

"Instant energy," he said.

Lew nodded.

"Angie's making dinner. It'll be ready whenever you want. Want some?"

Franco held out the bag. Lew took two. Franco stood there chewing and Lew sat there chewing.

"Okay, so we're goin' to find this guy Pappas?"

"Yes," Lew said.

"Say, listen, Angie's worried about you. We run into trouble looking, I've got guys who'll be there whenever you give the word. Billy Bavitti, Marty Glickman, Tony Danitori. Guys you know."

"Thanks, Franco. If we need them . . ."

"You'll tell me. Want me to leave you what's left in the bag?"

Lew took the bag from him and he left. He sat eating potato chip crumbs and looking at the envelope. When the bag held nothing more to search for, he picked up the envelope and opened it, pulling out a stack of reports, leaving salty grease smudges. The unmarked envelope had been dropped off by Milt Holiger who, like Lew, had been an investigator for the Cook County State Attorney's Office. Catherine had been Milt's favorite prosecutor. Unlike Lew, Milt was still there. He had done a lot of work for Catherine. Milt and Lew were working friends.

Lew had called only two people when he decided to come back to Chicago, his sister and Milt, whose help he needed. By giving him what was in the envelope and violating the confidentiality of the State Attorney's Office, Milt had taken a big chance. He and his wife Ruthie had a son in his second year at Northwestern and a daughter who had been accepted by Vanderbilt.

The only question Milt had asked Lew was, "Will this help you find who killed Catherine?"

Lew's right hand had a slight tremor, real or imagined. He did not want to be here. He would find the person who had killed Catherine. That would close one door behind him but the slow circling ball of depression would stay safely inside him. And if he somehow managed to lose it, he was afraid he would lose what he had left of Catherine.

The copy of a brief, neatly typed Illinois

traffic accident report was on top of the pile. The investigating officer, a detective named Elliot Cooledge, had gotten the call at 3 P.M. and arrived at the scene, Lake Shore Drive and Monroe, at 3:22 P.M. Traffic was backed up. Catherine's body was on the side of the drive. Cooledge talked to two people standing over her. Both the man and the woman who had been witnesses stated that it had been a hit-and-run driver. Cooledge called the office of Emergency Communications and requested a Major Accident Investigation Unit be dispatched immediately.

The next report was by a Major Accident Investigation Unit detective named Victoria Dragonitsa. It was nine-pages long. Distilled, the report said that the hit-and-run driver was in a small red sports car, probably foreign. Both the witnesses agreed that the car appeared to be deliberately targeting the victim who, they thought, saw it coming a second or two before it struck her. The red sports car speeded up after hitting Catherine. Her body bounced and thudded to the side of the drive. Neither witness had clearly seen the driver, but both, in spite of the sun on the windshield and the fact that they were watching a woman dead or dying, said there was only one person in the car.

The driver was thin, not very tall and wearing a baseball cap. The woman witness, Eileen Burke, said the driver was wearing glasses. The man, Alvin Fulmer, said he saw no glasses. Both witnesses said Catherine had not been carrying anything other than the black purse flung over her shoulder.

Lew put the report down on the bed on top of the traffic accident report. The grease-stained envelope lay next to the slowly growing pile.

Why was Catherine heading toward their apartment building at three in the afternoon on a weekday? Lew and his wife both usually worked till about six, got something to eat in the Loop, walked home together talking about the real and false anger, real and false tears of people who had compiled a trail of evidence that proved they had stolen, robbed, beaten, maimed or murdered. They tended to agree on movies and television shows. The night before she died they had argued over the film *Sea of Love.* For Lew, Al Pacino could do no wrong. Catherine had punctuated that conversation with the word *ham.* Their voices had not been raised as she set the table and he boiled the water for the spaghetti. The contents of a jar of Prego sauce was heating in a metal pot. It started as smiling banter, went flat, serious and determined as they dug into the pasta and the argument. Then, when it looked as if it would burst and hurt, Catherine has smiled and said, "How about an armistice and some more Italian bread?"

What could he give and who could he give it to to relive that night, any night? He could find her killer and pray to his imagination, but that wouldn't be enough, not nearly enough.

His own parents had never fought, at least not in front of Lew and Angie. At dinner, both of them had an unwritten list of things to say at dinner. Most of the things were about aunts, uncles, cousins on both sides of the family. Almost all of the conversation came from Lew's mother while his father ate and nodded, grunted with understanding and smiled at the right times. Lew's father had eaten, torn pieces of bread from the loaf, and looked tired. Was that long ago?

If Catherine had been going home for the day, why didn't she tell Lew and why wasn't she carrying her briefcase?

Two more documents to go. He skipped the next one and went to the twelve-page printout he had requested. It included all the automobile violations on Lake Shore Drive that day between 2 P.M. and 5 P.M. The printout covered everything from

Wilson Avenue North to 61st Street.

The listing of Catherine's killing was on the fifth page. It was no longer than any of the others: hit-and-run vehicular death. 3 P.M. Victim: woman, white, Catherine Fonesca, thirty-five. Vehicle: red sports car. Last seen heading south.

Lew flipped through the report, looking for a red sports car or even a red car in one of the notations other than the one about Catherine. There was one listing that might be a match and the timing was right. At 3:18 P.M. near the 55th Street exit in Hyde Park, a speeding red sports car brushed its passenger side against a green Toyota driven by a woman named Rebecca Strum, eighty, who almost lost control.

Rebecca Strum's name was familiar, not just to Lew but, he knew, to probably millions of people around the world. He had seen two of Rebecca Strum's books on the bookshelf near the kitchen in Franco and Angie's house. She was a visiting faculty member at the University of Chicago. She had won a Nobel prize for her writing and lecturing on the Holocaust. She was a death camp survivor. The driver of a red sports car had killed Lew's wife and may have come close to killing the person frequently recognized as the most important woman in the world.

Before picking up the last report, Lew closed his eyes and clasped his hands together. The tremor was still there. He opened his eyes and saw his hands. Had he been praying? He picked up the report. If there is a god or gods, He, She, It, or They had nothing to do with what Lew had decided to do.

The last report was the coroner's. Lew had seen hundreds of these reports. He had always tried to be as clinically dispassionate as the people who had dictated the reports appeared to be. This one would be different.

Catherine had almost certainly died almost instantly. Her hip and left foot had been broken and her skull had been cracked in six places as her body tumbled. Internal bleeding was massive. Her brain had ruptured and filled with blood. That's what it came down to. That was it.

Angie, Franco, Uncle Tonio would try to get him to go to the cemetery, but Lew wouldn't go. Catherine was not there, only broken bones and decaying body.

If there was a soul, it wasn't hanging around her grave. He hoped it wasn't. If there was a soul, as he had been taught and rejected by the time he was ten, it would come to him. He would welcome it, but he didn't expect it.

Lew slowly put the report on the pile, returned the documents to the envelope, put the envelope in his carry-on and went through the door. The smell from the kitchen was a kickback memory to better times, his grandmother's garlic pasta with shrimp. He followed the smell and the sound of a young woman's voice into the kitchen.

Angie and Franco were at the table watching CNN where someone who looked like Catherine was saying that thirty-one people had been killed by terrorists in New Delhi. Angie and Franco looked up at Lew, whose eyes were fixed on the woman reading the news. She was a young, pretty, long-haired blonde with perfect skin and a very red mouth. She really didn't look like Catherine. She only blurred his memory of his wife.

"You okay?" asked Angie, getting up.

He nodded yes and said, "Garlic pasta and shrimp?"

"When do you want to eat?" she said.

"When Franco and I get back I think I need to do something first."

"When you get back?"

"When I get back," Lew said.

Franco pushed back his chair and got up.

She wanted to ask Lew where they were going, but held back. Franco would tell her everything when they returned.

When they left the house, Franco asked, "Okay if we take the truck or you want me to get one of the cars from Toro's?"

"Truck's fine."

"Good," he said.

The sun was still up. No clouds. Cool October Chicago weather. The next day the temperature could rise or fall twenty degrees. It might even snow.

When they got in the truck, Franco asked, "Where to?"

"Pappas."

Franco grinned, drove past Cabrini Hospital, made a left on Racine.

"Angie's office," he said, leaning over Lew to point out the sign, ANGELA MASSACCIO, REALTOR, in black letters on the window above Gonzalez's Hardware Store.

"She's doing great," Franco said. "Want the radio?"

"No."

When Lew had to drive, he liked to drive alone or with Ames McKinney who was silent unless Lew asked him a question. Lew liked to listen to a voice, any voice turned low. No music. Talk. Evangelists, Pacifica

Radio, NPR, Limbaugh, Springer, any talk show. Company he could ignore or turn off.

"Think I need a haircut? Angie thinks I need one."

Lew looked. Franco could use a haircut. Lew told him. Lew cut his own hair, what remained of it, with a comb, scissors and disposable razor. His father had taught him how, saying only "Like so. Like so. Like so," as he cut, clipped and combed. For the past four years he had given himself haircuts looking into the pitted mirror of the men's room of the building he lived in behind the Dairy Queen on 301 in Sarasota.

Ten minutes later they were heading west on the Eisenhower Expressway.

Franco knew Pappas's address, remembered it from the fax Rich had sent him, but he wanted to be asked.

"You remember the address? I do." Franco beamed.

"My job. Hey, I know the streets. You know how to find people. We're gonna be a great team."

Lew didn't remember becoming part of a team.

"Yes," Lew said.

Lew thought about Rebecca Strum, wondered if when she was a young girl in a concentration camp they had given her a tattooed purple number.

"What do we do when we get there?" Franco asked.

"We talk. We listen."

"That's the plan?" asked Franco.

"There is no plan."

"Sounds good to me," said Franco, adding, "Yellow light on?"

"Why not," Lew said.

"Indeed," Franco said, flicking a switch on the dashboard.

The spinning light on top of the roof of the truck flicked yellow on the truck's hood. Franco began to weave through early rush-hour traffic. Lew tightened his fists and looked at the dashboard clock. Three in the afternoon. The time when Catherine was killed. Lew fought to hold onto that memory of Catherine's face, smiling as if she had a secret. He fought to hold onto it, knowing that another image of her was forming, an image of her crushed and bleeding face.

He tried. He lost.

The house was surrounded by a ten-foot-high wall of stone painted a conservative burnt ash. The metal gate was simple, wrought-iron painted black, each spike sharply pointed and level with the wall. There was a white button in the wall to their left. Lew pushed it and a man's voice from nowhere said, "Yes?"

"We're looking for John Pappas," Lew said.

"State your business and leave," the man said.

Franco leaned over and whispered in Lew's ear, "That's from *The Twelve Chairs*."

"Two men driving your car were following me this morning," Lew said.

"So?"

"I'd like to know why."

"Idle curiosity," came the voice, "or are you going someplace with this?"

"My name's Lew Fonesca. I want to know who killed my wife."

"I don't know who killed your wife," came the voice. Something in the voice, even filtered through the speaker, made Lew say, "But you know who did."

"Come in," the voice said wearily. "I'm clicking. Just push the gate and be sure it clicks locked behind you."

Franco and Lew pushed the gate open, stepped inside and Franco pushed the gate closed behind them.

"I'm supposed to be impressed," said Franco as they walked down a wide brick-lined path toward the big two-story wood-frame house set back on a broad green lawn with a spotting of orange and yellow leaves from a nearby tree. A breeze rustled. More leaves floated down.

"I've seen bigger houses with cars in garages that looked great and had to be towed because there was crapola under the hood and the owners were always afraid of what it would cost to fix 'em."

"You don't like rich people," Lew said.

"Not until and unless I become one," said Franco. "Then I'll join 'em."

Franco reached down and touched the gun tucked in under his jacket.

While Lew was knocking the second time, the door opened.

Standing in front of them was the driver who Franco had pulled from the car on the Dan Ryan. He didn't look surprised to see them. He motioned for Franco and Lew to come inside. The house smelled of something baking, something sweet and familiar.

They followed the driver up a flight of highly polished light wood stairs. On the landing, he went to a closed door and knocked.

"Come in," came a deep voice with the touch of an accent. "Come in."

Sitting in an armchair, hands on his lap was the one-eyed young man. At the window, his back turned, was a man with white hair, wearing dark slacks and a yellow sweater over a white shirt with a button-down collar.

The room was a combination den and office — antique wood desk and chair, two matching armchairs, a sofa that challenged the rest of the room but seemed right. There were three painted portraits on the wall to the right, all of one woman.

"John Pappas," Lew said.

The man at the window slowly turned. He was lean, dapper, had a weathered face and too-perfect false teeth as white as his equally full head of white hair. According to his driver's license, Pappas was fifty-seven years old.

"Have a seat," he said with a smile, pointing a hand at the sofa.

Behind them the driver, arms folded, leaned back against the wall near the door. The one-eyed man in the armchair looked at him and then back at Pappas.

Lew and Franco sat. So did Pappas after hitching up his pants, a low glass coffee table between them.

"We begin by being polite," he said. "Though you have met, I don't believe you know the names of my sons. This is Dimitri."

He turned his head toward the driver.

"He prefers to be called Dimi. Why? I don't know. That's what they called the young priest in *The Exorcist,* right?"

"Right," said Franco.

"And that," Pappas said, looking over his shoulder at the one-eyed young man, "is Stavros. He has no diminutive."

Pappas raised his right eyebrow, looking for a sign of recognition at his vocabulary. He got none from Lew and Franco.

"You're Greeks," said Franco.

"Your powers of observation are quite remarkable," Pappas said. "So, you have questions, ask."

"Who killed my wife?"

"Perhaps the person who would like to kill me and would not hesitate to . . . please make an effort to sit still."

The last, delivered with a smile, had been aimed at the fidgeting Franco. Franco folded his arms, looked at Pappas and decided to make the effort.

"Thank you. Conversation is a medium," said Pappas, sitting back. "Like film, video, a blank canvas or an empty screen, when used with respect, it deserves our full attention. Am I right?"

It was Stavros's turn to say, "You're right."

"See," said Pappas. "Stavros went to college. He's the artist who keeps our home and business running and repaired. Dimi is our heart, our emotion. I am the creator. In many ways, I have been most magnificently blessed. In others . . ."

He shrugged and continued.

"So, the artist can engage the medium and create art. Let us strive for conversational art."

"Let us," Franco said.

Pappas raised his right hand and his sons left the room.

"They are going to get us coffee and something special. They will also check the video monitors to see if anyone is watching the house. One does not know when an enemy might approach and mark it well, for in truth there is an enemy out there and the enemy has a name. I am under siege in my own home. This is my Troy. And I must be sure I don't let a gift horse enter. You understand?"

"Yes, you're paranoid," said Lew.

"And you are not," he said with a sigh. "You should be."

"I'm depressed," Lew said. "That's all I can handle."

Pappas nodded and folded his hands against his chest.

"The one who has made me a prisoner in my own home and may have killed your wife is called Posno. His full name is Andrej Pos-nitki. I think he is Hungarian, but that doesn't matter. When she was so foully murdered, your dear wife was gathering evidence against Posno, evidence that he committed murder, evidence of his life of crime which, I am sorry to admit, I partici-pated in, though only at the edges."

Pappas raised his right hand and let it float toward an unmarked periphery.

"The important documents supporting her evidence could not be found in her of-fice desk or your apartment. Posno's plan when your wife died was to find you and torture you, something he is very, very good at, and get you to tell him where those documents were, if you even knew. But you were not to be found. You fled, vanished, flew."

Pappas let his right hand, fingers flutter-ing, move up. Then he brought his hand back to his lap.

"Posno is not a genius, but he is clever and determined. He has almost certainly found you the same way I found you. Stavros found your name on the Internet. Something about your being involved in the shooting of some professor. That was a week ago. I sent Stavros to Sarasota to keep an eye on you."

"Funny," said Franco.

"Oh, I see," said Pappas with a smile. "Because my son has only one eye to keep on you. You want to know how he lost that eye? He was shot by the man who is looking for you. Now, I'll tell you how to find him."

"Why do you want to help me?" Lew asked.

Pappas rose from the chair and went to the window.

"Nine years ago your wife was the prosecutor in a murder case. I was arrested, charged. My record, I must tell you, is not without blemish but this crime I did not do."

He put his right hand on his chest.

"She talked to the witnesses, got experts to look at the signature on a hotel register . . . That's not important. She believed me, dropped the charges against me in exchange for my testifying against Andrej Posnitki, who had set me up. It was a sweet deal if you ignore that Posno is a maniac who, between the three of us, is responsible for the demise of more than forty-one people. Still I owe your wife and when my family has a debt, we pay it no matter how long it takes."

"I appreciate that," Lew said. "Posno

wasn't convicted."

"Good lawyers, lots of money. He got off. Since then he has found my presence on this earth intolerable. Putting him in prison or, better yet, death row, would greatly ease my paranoia. Your wife would not give up, as you well know. She continued to build a new case against Posno. So finding your wife's records might well keep us both alive. She didn't tell you about all this?"

"We didn't talk about cases except the ones I was working on for her," Lew said.

"Smart," said Pappas, pointing to his head and looking at Franco. "You don't know. You can't testify."

There was a gentle double knock at the door and Pappas, with a smile, said, "You're gonna like this."

One-eyed Stavros backed in balancing a large, round golden tray. He walked over and placed the tray on the glass table. The other son, Dimitri, came in with a smaller tray, balancing three small cups of almost-black Greek coffee. There were also three small plates with a fork on each. Pappas, Franco and Lew each took a cup and a plate.

Stavros leaned next to his father and whispered in his ear. Pappas nodded and whispered something back to him. It was

Stavros's turn to nod.

The brothers left the room, closing the door softly behind them.

"Glykismata," Pappas said after a sip of coffee. "Greek deserts. This one is *amygdalopita,* nut cake covered in clove syrup. These are *loukoumathes."*

He pointed to six round balls, which he said were Greek donuts covered with honey and cinnamon.

"Good with coffee," Pappas said with a knowing nod. "And these cookie twists are *koulourakia, glaktobouriko,* egg custard baked in phyllo, and baklava. Everything baked today by my mother. Did you know Aristophanes mentions baklava in one of his plays?"

"No," said Lew.

"Ah," said Pappas with a shrug. "Why should you? Take."

They put down their coffees. Lew took one of the cookies. Franco piled his plate. Pappas smiled.

"These are great," said Franco, his mouth full.

"You'll meet my mother on the way out," Pappas said, his eyes meeting Lew's. "As long as you have the blessing of your mother, it does not matter even if you live in the the valley of the dead. That's a Greek saying. I have her blessing and, pardon me for saying it, you are treading in the valley of the dead. It is not a good place to be."

He looked around the room and added, "Though I am under siege, I still have resources, which is why Posno has not gotten to me. I live in this comfortable prison. I would like to walk beyond the glass-covered walls that define my exile. To the extent that I can, I will extend my protection to you, but you must be quite careful. Find that evidence."

He held up a finger and added, "Put Posno away. You like those, huh?"

Lew was eating one of the phyllo desserts filled with custard.

"Yes," Lew said.

"Good," he said. "You have anything else you wish to ask me?"

"You know any jokes?" Lew asked.

"Jokes? Sure."

Pappas was smiling, puzzled by the question. Franco's cheek was full of baklava, his fingers honey-sticky, his eyes moving from Lew to Pappas as if they were suddenly talking Greek.

"You want me to tell you a joke?"

"Yes."

Pappas told Lew a joke and smiled, his teeth a huge wall of white. Lew took out his notebook and pen and wrote down the joke.

"Okay joke?" Pappas asked.

"Yes," Lew said, putting the notebook back in his pocket.

"You didn't smile," he said.

"I don't smile," Lew said.

Franco finished his baklava and wiped his fingers with a napkin.

Pappas shook his head, put down his plate and empty coffee cup and walked to the window, looked out, sighed and turned around.

"When you arrived, my sons covered your license plate with clay in case he came by this afternoon, the circling vulture Posno, appearing whenever he wishes, reminding me that I am his prisoner and that the day of execution is coming."

Franco put down his plate and cup and moved to the window.

"I do not think he knows yet about your tow truck, but he'll wonder, and with good cause, why your license plate number is covered. He almost certainly has a photograph of you, Mr. Fonesca, but not . . ."

"Franco," said Lew's brother-in-law.

"Franco," Pappas repeated. "I suggest you go out the front gate as you came, get in your truck and drive around the first corner. Mr. Fonesca will join you there."

"No," said Franco. "I'm going down there and if anyone gives me trouble I'll ram the holy shit out of this Posno's car."

"Not advisable," said Pappas with a shake of his head. "He is not likely to use a weapon unless you provoke him. You are not his prey."

"Lew?" Franco asked, fist clenched, turning to Lew as he stood. "The son of a bitch mighta killed Catherine."

Lew looked at Pappas, who pursed his lips.

"It may not be Posno," said Lew.

"It may not be," Pappas agreed with a shrug, "but I can think of no one else who would park in front of my house."

"We do it your way," Lew said to Franco. "Front door. Both of us, but no ramming. Let's go."

"As you wish," said Pappas, leading the way out the door.

"That's from *The Princess Bride,* the 'as you wish,' " Franco whispered as they followed Pappas down the stairs. "Lew, let's just get the bastard."

At the bottom of the stairs stood a short, thin, overly made-up woman with electric badly dyed red hair. She was holding a shoebox-size white box tied with a string. Pappas introduced her as his mother. She smiled and handed Lew the box. The smell

81

of baked phyllo and honey made it clear what was inside.

Pappas handed Lew a Greek fisherman's cap and moved to his mother's side, arm around her shoulder. Lew handed it back, took his Cubs cap from his pocket and put it on his head.

"Stylish," said Pappas.

"Thank you," Lew said to the woman, looking into her eyes.

Her smile faded.

"Sure," she said.

"We'll be watching over you," said Pappas as Lew and Franco went through the door. It closed behind them. The night had come. The air had gone cool and the wind whistled by. The box in Lew's hand was warm.

There was a car about twenty yards behind the tow truck, a black Lexus, and there were two people inside.

"I don't like this, Lewis," Franco said when they were in the truck with the doors closed. He took the gun out of his pocket and placed it in a panel slot in front of him.

"I know," Lew said, who sat with the box on his lap as Franco made a leisurely U-turn and looked down at the car with the two men as he drove toward the Eisenhower.

"Nice people," said Franco. "I mean the

Pappases. That John's a little . . . you know?"

"Very nice people," Lew said. "Pappas lied. Catherine didn't have any case going against anyone named Andrej Posnitki. She would have told me."

"They're following," said Franco. "Well, the old lady was nice."

"*Her* I remember," said Lew. "Not Catherine's case, Peter Michaels's case. Milt Holiger did the legwork. Bernice Alexander Pappas. Five or six years ago. She got off. Lack of evidence. Witnesses disappeared."

"What'd she do?" asked Franco, pulling onto the Eisenhower and heading toward downtown.

"Killed her husband and her husband's cousin with a very sharp baking knife."

"Maybe she . . ."

"Stabbed them about a dozen times each in the neck and face," said Lew, removing the string from the box.

The fresh-baked scent penetrated the smell of grease.

"Shit," Franco said, reaching for the box and putting his hand inside. He came up with a cookie. "You never know."

"You never know," Lew agreed.

"But she can bake. And you gotta admit, Pappas may be a phony, but he's a good son."

"He was an assassin for hire, probably still is," said Lew. "Suspect in at least fourteen murders."

"With this Posno guy?"

"Maybe."

Franco bit, chewed and went silent for a beat and then, "So Catherine never helped them?"

"No. Why would she?"

"I don't get it," he said. "What do we do now?"

"Go home."

"Don't think so," said Franco. "That Lexus is right behind us. Want me to lose them?"

Lew reached for the car phone, punched in Angela's home number, and when she came on he asked her a question and when she answered, he asked her for a favor. Lew hung up and told Franco what to do.

Less than half an hour later they were back in Little Italy, driving slowly. They pulled into a one-car driveway and got out of the truck. The outside houselights were on and the lights beyond the windows sent out orange-white beams.

"They parked across the street," Franco whispered.

The front door was open. They went in. Franco locked the door behind him.

"Now?" he asked.

Lew turned out the living-room lights so they couldn't be seen from the street. Timing could have been better but it wasn't bad. No one got out of the Lexus, whose lights and engine were turned off.

When Lew had called Angie from the truck he had asked her if she had an unoccupied house for sale in the neighborhood. She did. He asked her to go there, take the FOR SALE sign down, turn on the lights and leave the door open. She had. If they didn't already know, Lew didn't want to lead whomever was in the Lexus to his sister's house.

Franco had called one of his cop friends from the truck.

"I've got a joke, Lewis," he said.

"Yes?"

Five minutes later a Chicago P.D. patrol car glided down the street and pulled next to the Lexus. Two uniformed street cops got out, one on each side of the car, hands on their weapons. They had left their headlights on. White light surrounded the Lexus. Lew opened the front door a few inches.

"Please get out of the car," said the beefy officer who had been driving.

Two men, one man in his forties, wearing a suit and tie, and the other, a man about thirty, wearing a sports jacket, white shirt, no tie, his hair tied back, slowly got out of the car, careful to keep their hands in sight.

The man in the suit, who had been the passenger in the Lexus, looked at the partly open door beyond which Lew stood.

"Hands on the roof, spread your legs," said the cop.

They knew the drill. The younger cop moved forward and patted them down. He didn't miss a space. Found nothing.

"Identification," said the beefy cop. "Slow, so slow I can almost swear you're not moving."

The two men exchanged looks and reached into their jacket pockets, pulling out their wallets. The younger cop took the wallets and brought them to the beefy cop.

"Santoro," the beefy cop said, looking up from the open wallet.

Santoro, the passenger, didn't respond. He kept looking at the door as if he could see Lew in the darkness.

"And Cruz."

"Aponte-Cruz," said the man with the tied-back hair.

The beefy cop handed the wallets to his partner who knew what to do, call in their identification. He moved back to the police car.

Franco and Lew left the house, moved to the tow truck and climbed in.

"What are you doing here?" the beefy cop asked Santoro.

"Here?" asked Santoro, watching Lew. "We just parked for a few minutes, talk a little before we get something to eat. Here's as good as any place."

"You're loitering," said the beefy cop.

Santoro looked down at the hood of the Lexus and shook his head with a smile.

Franco backed the tow truck into the street. Franco and Lew looked down at the men named Santoro and Aponte-Cruz. Santoro met Lew's eyes and smiled. Lew couldn't read the smile.

3

Dinner, rigatoni with shrimp, had reminded him of his grandmother's cooking, Sundays at her house. She hadn't learned any of her recipes in Sicily. She had learned them from cookbooks, mostly written by second- or third-generation American recipe gatherers, most of them Jewish. Her food was good. Lew's mother had not carried on the tradition, but Angela had picked it up like a loose football and run with it. Franco had been a lean Massaccio when they were married.

Franco's friend Manny Lowen, the beefy cop, still in uniform, had come by. He had a bowl of rigatoni with grated Parmesan and told them that the two men in the Lexus were Claude Santoro and Bernard Aponte-Cruz and that Santoro owned the car.

"Santoro's a lawyer," said Manny, working on a coffee and one of the last of the Greek deserts Angie had put out on a plate. "No criminal record. Lots of money. Lots of friends. Office up high on LaSalle Street. You want to find him, he won't be hard to find. He's in the phone book. The other guy, Aponte-Cruz, another story. He's a leg breaker for rent. Did four years downstate for breaking up a restaurant owner on Elston Avenue in front of witnesses. Owner came out on the other side with a limp, a twitch and a tendency to look over his shoulder a lot."

When Manny had left, Angie said, "You need my car tomorrow?"

"I can drive him," said Franco, failing to resist the last Greek cookie.

"Lewis?" Angie asked.

Lew didn't like driving anywhere. He didn't like driving in Chicago in particular. These weren't streets. They were bumper-to-bumper miles of memories. He accepted Franco's offer.

The phone had rung while they were still at the table and Franco had answered.

"Franco . . . got it . . . fifteen, twenty minutes tops."

He hung up, said, "Work," and kissed Angie on the cheek as she patted his hand. "Lewis, see you in the morning."

And he was gone.

"Can I ask?" Angie had said, folding her hands on the table when Franco had left.

"Yes."

"You going to see the rest of the family?"

"Not this time."

"Uncle Tonio?" she asked.

"Maybe."

He started to reach for the last baklava on the plate and changed his mind. What he really wanted was a DQ chocolate cherry Blizzard. He knew his comfort food and that was it, something he had not tasted before Catherine was killed.

"You're thinking about giving up, aren't you?" Angie said. "Thinking it wasn't such a great idea, your coming here?"

"Something like that," Lew said.

"Don't," she said.

She got up, came around the table, hugged her brother from behind and kissed the top of his head. There was nothing more to say. Not now. He helped Angie clear the table and put the dishes in the dishwasher. Then he went to Teresa's room where he called Ann Horowitz.

"It's me," he told her when she answered the phone.

"We start with a joke," she said. "You have one?"

"How many advisors to the president does it take to change a lightbulb?"

"I don't know, Lewis," said Ann Horowitz. "How many?"

"I don't know. The president has appointed a committee to investigate and they'll let us know the answer as soon as possible."

It was almost ten at night in Chicago, which meant it was almost eleven in Sarasota. Ann and her husband went to bed around midnight and Lew had been told he could call until then. Now he said, "I don't know what I'm doing here."

"You are trying to find out how your wife was killed," she said, "and who was responsible."

"You're eating," Lew said.

"Frozen Twix and green tea," she answered.

"How is it?"

"So-so," she said, "but I like to try new things."

"I don't," Lew said.

"Where did you get the joke? Did you make it up?"

"No," he said. "A Greek hit man told it to me. His mother baked us Greek pastries."

"Good?"

"Yes," he said.

"The trick is not just in the ingredients," said Ann. "It's in sharp, even cuts of the phyllo."

"She killed her husband and his cousin with a very sharp baking knife," he said.

"Tonight?" she asked calmly.

"No, about six years ago. Tell me again, what am I doing here?"

"I assume you're not asking a what-is-the-meaning-of-life kind of question."

"No."

"Good," she said. "You are there to bring to an end a part of your grief and to come back and tell me whatever it is you have not yet told me."

"I . . ."

"Not all of it," she went on. "I will not deprive you of your grief and depression. Without them you fear you would be looking into dark emptiness, that there would be no more Lewis Fonesca for Lewis Fonesca believes he is defined by his grief and depression. I know, not because of my brilliance as a therapist but because you have told me repeatedly. I don't need to have you do it again, so I've done it for you. You are a tough town, Lewis."

"I know."

"It's not a compliment. Okay," she said with a sigh, taking a crunchy bite of Twix. "I'll give you some reasons for finding out what happened to Catherine. You pick one or more or all of them. Ready? No, of course you're not ready, but you need the halftime pep talk. So, first, you owe it to her. It's selfish to cling to the darkness and videotapes on your cot, memorizing the lines from *Mildred Pierce.* Your Catherine deserves to lie in peace with the final line written by you. Call it a loving eulogy. Or try this, someone is responsible for your wife's death. You don't want them to forget what they have done. Also, you don't know what or who you might find. Your sense of the world, your two-room world, may be forever changed by what you find. And that could be good."

"Or bad."

"Or bad," she agreed. "Or something that can't be defined by good and bad."

"All right," he said.

"Good. Remember, no matter what you find, you can always come back here to your misery."

"That's comforting," Lew said.

"And in your case, I know you mean that. Are you going to go to the cemetery?"

"No. There's nothing there but a stone cross."

"It's not what is there, Lewis, but what you bring there with you. *The Daily Show* is coming on. Good night."

She hung up. Lew was sitting in the pillowed wicker chair in Teresa's room, the phone in his lap.

When Ann hung up, he sat there thought about Catherine's missing file, the one Pappas and Andrej Posnitki and, for all Lew knew, maybe Claude Santoro wanted as well. All of the things in Catherine's and his apartment had been been boxed, taped and taken to his uncle Tonio's warehouse on Fullerton by Angie, Franco, Tonio and some of Tonio's men after Lew had left Chicago. Lew hadn't wanted to look at any of it then. He didn't want to now.

Milt Holiger had told Lew that he and two Assistant State Attorneys had gone through all of the files in Catherine's two cabinets and the contents of the drawers of her office desk. Nothing was surprising in them, nothing about an upcoming case that might lead to someone running her down. Lew believed him. Milt was good, but Lew was another set of eyes, another history.

"The active files," Milt had said, "were turned over to other lawyers in the department. The closed-case files have been crated and stored."

Lew decided that in the morning he would move again, go through the motions, do the one thing he did well, find people, let them talk. He got up. He hadn't unpacked anything from his duffel bag. He didn't intend to. He unzipped the blue cloth bag, took out clean socks, underwear, a folded white button-down shirt, a folded blue shirt, a rolled-up black T-shirt with the faded words THE TRUTH IS OUT THERE, and a Ziploc plastic bag containing his toothbrush, toothpaste and disposable razor. He laid them out on one side of the bed next to his zippered denim jacket.

Teresa had a small bathroom inside her room, no bath, just a shower. Angie had put out a pair of towels on the sink. Ten minutes later Lew turned out the light and lay in bed, looking up at the ceiling at the swaying shadows of the branches of the tree outside of Teresa's window.

Just before he fell asleep a name came to him: Rebecca Strum.

A thousand miles south in Florida, the hurricane season had begun.

Lew was up early, the sun warm across his eyes. He covered his face with his arms, but thoughts, names, memories cometed through his mind with fleeting images he almost recognized. This time he wasn't dealing with someone else's missing husband, wife, mother or child. He wasn't losing himself in someone else's loss. This Chicago pain was all his.

Dressed in jeans and a long-sleeved, reasonably ironed blue shirt with a collar that could have used a couple of stays, Lew tucked his Cubs cap on his head, put on his white socks and sneakers, checked for the first signs of daily stubble on his cheeks and neck and looked at himself in Teresa's mirror.

Catherine said that he looked particularly good in blue shirts. She seemed to mean it. He didn't think he had looked particularly good when she had said it and he certainly didn't think so this morning.

Lew put on his denim jacket.

Franco was sitting in his overstuffed chair in the living room. The chair had been sat into exhaustion by three generations of Massaccio and Fonesca men. Franco was drinking coffee from a white mug with a black-and-white photograph on it of the DiMaggio brothers — Joe, Vince and Dominick — in uniform, arms around one another's necks, grinning the toothy DiMaggio grin.

"Hey, Lewis," he said, getting up. "Angie had a client coming into the office early. Coffee's on. Want some eggs, something? How about I put some butter in a pan and fry you up some spaghetti and meatballs?"

Lew checked the wooden clock on the wall, Roman numerals. It was a little after seven. Lots of time. The imagined smell of a recooked dinner jolted him with the memory of his standing over a black iron skillet and preparing almost the same breakfast Franco had just offered.

"That breakfast I smell?" Catherine had asked, wandering in, still in a blue-and-white–striped nightshirt.

She stood behind him at the stove, kissing his cheek and looking down at the sizzling skillet.

"Smells good," she said.

This was a few weeks before his wife had been killed.

Something about the way she spoke, the lack of a morning hug, the surface-only kiss, came back to him. Was he imagining it? Should he have said something?

In his mind's eye Lew looked over his shoulder at Catherine who, cup of black coffee in front of her, sat at the tiny kitchen table. She drank slowly, looking out the window at the morning traffic. The morning was overcast. Normally, the downtown Chicago skyline was a panorama in front of them. Not that morning. She ran her fingers through her disheveled hair. Normally, she turned on the television on the counter to watch the morning news. She did not turn on the television set. That morning had been forgotten until now.

"No, thanks," Lew said to Franco. "Just coffee."

"Want the last of Norman Bates's mom's pastries? We saved it for you."

"Sure."

An hour and a half later Franco and Lew were at the law offices of Glicken, Santoro and Turnbull. The offices were on LaSalle Street in the heart of the Loop, fifteenth floor. Franco had parked the tow truck in a four-story garage two blocks away where the hourly rate was eight dollars an hour for off-the-street and six dollars an hour for daily customers. Franco would be charged neither. He knew the night manager and the day manager who steered breakdown calls his way and got a finder's fee.

Lew tucked his blue Cubs cap into his pocket.

The large, gray-carpeted reception area had six black leather armchairs and a reception desk with a telephone, computer, pad of lined yellow paper and three pens ready for the day. On the wall were large side-by-side color photographs of the partners smiling confidently. Glicken was dark, curly-haired and definitely Jewish. Turnbull was

Black. Claude Santoro was either Hispanic or Italian.

Lew never found out.

Santoro's name was on the door on their right in the small waiting area. His door was slightly open. The lights were on. No voices.

Lew knocked and then knocked again. Franco reached past him and pushed the door all the way open. Santoro was seated behind the desk in front of them. His eyes were open. He seemed lost in thought. There was a black hole over his right eye, another in his neck and a third just above his mouth. All were ringed by blood.

"He's fucking dead," said Franco.

Lew said nothing. Blood had oozed out of the bullet holes and dried up.

Franco reached for the phone on the desk in front of the dead man.

"No," Lew said.

Franco jerked his hand back.

"Hey, Lewie, come on. We've got to call the cops."

"Don't touch anything."

"Okay."

Lew sat across the desk from Santoro.

"We call the police right?" Franco said.

Santoro's eyes were open, fixed on Lew's face. They were staring each other down. Santoro would win. He was dead.

"Lewie, you all right?"

"Yes."

"We call the police, right?" he said.

Lew didn't move.

"Or we get the hell out of here fast. Lewis, come on. Lewie, what's going on here?"

What was going on was that there was no way of getting around the truth. If Santoro's death was not connected to Catherine's, Lew faced a very large coincidence.

He got up and moved around the desk behind Santoro.

"You can wait outside," he said, looking at the top of the desk.

"You think I want out because of the dead guy?" Franco asked, shaking his head. "I've seen dead guys, kids on the roads like road-kill. I'm a tow-truck driver, remember?"

"I remember," Lew said.

"You want help?" he asked, looking at the closed door to Santoro's office.

"No," Lew said.

There was a fresh, lined, yellow legal pad with a pen next to it. The top page was blank. There was an empty in box, an aluminum football with a clock imbedded in it, facing Santoro. Next to it was a fresh box of Kleenex with a red wood cover. At the right was a flat, black cell phone holder-charger. There was no phone. Franco mumbled something to himself. Lew took a small stack of tissues.

"You know what your sister'll do to me if we get arrested?"

"No."

"I don't either," said Franco, clearly frustrated. "But I won't like it. I know that."

Franco's near panic had been transformed into quiet resignation. He would not be surprised if the killer burst through the door, guns in both hands, firing away. He wouldn't have been happy either, but he wouldn't be surprised.

There were four desk drawers. Lew opened and went through them, flipping papers with the tissues. Then he went through Santoro's pockets the same way. A little more than four hundred dollars in his wallet. Lew put the wallet back.

He wanted to touch Santoro's shoulder. Then he paused and looked down at the dead man.

"Lewis, you okay?"

"Yes, let's go."

"I can live with that," Franco said, moving ahead of Lew to the door. "You find anything?"

Lew reached past him, opened the door with the tissues and wiped down the knob. Then he realized that while he was erasing their fingerprints, he might well be removing those of the person who had killed Santoro.

They walked past the reception area, into the hallway outside and then to their right, back toward the elevator.

"Find anything on him?"

It wasn't what Lew had found, but what he hadn't found. Santoro's phone was gone. He had no appointment or notebook in his pockets. Whoever had killed him had taken any phone and notebook he might have had.

"No," Lew said.

"Stairs?"

"No."

There were surveillance cameras in the building's lobby, at the entrance and even one in the wooden mesh grid of the elevator's ceiling. They were on tape. That would be fine. If Lew were right, the tape and medical examiner would prove Lew and Franco had entered the building at least eight hours or more after Santoro was dead. That wouldn't stop the police from having questions.

The elevator pinged and the doors slid open almost silently. In front of them stood a large black man in his forties. He was wearing a blue suit and matching tie and carrying a briefcase. He looked exactly like his photograph on the wall of the reception room of Santoro's law firm.

The man was Turnbull of Glicken, Santoro and Turnbull, or, to be more current, Glicken and Turnbull.

He took Lew and Franco in and moved toward the offices Lew and Franco had left seconds earlier. Franco and Lew stepped in and Lew hit the Lobby button.

They were only a few blocks from the County Office Building. Lew headed toward it with Franco at his side, looking back over his left shoulder.

"I'm not gonna ask," said Franco.

People hurried to their offices or jobs serving the people going to their offices. Lew could tell by how they were dressed, by the color of their skin, which were the served and which the servers. Lew was definitely a server.

They stopped on the broad stone courtyard in front of the building where Lew had worked, where Catherine had worked. Too many demons were being faced too quickly and he had been in the city for less than twenty-four hours.

Franco looked at the three pay phones in front of the building and then at Lew who nodded.

"Just say, 'Attorney Claude Santoro murdered in his office' and hang up."

Franco moved toward the phones to call 911.

4

"I had a dream last night," Franco said as they watched the doors, waiting for Milt Holiger to come out.

Lew had used Franco's cell phone to call Milt and ask him to come down. Holiger had said he would be down in a minute. About five minutes had passed.

Lew's body had changed. Four years in Florida had made a cool Chicago October morning feel like the inside of an ice-cream truck. The dead man they had found a few blocks away contributed more than a little frost.

"You want to hear it?"

"Sure," Lew said without looking at Franco.

"Craziest damn . . . anyways, you and me and Ange were watching the Bears playing the Eagles. Bears have the ball. Got it?"

"Got it," Lew said, eyes fixed on the glass doors.

"Bears quarterback gets the snap, steps back, throws. Ball sails right into the hands of the referee. Ref cradles it like a pro and starts chugging it toward the goal like Thomas Jones. The other refs block for him. Touchdown. Refs celebrate. Crowd goes nuts. Now what the hell does that mean?"

"It's not just the good guys and the bad guys you have to watch out for, you've got to keep your eyes on the peacekeepers because they might steal the ball."

Franco looked at Lew who didn't look back.

"You think?" he asked.

"No," said Lew.

"I'm talking a little nuts like this because of the dead guy, right?" asked Franco.

"Probably."

"You feel . . . ?"

"Yes," said Lew, eyes still focused on the door.

"You don't show it," Franco said.

"No."

"It doesn't mean you don't feel it, right?" said Franco. "Yeah, I know. I sound like Angie."

Milt Holiger came through the door. He plunged his hands into his pants pockets. Lew remembered that Milt's hands and feet were always cold.

"Heredity," Milt had once explained. "Father, brothers, uncle. We all wear socks in bed."

Milt was stocky at forty and working to maintain and nurture his still controllable belly. Lots of brown hair with perfect sideburns, Milt looked like the generic weary television series police captain or lieutenant whose shoulders were stooped from hunkering down to ward off the blows of word and fist.

Milt dodged a pair of arm-gesturing lawyer types and walked to his right.

"That him?" asked Franco.

"Yes."

"Where's he goin'? Doesn't he see us?"

"He sees us. He's dropping bread crumbs," Lew said, following Holiger through the morning crowd.

Three blocks later they joined Holiger at a table in the rear of a dark narrow inauthentic deli that served neither good Jewish or Italian food. Holiger looked at Franco.

"My sister's husband," Lew said. "Franco."

They shook hands. The morning crowd had dwindled down to six customers besides the three of them. The place smelled as if it had been fried in something sweet and fatty.

"Better off not having people in the office

see us together," Milt said. "I give you information, someone connects the wires and I've got trouble."

"You mean you can't help anymore?" Lew asked.

"Who said that?"

He put his right hand to his chest. A heavy-legged waitress in a uniform that had once been yellow but now was a forlorn amber placed cups of coffee in front of them. They all ordered toasted onion bagels with cream cheese.

"Okay," said Milt, picking up his cup. "What do you need?"

"You're sure there was nothing in the things Catherine left at the office that might make someone want to kill her?"

"Nothing," said Milt. "Of course you never know, but nothing, no secret deposition, overlooked piece of evidence, name of a bombshell witness, nothing."

"Active cases?" Lew asked.

Franco was working on his second cup of coffee, his eyes moving from Lew to Milt to the front door of the deli behind the gray shadow where they sat.

Lew, I —"

"I know," Lew said. "But things changed about an hour ago; a lawyer named Claude Santoro was found murdered in his office on LaSalle Street."

"Excuse me," said Franco, getting up. "I'm going to the men's."

When Franco was gone, Lew asked, "You've heard of Santoro?"

"Not a criminal defense lawyer far as I know," said Milt. "Want me to check him out?"

"Yes."

He took out his notebook and wrote.

"Andrej Posnitki, Posno," Lew said.

Milt wrote and said, "Rings no bells. What else?"

"John Pappas," Lew said.

"Maybe."

"He's the son of Bernice Pappas, father of Dimitri Pappas and Stavros Pappas."

"Yep," said Milt writing quickly, "I remember now. A noble family. The old woman, kids. Yeah, I remember John."

"See what you can find on all of them."

Holiger looked at his list and read: "Santoro, Posnitki, the Pappas clan. Anything else?"

"Not for now," Lew said.

Holiger closed and pocketed his notebook as Franco came back and sat next to Lew.

"I'd ask you to come to the house for dinner with me and Ruthie, or we could take you out someplace," Milt said. "But I know better. If you decide down the line while you're in town to take up the offer, you've got my number."

"Thanks, Milt," Lew said.

"No, Lewis, I mean it. Ruthie would like to see you."

"I'll —" Lew began.

Holiger held up a hand and said, "Whenever you're ready."

He got up. So did Franco and Lew. Milt said, "Good to meet you, Franco. Take care of yourself, Lewis, and call me tonight about this."

He patted the pocket of his jacket where he had placed his notebook.

"Now?" asked Franco when Milt was gone.

"Uncle Tonio's," Lew said.

"Right."

"You ever hear of Rebecca Strum?" Lew asked as they walked to the garage where Franco's tow truck was parked.

"Sure, yeah," he said. "You kiddin'? Angie's a reader, read all of her books. They're lined up in the case in our bedroom, a couple in the built-in case in the dining room. Everybody knows Rebecca Strum."

John Pappas stood against the wall in the kitchen watching his mother lay out the ingredients for her famous *Kibbeh Bissanieh,* baked lamb and wheat. It was one of his favorites. He enjoyed the smells of the kitchen, the clanking of mixing bowels and wooden spoons, the sound of cracked wheat being crushed.

His mother, wiping her hands on her apron, looked over her shoulder at Pappas for an instant smile and then went back to work. She sang a medley of random lines she remembered from almost forgotten songs.

" 'Born free,' " she sang, " 'Free as a rainbow round my shoulder, free as that old devil moon in your eyes, free as the wind and the rain in your hair.' "

Pappas plucked a pine nut from a small pile in his left palm and dropped it on his tongue.

Stavros and Dimitri were born into the world of their father and their grandmother. Their mother had disappeared when Stavros was learning to talk and Dimitri learning to walk. Stavros remembered her as tall, thin, pale with red hair. Dimitri remembered her not at all. Her name was Irene and she was not to be spoken of. The few times the name Irene had come up — a television character, a waitress in a restaurant — John Pappas had looked at his sons, seeking a reaction.

111

He got none.

It was not a world they would have chosen, but they had accepted it without childhood whimper or teenage rebellion. This was a family in which nothing but complete loyalty would be tolerated.

The brothers didn't want to walk in their father's shoes. They didn't know what might be lurking in those shoes and they did not want to know.

They did what they were told, what they had to do, to protect father, grandmother and each other. But in the end, Stavros and Dimitri, though they might well be willing to die to preserve the family, most certainly did not want to be a part of the family business. John Pappas accepted this. The line of assassins went back forever. It would probably stop with him. It was time.

Bernice Pappas added the mixture of water-soaked bulgur wheat, onions, ground lamb, pine nuts, salt and pepper. She tasted the mixture, found it acceptable and kneaded and laid it out on a baking pan. She looked down at what she had done and smiled as she turned her head toward her son and placed the pan in the oven.

"Will they have the balls to kill him?" she asked, closing the oven door, wiping her hands on her apron and looking at her son.

"Yes," said Pappas, lifting the palm of his hand to his mouth to get the last four pine nuts.

"Posno has to die," she said, moving bowls, wooden spoons, cutting boards to the sink.

"I know," said Pappas.

They had agreed to this a long time ago and many times since. He always listened dutifully when his mother brought it up again. It did have to be done. Posno was too great a threat to him and the family.

"Get rid of him before he gets you killed," she said, searching for something in the refrigerator. She retrieved a small bottle of spring water and moved to the kitchen table where she sat in a wooden chair.

"Yes," Pappas agreed.

He could already smell the *Kibbeh Bissanieh* baking.

What, he wondered, was Posno doing now?

Andrej Posnitki followed the Pappas brothers. He was careful. He would not and could not be seen. It was the reason he had survived his entire life. He was careful. He was ruthless. He thought neither of the future nor the past.

Posno drove a new Prius, which didn't

deliver nearly the hybrid mileage he had been promised. He accepted this fact. He knew he was capable of convincing the automobile dealer on Harlem Avenue to take the car back. Posno could be very convincing, but he also had a simple philosophy: Almost everyone can't be trusted. If you were to right each wrong done to you, you would never get through the day and there would be a trail of the broken and the dead. Save your wrath for the big threats to your existence and your work.

Somewhere in the files of Catherine Fonesca, wherever they might be, was information that would end the existence of Andrej Posnitki. He would not let that happen.

Uncle Tonio was a dealer in merchandise.

Toys, DVDs, wallets, purses, chairs, you name it, from sources in China. Knockoff computers, watches from Japan. Rugs that looked like handmade Turkish from Poland. Lamps that looked like Art Deco 1935, but were made in 2006 in India. Leather sofas, both real and synthetic, from Indonesia. Ancient Peruvian jewelry made last year in Lima. In his fifty-one years in business, there was little that one imagined or made to fit in a crate that had not passed through Uncle Tonio's warehouse on Fullerton.

Lew didn't think anyone in the family, even his father, knew what most of the merchandise was or had been.

Every few weeks when Uncle Tonio came to dinner he brought a gift. Once, Lew remembered, it was two cartons of Cheerios. They ate it for a year. Another time the gift had been a small wooden tomato crate packed with forty dolls that looked like Barbies, but weren't. They were all dressed in yellow tennis outfits complete with yellow visors and a plastic tennis racquet. For years Angie had given them away to her friends for birthdays and Christmas.

Lew's cousin Mario and most of the family assumed there was something not quite legal about Tonio's business. When they said it aloud, they did it with a knowing smile of pride. Maybe the family actually had a Mafia connection? Maybe Uncle Tonio had known Capone, Nitti, Giancanna?

Tonio did nothing to dispel the belief. He encouraged it.

"So," someone might ask over dinner, "what's new, how's business?"

Tonio would keep eating, looking at his food, raising his fork as a prelude to answering and say, "You know, pretty good, not complaining. Pass the pepper."

If Uncle Tonio was a family legend, his

warehouse on Fullerton held the awe of a haunted castle. The two-story concrete building was about the size of a football stadium. It didn't stand out in the neighborhood. Most of the buildings in the area were big, constructed for storage and shipping. The brick ones dated back to the late 1800s. One had been an icehouse till the 1940s.

Uncle Tonio's warehouse had been built at the beginning of World War II to hold military vehicles — half-tracks, jeeps, trucks, staff cars. No one lived within six blocks of Uncle Tonio's. During the day, the warehouse and the neighborhood were benign, a set for a television cop show chase, complete with fissures and buckles in the pavement and a very nice quartet of train tracks long gone to rust.

At night, the warehouse made the transformation to haunted castle, dark except for small night-lights on some of the buildings, looming, moaning distant sounds from traffic on the expressway and the occasional bark of guard dogs inside some of the surrounding buildings.

Franco parked in front of the loading dock that was also the main entrance. Uncle Tonio's warehouse looked exactly the way it had more than twenty years ago when Lew had last seen it. It also looked nothing like it had twenty years ago. It was just as massive, but the man saw what the boy had not. The warehouse was sagging, with small, narrow and not clean windows. The concrete block walls were cracked. Lew stood still in front of the loading dock.

"What?" asked Franco.

"The castle's gone."

"What?" asked Franco, walking past Lew. "Castles? You worry me, Lewie."

Lew moved to Franco's side and they climbed up the steps of the dock. The rusting handrail shook. Franco had called Uncle Tonio who said he would meet them. And he did.

Uncle Tonio was at the open double door in front of them, arms at his side, legs apart. He wore what he always wore, dark slacks, a sweater in the fall and winter, and highly polished shoes, a long-sleeved light blue or white shirt and a colorful tie with matching suspenders. Uncle Tonio's supply of sweaters, shirts and ties was nearly infinite, probably the tax-free tariff of hundreds of shipments. He never wore the same clothes twice.

Tonio's hairline was now, as always, receded as far back as Lew's. Tonio was lean and no more than five foot eight. He was, Lew thought, what Lew would be at seventy-two with some big differences. Tonio's eyes danced. He bounced on his heels. His natural look was a smile.

"Come here," he said, stepping in front of Lew, examining his face and giving him a hug.

Tonio smelled, as he always had, of peppermint.

He touched Franco's arm and said, "Come on."

They followed him inside. Tonio closed the doors behind them. Light through the few dirty windows and fluorescents tingled ahead of them as they followed the quick-paced Tonio down a wide aisle of wooden pallets on both sides. The pallets were stacked with cardboard and wooden boxes, fifty- and one-hundred-pound thick brown paper bags. The walls of merchandise were three or four times as high as Lew. Lew remembered that there were three more such aisles, each almost as long as a football field.

"Just got in from China," Tonio said, nodding at a pallet full of brown boxes. "Fifty-thousand pair of women's underpants, choice of pink, white, black. Would you believe there's this big town over there where all they do is make women's underwear?"

He didn't wait for an answer. He disappeared to the left. Lew and Franco followed. In front of them was a light.

"There," he said. "Herman opened it for you."

Franco and Lew shook hands with Herman. Herman was lean, black, hair still dark, and had served in Korea with Tonio.

"Good to see you," Herman said.

Lew nodded.

The irony of Tonio and Herman's friendship was that Tonio was a dark Sicilian and Herman a light-skinned offspring of the melting pot removed from Africa by six generations. People sometimes mistook them for brothers.

That was fine with Tonio and Herman. Herman had twice saved Tonio's life. They never spoke about Korea. Not to strangers, friends, family or each other.

In front of them was a steel-mesh-enclosed area with its sliding door open. The lock and key were in Herman's hand. Ceiling lights in the room were bright. The wall to the left where they entered the enclosure was lined with neatly sealed cartons labeled with black Magic Marker: KITCHEN; BATH; LAUNDRY ROOM; DINING AREA; LIVING ROOM; BEDROOM; OFFICE; LEW'S CLOTHES; CATHERINE'S CLOTHES. On the other two walls were Catherine and Lew's furniture: bed; sofas; chairs; tables; desks; lamps; file drawers. It could have been a furniture show room.

"Sliders," said Tonio. "Take a look. When we lock up, we slide 'em closed. Temperature inside is a steady seventy-four degrees. Nobody but family goes in, nobody but Herman."

"Thank you," Lew said.

"Hey, I took care," said Tonio. "Angela supervised the packing and moving."

They stood looking. Lew recognized everything but it all looked unfamiliar. He had come in search of a piece of the past that might lead to who had killed Catherine. But here was his life with Catherine, a small lovingly kept museum.

"Franco," Tonio said, touching Franco's shoulder. "Let's leave Lewis alone. Lewis, you know how to make your way back to my office from here?"

"Yes," he said.

"When you're ready. Want something to drink, eat?"

"No," Lew said.

"I could use something to eat," said Franco.

"We got it," said Tonio.

When the last echo of their footsteps and

120

voices were gone, Lew spent another minute or five looking at chairs, tables, bookcases, cabinets. Then he made himself move to Catherine's file cabinet and kneeled.

Half an hour, one drawer, and one slightly aching back later, he stood to stretch.

"Find anything?"

Lew didn't turn. He recognized the voice. "No."

"What's in your hand?"

Lew held up a framed photograph of himself and Catherine at a lodge in Wisconsin. It had been in the front of the drawer, either put there by Catherine or packed there by Angie.

"Wife?" asked Dimitri.

"Yes."

"Someone killed Posno's lawyer," Stavros said.

Lew turned. Stavros's single unblinking eye was focused between Lew's eyes. Dimitri, at his side, was still looking at the photograph in Lew's hand.

"Posno's lawyer?" Lew said.

"Followed you when you left our house last night," said Stavros. "Posno's lawyer and another man."

"Aponte-Cruz," said Dimitri.

"Aponte-Cruz," Stavros repeated. "Now, the lawyer is dead. Our father doesn't want anything to happen to you."

"Why?" Lew asked.

The brothers glanced at each other.

"Our father likes you," said Stavros.

Lew shook his head. That wasn't the answer.

"He wants you to find whatever your wife had on Posno," said Stavros. "He wants to be sure Posno doesn't get it before you do."

"What do you want?" asked Lew.

"Me, personally? I want Posno dead," said Stavros. "He took my eye. I'd settle for his eye. Is it here, your wife's files on Posno?"

"So, Posno killed his own lawyer?" Lew answered the question with his own question.

"Maybe," said Dimitri. "Maybe lots of people didn't like him. He was a lawyer."

"You're here to protect me from Posno," said Lew.

"Right," said Stavros.

"But you have guns pointed at me."

"Things get complicated," said Stavros nervously.

"I know," said Lew.

"Keep going through the drawers," said Stavros. "We'll watch. You find something, you give it to us and we go away."

"Just be —" Dimitri began.

He stopped speaking because a thick arm

was around his neck. Franco lifted him about a foot off of the ground, took the gun and threw it to Lew and let Dimitri fall on the concrete floor. Stavros, at the same time, was seated on the floor, his head back against the steel meshing. Uncle Tonio had punched him in the kidney, hard. Stavros had gone down groaning.

"Got by us," said Tonio. "Sorry. Saw their car parked near the dock. Franco recognized it."

"We were eating Polish sausage sandwiches," Franco explained, eyes moving between the brothers on the floor. "Saved you one."

"Thanks," Lew said.

"These?" asked Tonio, looking at Stavros and Dimitri. "What?"

The brothers had made it to their feet. Stavros was shaking his head.

"Nothing," Lew said. "Let them go."

"Hold it," said Stavros, leaning back against the meshing. His good eye rolled, still trying to focus. His glass eye looked at nothing. "Dimi, you okay?"

Dimitri nodded yes.

"We're not very good at this," said Stavros with a sigh.

"No, you're not," Lew said.

"We're not tough either," added Dimitri.

"We've never hurt anyone."

Stavros turned his head so his good eye was aimed at Lew.

Lew believed them.

"I want to design Web pages. Dimi wants to play the viola in an orchestra. We don't want to carry guns and be in car chases and follow people on airplanes."

"Our father needs us," said Dimitri, gagging. "He needs us."

"Yeah," agreed Stavros. "Posno goes down, our father is safe, and Dimi and I head for California."

"A one-eyed actor?" said Franco.

"Go," said Tonio, helping the groaning Stavros to his feet. "And do not come back. You hear what I'm saying?"

Franco lifted the still-gagging Dimitri and stood him up.

Stavros and Dimitri nodded that they understood. Tonio picked up Stavros's fallen gun and handed it to Lew who now had two guns he didn't want.

"How did you lose your eye?" Lew said.

Stavros brushed his hair back with his hand.

"Told you, Posno."

"When, how, the story," Lew said.

"Okay, Dimi and I went with our father to a doctor's appointment in Cicero. Afternoon. Dimi was the driver. I was the shot-gun. That's what our father called me. I didn't have a shotgun. I had a gun in the holster under my jacket and another in my pocket. Posno could come anywhere, any-time, our father always said. Watch, be ready."

"We weren't ready," said Dimitri.

"We parked in front of the office build-ing," said Stavros. "Pop went in. Dimi stayed behind the wheel. Street looked empty. I got out and stood by the door where I could keep an eye on things. Only then I had two eyes. Maybe five minutes later, three shots."

"Maybe four," said Dimitri.

"Maybe four," Stavros agreed. "Four shots from I don't know where. I felt an itch I had to scratch under my eye but I pulled out both guns and started to shoot. I didn't know where I was shooting. Even if I did, I'm a rotten shot and by then I only had the one eye."

"You see the shooter?" Lew asked Dimi-tri.

"No," he answered. "I ducked down. Almost got killed. Stavros put two shots through the windshield."

"Couldn't see. Couldn't shoot all that

straight even when I had two eyes," Stavros said.

"Then?" Lew prompted.

Franco and Uncle Tonio listened and kept an eye on the brothers.

"Pop came out," said Dimitri. "Heard the shots. Pop had his gun out. He saw Stavros on his knees, his hand over his eye, blood coming down. Pop went nuts. He was looking around like a looney. I think he said, 'Where?' "

"He said, 'Where,' " Stavros confirmed.

"So Pop looks at me," Dimitri went on. "I point ahead of the car. Pop goes running that way. I get out of the car and said something."

"You said, 'Stavros, stop shooting at me,' " said Stavros.

"Your father?" Lew said.

"Turned into an alley," said Dimitri. "Couldn't see him. Shots. Pop comes back, gun in his pocket and says, 'Posno.' "

"They put me in the car and took me to the hospital," said Stavros.

"What does Posno look like?" Lew asked.

"Like a bald Sylvester Stallone with a beard," said Stavros. "Broken nose, white scar on his chin. Doesn't smile. Pop says he doesn't have the beard some of the time."

"Wait," said Tonio. "How'd you two get in here?"

"Broke a window in back," said Stavros.

"Herman, how much is a window?" asked Tonio.

"One hundred and fifty would be fair," said Herman.

"I'm not trying to be fair," said Tonio. "I deserve a small profit for having my place of business violated." He looked at Dimitri and Stavros. "Two hundred and fifty dollars."

With fifty dollars from his brother added to the two hundred he had in his wallet, Stavros came up with the cash and handed it to Herman.

"Now?" asked Franco.

Lew nodded.

Franco and Uncle Tonio marched the wounded brothers through the warehouse and out onto the loading dock. Lew followed, a gun in each hand. Stavros and Dimitri walked wounded across the shipping dock, went down the stairs, got in their car and drove away.

"I'll take those," said Herman.

Lew placed the guns in Herman's hands.

"They should go to the police to be checked against the bullet that killed a lawyer named Claude Santoro," Lew said.

"Our fingerprints are all over them," said Franco.

Herman tucked one of the guns in his pocket, took the other, disassembled it, looked down the barrel. He did the same thing with the second gun. The entire process took him no more than two minutes.

"Neither of these guns has ever been fired," Herman said, handing the weapons to Tonio who looked at Lew.

"Want me to put them someplace safe?" he asked.

Lew nodded.

"You want that sandwich?" asked Tonio.

"Sure," Lew said.

A few minutes later, seated behind the desk on the same wooden swivel chair Lew remembered as a kid, Uncle Tonio told them about the time Sam Giancanna had bumped into him when Tonio was coming out of Donellini's.

"I fell on my ass," said Tonio, holding a potato chip up to the light. "Guy with Giancanna picks me up. Giancanna apologizes. I know who he is. I say, 'Sure, no harm.' Giancanna nods. Guy with him reaches under his jacket. I figure they're going to make me full of holes. Guy hands me a bunch of twenty-dollar bills folded over. I thought about handing the money back."

"Not a good idea," Franco said.

"No," Tonio agreed. "I pocketed the money. Took Herman back to Donellini's the next night and spent it."

"*Vitello Picata* and pasta," said Herman, who sat on a wicker chair that would have dropped a heavier man, like Franco, into a comic pratfall.

"Think there's a fixed rate for everything?" asked Franco, chewing on a sausage sandwich. "I mean like this Posno. You know, like four or five thousand for a broken arm or leg? Maybe a hundred thousand to kill you?"

"Twenty thousand," said Herman.

"And that's on the high side," added Tonio. "You want it done nonprofessionally, you can get it for less than five hundred dollars, a crackhead for less. A good pro, you get to choose your method and whether you want it to look like suicide. Want something exotic, you pay a price, you get it."

"Can opener," said Herman.

"Right," said Tonio, remembering. "We read this book by —"

"John Lutz," Herman completed.

"Right," said Tonio. "Guy kills another guy with a can opener."

"How?" asked Franco, his cheek bulging with the last of his sandwich. "Wait. I don't want to know."

"Lewis," said Tonio. "You got someone you want killed?"

"No," Lew said, getting up. "I've got someone I want to talk to."

"Who?" asked Franco, rising.

"Rebecca Strum."

5

"Maybe you should call her, be sure she's home," said Franco as they headed south down Lake Shore Drive.

"We'll try," Lew said.

The phone beeped as they passed Soldier Field. Franco picked it up and handed it to Lew.

"Milt," Holiger said. "Lewis, I'll give you the ruthlessly edited version of what I've got. Can't do more now."

Lew could hear street sounds behind him.

"Santoro, the dead lawyer. Can't find a connection. Never represented Pappas or Posnitki. Never faced them as witnesses in court as far as I can tell. I'll keep digging."

"No Posno?"

"Name came up on a couple reports, a few newspaper articles, on Web sites. Just the name. No arrests. No convictions. Same photograph of him appears on three Web sites."

Milt described Posno. The description matched the one Stavros had given. He gave Lew a Web site address. Lew wrote it in his notebook.

"Thanks, Milt."

"Lew, the police want to talk to you and Franco. They have you on video at Santoro's building and one of Santoro's partners says he saw the two of you outside their office. You're not suspects. Santoro was shot long before you got there. But you left the scene."

"We called 911."

"Right," said Milt. "Might want to call the detective handling the case, Alan Dupree."

"Little Duke," Lew said.

"Yeah. Know him?"

"Yes," Lew said.

"I've got to go," said Milt. "Call me later."

He hung up. Lew held the phone in his hand and told Franco what Milt had said. Then he pulled out his notebook, found a number and punched it in. He asked for Detective Dupree. A woman came on.

"Your name?" she asked.

He told her.

"Please hold," she said.

Lew held, heard a double click and Little Duke's raspy voice. Dupree was black, about six-two and one hundred and eighty-five pounds. His body was lean and hard, his hair short and curly, and he would have been handsome if it hadn't been for the pink raised scar that jutted from the right corner of his mouth to below his chin line.

Little Duke was a workaholic, a cop who doled out street-corner and bar room justice. Crime in his area was a personal affront. Dupree had been the principal detective in four of Catherine's cases. Lew had done the legwork and research on the cases for the State Attorney's Office.

"Lewis Fonesca?"

"Alan Dupree."

"We need to talk," he said. "Where are you?"

"Where do you want me to be anytime after four?"

He told Lew and added, "You've got another guy with you. Bring him too."

"I'll bring him," Lew said.

Lew looked at Franco who shrugged. Little Duke had hung up.

They found Rebecca Strum's apartment building in Hyde Park about four blocks from the University of Chicago campus. Franco parked illegally, turned on the flashing red light.

"Nobody tows a tow truck," he said. His mantra.

No doorman. Neat, clean, no-nonsense empty lobby with lots of glass and no framed prints on the walls. There were three black benches with no backs.

Next to the elevator was a telephone and a list of tenants with a number to punch in. The elevator slid open and two people came out. The man was lean, short, a pink-faced man wearing denim pants and a red-and-brown flannel shirt. The woman was tall, young and very pretty with smooth black hair. She wore denim pants and a blue sweater. She towered over him.

As the pair passed, the man, excitedly and with much hand movement, said, "If Samuels really meant what he said, if he followed through to the logical, the only conclusion, he would realize that his entire premise had been toppled."

"Victor," the young woman said patiently, "that would not be the only conclusion."

They had paused at the entry door. Franco motioned Lew to join him in the elevator.

"All right," said the man with resignation. "You're the professor. Explain."

Lew got into the elevator just as the woman said,

"It's the Posno fallacy."

Franco reached over to hold the closing elevator doors. Lew stepped out. The couple had already gone outside. Franco and and Lew hurried after them.

They were standing on the sidewalk, facing each other. He was talking again, arguing over whether Mahler was superior to Bruckner.

"You said something about Posno," Lew said.

"Yes," the woman said. "You think Posno was right?"

The man looked at Franco and plunged his right hand into his pocket.

"Who is Posno?" Lew asked.

"You don't know?"

"No, enlighten me."

"Posno," she said, "is a maniacally ambitious, talented economics professor at Sanahee University, a self-proclaimed expert on not only micro- and macroeconomics, but politics, philosophy and astrophysics."

"Andrej Posnitki," the young man said, eyes on Franco. "Grad students and faculty call him Posno to evoke a name that suggests a mythical monster."

"Grendel, Cronos, Scylla," she said.

"Where can we find him?" Lew asked.

"Library," said the man.

"Which library?" Lew asked.

"Almost any library," said the woman. "Andrej Posnitki, Posno, is a character in

Campbell Restin's novel *More Fool That.*"

"Won the Ledge Award, the Millman Award and was a strong contender for the National Book Award in 1978," the woman said.

The man and woman moved down the sidewalk. His voice rose with animation with the name *Bruckner.*

"What the hell's going on, Lewis?" asked Franco.

"We're looking for someone who borrowed a name," Lew said. "Or a mythical monster."

The corridor on the eighth floor smelled of Lysol and gardenias. The carpeting was gray, the walls muted white. They moved to Rebecca Strum's door.

"I don't believe this, Lewie. Anyone can just go up an elevator and knock at Rebecca Strum's door. She's . . ."

"Famous," Lew said, using the brass door knocker and stepping back. The door opened almost instantly.

Rebecca Strum, no more than five feet tall, hair thin and white, skin clear, a thin book in her left hand, stood looking at them with a smile that made Lew think she knew why they had come to her door.

"Yes?"

"My name is Lewis Fonesca. This is Franco Massaccio. You had a car accident four years ago, a car bumped into you on Lake Shore Drive."

"I remember," she said, pulling up the drooping sleeve of her olive-colored sweater.

"About ten minutes before that my wife was killed on Lake Shore by a hit-and-run driver in a red sports car."

"I'm very sorry for your loss," she said. "Red sports car?"

"Yes."

"Come in."

They followed her into the living room. The windows looked out toward downtown Chicago. The room was neat, uncluttered, only one picture on the wall, a large blown-up photograph of a harbor surrounded by tree-covered hills. The rest of the wall space was lined with shelves filled with books evenly lined up, most of them hardcovered. Facing the window was a desk nestled between two bookcases. On the desk was a pad of yellow lined paper, about half the pages tucked under it, and an open laptop computer. Nothing else.

They sat on three identical chairs padded with green pillows and matching arms. Rebecca Strum kept the thin book in her lap and said, "Coffee?"

"No, thank you."

"No," echoed Franco, looking at the shelves of books.

"Can you tell me again what happened?" Lew asked.

"It was more than four years ago," she said. "Why now?"

"I've been asleep," Lew said.

She nodded in understanding and said, "The driver was a man, Asian, probably Chinese, about forty-five. His eyes were moist. I think he had been crying. He may have been drinking, taking drugs or suffering from a mental disorder or possibly a trauma. His driving was erratic, weaving back and forth. He . . . never mind."

"What?" Lew asked.

"The look on his face was very much like yours right now, the same look of grief and mourning of people who have had their pretenses, illusions, masks, torn from their faces. Gaunt, haunted in despair, a legion of brothers marching to hell."

"You wrote that," Franco said.

"Yes."

"*The Dirt Floor,* right," said Franco. "That's the only thing I memorized and I wasn't trying. My wife is the real fan. No *fan* isn't the right word. Respecter, admirer?"

Rebecca Strum nodded and smiled.

"In the window of his car the red sports car," she said, "there was a yellow-and-red parking permit about the size of a sheet of typing paper cut in half."

"Did you tell the police this?" Lew asked.

"I didn't remember till several months ago when I saw a permit on a car exactly like it parked on 51st Street. I didn't think the police would be interested in a minor traffic accident after four years. Had I known your wife had been killed by this car, I would have called the police. Not a sin but a misdemeanor of omission. 'Had I but known' is the historical cry of people who do not accept their responsibility, their guilt. How can you heal if you don't accept that you are ill? The Germans in the town next to the concentration camp where my family died and I . . . I'm sorry."

She placed her book next to her on the arm of her chair and tugged at her sleeve. She had pulled it back just enough for Lew to see the first three numbers tattooed on her right wrist.

"Now, may I anticipate your next question?" she asked. "First, yes, I would recognize the man in the red sports car. I told this to the detective who talked to me after the accident. Second, the parking pass in the window of the car on Fifty-first was for

Mentic Pharmaceuticals in Aurora. Now, I'm sorry but I must finish rereading this today," she said, putting a hand on the book. "Dante's INFERNO. I'm having a discussion of it on campus tomorrow with some graduate students who will understand it but won't feel it. It's not their fault. Have you read it?"

"No," Lew said.

Franco nodded no.

"You might want to," she said, looking at Lew. "It's about the poet Dante's descent into Hell and Purgatory and then to Heaven."

She looked at the book and then at her shelves.

"At lectures, discussions," she said, "I ask people if they have read Dante, *Moby Dick* or *War and Peace, Crime and Punishment, The Iliad, Sister Carrie.* The answers are always the same. They say they have read them all. When asked to tell me something about the book, it becomes clear that the reading was far in the past and forgotten and perhaps they have deluded themselves into believing that they have read the classics. They feel guilty. They vow to themselves to immediately read something by Thomas Mann. You understand?" she said.

Lew nodded. Franco said, "Yes."

"It is human nature," she said, "to believe you have learned from the past, that you remember it when, in fact, you must make the effort to keep the past alive. I did it again, didn't I?"

"What?" asked Franco.

"I lectured to you."

"No," said Franco.

"Yes," she said. "I've been doing it long enough to recognize my somber certitude when I hear it."

She touched the number tattooed on her wrist. Lew's need to find out what had happened to Catherine should have seemed small compared to that number on Rebecca Strum's wrist, but it didn't.

"Is there anything else?" she asked.

"Posno," Lew said.

She looked puzzled.

"Posno? That's a character in some book I think," she said.

"Yes, Andrej Posnitki, Posno."

"I've never read it," she said.

Franco shrugged.

"Would you check the name on the Internet for us please?" asked Lew.

"Lewie," Franco whispered loud enough for her to hear. "You know who you're asking to —"

"No," she said, getting up with the help of

both hands placed just above her knees. "It's fine. Now I'm curious about why a man with a face worthy of Munch should want to know about a character in a novel."

She moved to the desk by the window and sat slowly, hands on the arms of the wooden desk chair. Lew stood over her left shoulder, Franco over her right.

"Years ago," she said, "Well, really not that many years ago, I used to do this for Simon Weisenthal."

Her dappled fingers danced over the keys of the laptop and images, lists popped up and then stopped.

"Thirty-seven-thousand six-hundred and seven hits," she said. "Not an unusually high number even for as obscure a fictional character as Andrej Posnitki. Colley Cibber, a very minor actor, poet and playwright, has more than ninety-nine-thousand hits. Cibber was an actor known most for the fact that Alexander Pope ridiculed him in *The Dunciad*."

"Posno," Lew said. "Are there any hits for Posno?"

Her fingers danced again.

"More than eighty-eight thousand," she said. "It seems to be a Dutch name. Let us see. Posno Flowers, Posno Sporting Goods. Is it possible to narrow the search?"

"We don't want to keep you from Dante," Lew said.

"Dante has waited more than six hundred years," she said. "He can wait and the students can wait a few minutes longer. Narrow the search."

Lew knew what that meant.

"Posno, crime, murder, trial," Lew said.

She tapped in the words, clicked on search, narrowed and said, "One Web site devoted specifically to what appears to be your Posno. Look."

On the screen in the upper left-hand corner in boldface was Posnitki, Andrej (Posno).

It was followed by three paragraphs. Lew and Franco leaned forward to read, but Rebecca Strum said, "I'll print it for you."

She pushed a button, and then another and a rumbling sound came from under her desk. A few seconds later she reached down and came up with a printed sheet. She handed it to Lew and got up, a little more slowly than she had from the green chair.

"Thank you," said Lew.

"One more thing," she said, and with her book moved across the room and through a slightly open door.

It took her no more than ten seconds. When she came out, she held a different, thicker book in one hand, a pen in the other.

"Your wife's name?" she asked Franco.

"Angie."

"Angela," Lew said.

Rebecca Strum nodded, opened the book, wrote something in it and handed it to Franco.

"I just had a box of them delivered yesterday," she said. "I don't have room and I'd rather it go to someone who will read it than have it lay in a box in the darkness of a storage room."

"Thank you," said Franco. "You're . . . she thinks you're great."

Rebecca Strum shook her head and let out a two-note laugh.

"My two children think I'm a petty tyrant posing as a martyr. My husband, long dead, resented my notoriety and I never noticed. I've been frequently duped by emotional and financial criminals and used by frauds I didn't even recognize who played on my ego. A full list of my indiscretions, omissions and petty vices would compare with anyone who has lived as long as I have. I'm not great. It's enough that I've lived this long and can still speak out and write and have visitors, especially those who don't expect wisdom and don't expect me to remember when I do not wish to remember."

She touched Lew's arm and Lew and Franco left, the door closing gently behind them.

"Can you fucking believe that?" asked Franco, looking at the book.

He opened it as they moved to the elevator.

"Listen to this," he said. " 'To Angela, Imagine that we are holding each other's hand and walking together through the forest of the night.' And she signed it."

"Nice."

No one was inside the elevator when the door opened and they stepped in.

"What do you know about Rebecca Strum?" asked Franco.

"Not much."

"Come on, Lewis. Work with me here. I've got a point."

The elevator dropped slowly, a slight metallic clatter beneath their feet.

"Husband's dead," Lew said.

"And?"

Lew looked away, felt the sheet of paper in his hand.

"She's hiding her grief with a smile. She's resigned herself to the unfairness of life and she's dedicated herself to trying to understand and comfort others," said Lew as the elevator stopped.

"You're saying it like you're reading it off a Wheatie's box."

"Jewish woman who lived through the Holocaust," said Lew as they stepped into the lobby. "What she's been through is a lot worse than what I've been through and she's taking it better."

"Pretty good," said Franco. "But you're wrong about one thing."

"What?"

They were on the sidewalk again. Across the street a pretty girl with a blue backpack was hurrying somewhere, talking on a cell phone. Her long dark hair bobbed with each step. Lew had the feeling he had seen her before, a thousand times before.

"Rebecca Strum isn't Jewish," said Franco as they moved back to the truck. "Her husband was a Jew. I think she's a Lutheran or something like that. Her father was a Communist, landed the family in a camp. You should read one of her books, Lewie."

When they got back into the Franco's truck, the phone hummed. Franco picked it up, said, "Massaccio Towing." He handed the phone to Lew.

"Fonesca, my name's Bernard Aponte-Cruz," said the man. "I was the one with

Claude Santoro last night. We should talk."

"When?"

"Now," he said. "Right now. Claude had something to tell you. That's why we followed you last night. We got your number from the side of the truck. He said he was looking for the right time to get you alone. He never got the time. Now the police think I killed him."

"What did he want to tell me?"

"I don't know, but it had something to do with the bank."

"Bank?"

"Claude was a consultant for First Center Bank. He specialized in banking and insurance law."

"He wasn't a criminal attorney?"

"No, never," said Aponte-Cruz. "And he was a good guy. I'm telling you. He was a good guy."

"You worked for him?"

"He was my brother-in-law."

"Why did your brother-in-law need you with him last night? Why didn't he just talk to me?" Lew asked.

"Someone called him. He didn't know who. A man, said he should stay away from you or he'd be killed. That's when Claude called me. I'm not such a good guy. Shit, my aunt and uncle, Claude's mother and father, they live in Yuma. I'm going to have to call them, tell them. Shit. Claude was their only kid."

"Why didn't he just talk to me?"

"He wanted to check you out. He was looking for a safe place to talk and Claude was sure he was being followed. We were about to go into the house you were in last night when the cops showed up. Then you and Tow Truck came out and . . . come on, you know this."

"What did he —" Lew began.

The phone went dead. Lew hung up and the phone rang instantly. Franco picked it up and said, "Franco . . . right, right, I got it. Hold on. He covered the mouthpiece with his palm and turned to me. "Job. Parking lot downtown on Washington. You want me to get someone else to take it?"

"No," Lew said.

Franco nodded and pulled onto the street. Lew read the sheet Rebecca Strum had printed out.

Posnitki, Andrej (Posno)
Murderer. Assassin. Thief. Born in Kaunus, Lithuania, 1949. Accused of murdering a Russian Orthodox priest in 1969. Fled to Budapest. Fled Hungary in 1976 to avoid arrest and almost certain impris-

onment following the murder of five anti-Communist dissidents at a cafe.

Posno came to the United States illegally, moved from city to city, changed his name frequently. He made his services available to a Russian criminal organization.

Andrej Posnitki has never been arrested.

Andrej Posnitki has murdered more than thirty-five people.

One of those people he murdered in the Budapest slaughter was my father.

If you have any information or recognize the man below, please contact: Relentless, Box 7374, Boise, Idaho.

At the bottom of the page was a head and shoulders drawing in black of a heavyset man, head shaved, a nose that veered to one side from being broken, and a neat, short beard.

Lew held up the drawing for Franco, who looked at it and said, "Looks like the guy who always plays bikers on TV shows or that wrestler, what the hell's his name, the Blast. No wait, looks a little like that Packer's linebacker from a few years ago. Even looks a little like my brother Dom if Dom took off a few pounds, shaved his head and face. Dom even has a broken nose, but it goes the other way."

Franco demonstrated by pushing his nose to one side.

"I don't think Posno's your brother."

"I don't either," said Franco. "I'm just saying . . ."

Lew was spread too thin, too many people to see, too many strings to follow into the cave. He needed help.

As they drove, he picked up Franco's phone, took out his notebook and found Milt Holiger's phone number. In Lew's life, he had been able to remember only three telephone numbers. Not his own, not his parents. He remembered Catherine's phone number before they were married. He remembered his friend Lonnie Sweeney's phone number, still did, though he hadn't talked to Lonnie for at least fifteen years. Or was it more like twenty years? The phone number of the Texas Bar & Grille in Sarasota where Ames worked. That he remembered. Oh, yes, the number of his aunt Marie, the old number she hadn't used in at least twenty years.

Numerically challenged, Lew kept a stained and frayed sheet of paper in his notebook. On the sheet were the phone numbers of people and memories he had fled in Chicago, and people who had squeezed or pushed through the door into his life in Sarasota.

Lew had tried many times over the years to memorize the multiplication tables. Never could. Still can't. Ask him how much seven times nine is and he has no idea.

Milt answered his cell phone after three rings.

"Lew?" he said.

"How did you know it was me?"

"Caller ID. I've got the number you're calling from and the name of your brother-in-law Franco."

"How's your time?" Lew asked.

"Moving inexorably forward," Holiger said. "What can I do for you?"

"Roadwork."

A blue Mini Cooper driven by a clown smoking a cigar passed by and waved. The clown was in whiteface with a bulbous purple nose. A sad look had been painted on his face. He held up his hand. So did Lew.

"If I can help, sure," Milt said.

Lew told him about the Asian driver and the parking permit, and Santoro's working for the bank.

"Take your pick."

"Bank," he said. "I can walk over there. I'll give you a call. Not much more on

Posno on my end. How about yours?"

"A little."

"I'll keep looking."

Lew carefully folded the sheet of paper and tucked it into his notebook, reasonably sure neither he nor Pappas or his sons would find Posno. Lew remembered the sweet, proud smile on the face of Pappas's mother, who had divided her time between the kitchen and murdering her husband. He imagined Posno, broad, bald, hulking, being thrown into the Pappas kitchen. John or one of the boys would lock the door and Posno would be alone with Pappas's mother wearing an apron, smiling, holding an oven tin with a red pot holder in her left hand. The oven tin is filled with sweet honey treats. In her right hand, she holds a long, very sharp knife, which is ideal for both slicing phyllo dough and Posno's throat. He is twice her size, but he doesn't stand a chance in her kitchen.

"Lew? You there?" asked Milt.

"I . . . yes," Lew said.

"I'll call you when I have something."

"Thanks, Milt."

The call ended.

"You see that clown back there?" Franco asked.

"Whiteface, tufts of red hair, down-turned

painted mouth, cigar."

"Huh? I meant the clown in the SUV who cut us off. You okay, Lewis?"

"Sure."

But Lew knew he was decidedly not okay.

6

Little Duke Dupree sat across from Lew and Franco in a window booth at the Tender Restaurant on 76th Street. Little Duke had parked where he could see both his car and Franco Massaccio's tow truck through the window.

They drank coffee, ate the Tender Restaurant's famous oversized chocolate coffee donuts. The donuts were brought to the table by a powerful-looking black man who walked with a limp.

The Tender had been Little Duke's suggestion, a very strong suggestion. People were talking in other booths and at tables. Neat, clean, good food, the Tender was an eye-blinding contrast to the South Side bars in the neighborhood Little Duke had roamed for more than two decades, keeping the peace when he could, showing that he was the sheriff carrying the biggest gun and reputation, most of it myth, some of it true.

Lew had seen him in reaction and action twice.

Little Duke Dupree dressed the part, black pressed slacks, black shoes, a black turtleneck shirt under a black cashmere sports jacket.

Franco and Lew were the only white people in the Tender. The same was true of the pedestrian traffic outside.

"Santoro," said Detective Little Duke.

It wasn't a question. It was a name put on the table for Franco's and Lew's reaction.

"We didn't kill him," said Franco, huge half-eaten donut in hand.

Little Duke looked at Lew and put both hands flat on the table.

"You could have gotten around the cameras in the building, come in during the night, got away. Then you could have come back, let the cameras pick you up. Visual and timed video that when you were in Santoro's office, he was long dead."

"We didn't do it," Franco said.

"I believe you," said Little Duke. "What were you doing in his office?"

Lew told him the whole story. He didn't start it with the date he was conceived or born and he didn't include the heart of the story, the people. Little Duke took no notes. From time to time Franco nodded in agreement or said, "That's right."

Lew told him about Pappas and his sons, Posno, Rebecca Strum, the Asian driving the car that had killed Catherine. He told it in ten minutes. Told the story but not the characters. Lew knew that Little Duke would check police reports, first, to confirm that Franco and Lew had a run-in with Stavros and Dimitri on the Dan Ryan Expressway and second to confirm that Santoro and Aponte-Cruz had been questioned by the police.

Little Duke closed his leather-bound notebook and put it back in his pocket.

"We've got Aponte-Cruz," he said. "No weapon. The appointment book was missing from Santoro's desk."

Lew knew where this was going.

"Yes."

Little Duke looked at Lew, his eyes unblinking.

"Want some advice?" Little Duke asked. "Don't talk religion with a Baptist and don't try to stare down a violent crimes detective."

"I wasn't," said Lew.

"He wasn't," said Franco. "He stares like that a lot."

"I do?" asked Lew.

"You do, Lewie."

"You have it?" asked Little Duke patiently.

Lew had witnessed that same patience the last time he had seen Little Duke Dupree. Lew had been trying to find a possible witness in a fraud case. Little Duke had accompanied him to a house not far from where they were now sitting.

Two young men, black, stood in their way. One of the young men wore a black sleeveless shirt with a white thunderbolt on the front. He had the body of a weight lifter, the tattoos of an ex-con and the attitude of a drug dealer.

Little Duke had been patient. Word was that Little Duke's wife had left him after being there too many times when he had been patient. Word was she was now dead. Lew had heard the word. When it was clear that patience and reason were not going to move the two men from the doorway, Little Duke's gun had suddenly appeared. He had slammed the butt into the face of both young men, who were unprepared for the instant change in the policeman from a Father O'Mally to Jack Bauer.

Little Duke had broken both of their noses and wiped the bloody handle of his gun on the thunderbolt T-shirt of the man who was kneeling and holding both hands to his face to slow down the bleeding. Little Duke had stepped past them. Lew had followed. They found the witness, a pregnant girl no more than sixteen, in a second-floor apartment.

In the booth at the Tender, Franco looked at Lew, waiting for an answer to the question Lew couldn't remember. Franco's left cheek was bulging with donut. Then Lew remembered.

"Do I have what?" Lew said.

Little Duke looked very patient. He held out his hand palm up. There was a thick gold band on one of his fingers. Lew reached into his back pocket and came up with Santoro's appointment book. He handed it to Little Duke, who tapped the edge of the notebook on the table and opened it.

"He didn't have any appointments until ten," Lew said. "We were gone by then."

"You didn't have an appointment?"

"No."

"So what were you doing there?"

"He was looking for me," said Lew.

"Why?" asked Little Duke.

Franco's eyes moved back and forth between the detective and his brother-in-law, amazed at Lew's sleight of hand.

"Hey," said Franco, "we didn't kill him —"

"What's in the book?" asked Little Duke,

ignoring Franco.

"Dinner and bar appointments with Bernard Aponte-Cruz," Lew said. "Appointments with people, dinners, addresses and phone numbers of theaters, friends, restaurants, bars . . ."

"Gay bars," said Little Duke, sitting back.

"I didn't check —" Lew began.

"I will, but we found enough from Santoro's apartment town house to figure it out."

Franco wiped his chocolate fingers on a napkin.

"Hey," said Franco. "Let's say Santoro wanted to break out of the relationship. Right. Aponte-Cruz is a hit man, right? People who hire him who are not exactly sympathetic to alternative lifestyles, right? Santoro threatens to expose him and —"

Little Duke looked at Lew and said, "Bernard Aponte-Cruz was not a hit man. He was the security guard at the door of the Chelsea."

"The disco place," said Franco.

"Disco is as dead as Santoro," said Little Duke. "The Chelsea's the right-now hot spot, painful music, kids looking for drugs or sex they won't find. Gays of both genders looking for sex which they will find, and Bernard Aponte-Cruz at the gate."

"Aponte-Cruz and Claude Santoro were queer with each other," said Franco. "I mean they were lovers or something?"

"Yes," said Little Duke.

"Him and his brother-in-Law? Okay," tried Franco, rubbing his lower lip with a thick finger and coming up with, "Aponte-Cruz threatened to expose that Santoro was gay and —"

"Exposure wouldn't mean much to Santoro," said Little Duke, looking out the window. "In this city, inside the Loop, it might bring him more business. Outside the Loop, a successful good-looking guy like Santoro, it would make him very popular."

Three men in their late teens or twenties saw him and hurried by.

"Okay," said Franco. "So Aponte-Cruz killed Santoro? You just go pick him up, right?"

"Aponte-Cruz is dead," Lew said.

Little Duke drank some coffee and nodded.

"Right. Aponte-Cruz was shot about four hours ago in his apartment," said Little Duke. "No gun found. Bullets are 9mm. Odds are it's the same gun that was used on Santoro."

"Why?" asked Franco.

Lew looked down and then met Little

Duke's eyes.

"Maybe someone didn't want Santoro to talk to me. Maybe someone who was responsible for my wife's death."

"Possible," said Little Duke.

"Why are you on Santoro's case?" Lew asked. "It's not your district."

"I asked for the case," said Little Duke. "People downtown behind desks owe me favors. I called one in. Claude Santoro was my wife's brother, her only brother. We'll forget about where I got this," Little Duke said, tapping the appointment book inside his pocket. "One condition. You find anything, let me know."

Little Duke, got up from the booth and dropped a twenty-dollar bill on the table.

"Thanks," Franco said.

Little Duke, eyes still on Lew, nodded, walked to the door and went outside. The chatter level at the other booths and tables became louder.

"You palmed the appointment book in Santoro's office," said Franco.

"Yeah."

"We're partners, Lewis."

"I thought you'd be better off not knowing," said Lew. "You could say you never saw the appointment book, and you'd mean it."

"Lewis," Franco said, shaking his head. "We're family, right?"

"Yes."

"You've gotta trust me a little here," Franco said. "You know?"

"I know," said Lew.

The limping waiter came to the booth, pocketed the twenty and asked if they were finished.

"Cops pay for their food here?" asked Franco.

"Some do," said the waiter. "I'd pay Little Duke to eat all his meals here. Nobody messes with this place. All but the dumb ones, the really dumb ones. I can handle them. Anything else I can get you? On the house."

"Half a dozen donuts to go?" asked Franco.

"Done," said the man, who limped away.

The tow truck was parked at the curb. A quartet of men was leaning against it, side by side. They were all in their twenties or thirties, all needing shaves, all with chins up, and all with T-shirts and attitudes, all of them black.

Franco stepped up to the one blocking the passenger side door and politely said, "Pardon me."

"I don't think so," said the young man softly, meeting Franco's eyes. "You are not pardoned, not for any fuckin' thing you did, are doing, or will do for the rest of your motherfuckin' life."

"We were with Little Duke," Lew said.

"I don't see no Little Duke," the man blocking the door said, looking around. "I don't see no duke, baron, earl or king. I just see two white guys shitting their pants."

Franco shook his head and grinned.

"You find this funny, chubby?" asked the man at the door.

In answer, Franco handed Lew his bag of donuts, grabbed the man by the neck and hurled him toward the restaurant. The man had trouble keeping his balance, doing a trick dance to keep himself from falling. Two of the others against the truck cursed as they took an angry step toward Franco. Franco was ready, arms out. The man he had hurled was heading back to join the others.

"Okay," said the fourth young man, still leaning back against the truck. "That'll do."

The three men facing Franco stopped.

The fourth man, the one they had heeded, was short, teeth even, serious.

"We were just having some fun," the young man said. "No one has to get hurt either side and we don't want a visit from Little Duke. Get back in your truck, thank your God, and play with your rosary on your way home."

Franco was breathing heavily now, leaning forward, arms at his sides, eyes moving back and forth from face to face. Franco wasn't sure that he wanted to go.

"Let's go," Lew said.

Franco shook his head, lowered his arms, took the bag of donuts back from Lew and moved around to the driver's side. Lew reached for the handle of the passenger side door. His eyes met those of the leader.

"Eric Monroe," Lew said.

"No," said the young man. "I'm his kid brother."

"You look just like Eric Monroe," Lew said.

Monroe let out a small laugh and turned his head.

"You can tell black men apart?"

"It's what I do," Lew said. "What's your brother doing?"

"Playing for some team in France, hanging on, signing autographs, playing first base now, getting older, saving nothing."

"He was good," Lew said.

"Telling me?" Monroe said, tapping the brim of Lew's Cubs cap. "He was the best.

Still pretty damned good, but —"

Franco started the engine.

Lew reached for the door.

The young man gave him room to climb in.

When he lifted his leg, the shot came. The first pop of a Fourth of July rocket. The bullet thudded into the door.

The four men ran to the wall of the Tender. Lew looked up.

"Get your ass in that truck and get down" shouted Monroe. "Someone's shooting at you."

Lew climbed in and closed the door. Franco hit the gas.

As they pulled away, Lew saw an old woman across the street. She had a shopping bag in one hand. With the other she was pointing.

"I saw him," she shouted. "I saw the shooter, saw him clear as healthy piss. White man over by the alley, over there. Saw him."

Her voice drifted away.

"Posno?" asked Franco as they drove.

"Maybe."

"Who else wants you dead?"

"Maybe the driver of the car that killed Catherine."

"Posno, right? Same thing," said Franco.

The phone buzzed as they hit Lake Shore

Drive and headed south. Franco dug into the bag for a donut.

"There's a bullet hole in your door," said Lew.

"Damn. Toro can take care of that."

"Went through," said Lew, looking at the hole.

"Yeah," said Franco. "What're you gonna do? Shit happens."

The phone hummed.

Lew ducked his head and reached down as Franco hit the speakerphone button and said, "Massaccio Towing."

Milt Holiger's voice came on.

"Lew?"

"I'm here, Milt."

"Bank lead is a bust," he said. "I went there. Santoro did do a lot of legal work for First Center. Estate settling, bequests, nothing involving Catherine, you. Dead end."

"Thanks, Milt," Lew said, still with his head down. He and Catherine once had a small savings account in First Center.

"I'm sorry. Anything else I can do?"

"I'll let you know."

Lew sat up as Milt Holiger signed off. In Lew's hand were the mangled remains of a bullet. He showed it to Franco.

"Is it 9mm?"

"I think so," said Lew.

On the way south, they passed a late-model blue Pontiac with its hood up and a man with his hands in his pockets watching the traffic move past. Franco pulled in front of the Pontiac, turned on his revolving light and said, "Gotta check."

He got out and called back to the man, "Need help?"

"Yes," he said.

Five minutes later, the Pontiac was being towed, the man was squeezed in next to Lew, and Franco was making arrangements to bring the car to a garage in Naperville.

"Name's Kerudjian, Theodore Kerudjian," the man said. "I repair copy machines, business, home, whatever."

He handed Franco and Lew cards.

"But what I really want to do is direct," he said. No response.

"That's a joke," said Kerudjian.

"You know other ones?" asked Lew.

"Sure, you want to hear some?"

Kerudjian turned his head toward Lew. The man was probably in his late sixties, maybe he was seventy. He was short, baldness firmly established against a desperate island of gray hair.

With enthusiasm and arm movement, laughing at his own timing and punch lines, Kerudjian told a string of jokes, pausing after each to say, "Funny, huh?"

"It's funny," Franco agreed.

Kerudjian looked at each of them. He had been the only one laughing.

"You're not laughing," he said.

Lew looked at the man whose surface of good humor had suddenly vanished. Without it, Kerudjian wore a look of defeat.

"Lewie doesn't laugh," said Franco, "and I'm a little pissed right now. Somebody shot a hole in my truck. You see it?"

"I didn't know it was a bullet. . . ."

"It was. It is," said Franco. "Someone was trying to kill Lewie. He's my sister's brother."

"Lewie?"

"Me."

"When . . . ?"

"About half an hour ago," Franco said.

"This is a joke, right?" asked Kerudjian. "I tell a joke, you top me, right?"

"No," said Lew.

Kerudjian smelled of distant garlic, ink, hints of sweat.

No one spoke till they got to the garage. They dropped the car and the confused Kerudjian, who had given Franco a credit card to pay for the tow.

"Not bad," said Franco as they got back into the truck. "And I get a referral fee from

Raphael. It's a long tow to Naperville."

John Pappas never left his house. Never.

This was, Pappas knew, in crisp, sharp contrast with Andrej Posnitki who was forever moving, flittering, following, threatening, maiming, killing and reciting second-hand poetry.

Seated in the kitchen, Pappas, who had lived with Posno for years, could hear his former partner delivering a flat monotone recitation of a poem neither he nor Pappas understood.

Everyone seated at the heavy, knife-scarred wooden table knew the truth about the siege that kept John Pappas in his house. His mother, Bernice; his sons, Stavros and Dimitri; and John himself knew that it really wasn't fear of Posno that kept him inside the house.

John Pappas was agoraphobic. It had started suddenly, on a Sunday morning while he was reading the *Tribune* at this table. Nothing particular seemed to have triggered it. He simply knew that he was afraid to go outside. There were ghosts out there, people he had killed. It didn't matter if they were real ghosts or memory-conjured and imaginary. They were beyond the protection of his home. Even thinking about leaving the house started an undulating wave of anxiety that moved toward him, an invisible flow under the level of control and consciousness. To keep the ghosts away, and to keep Posno outside, Pappas simply stopped considering opening the door and stepping out.

And he blamed Posno.

Sipping his coffee as he chewed a grainy sliver of warm *halavah* his mother had finished this morning, John Pappas wondered if Posno was now afraid of being inside. It would be an almost Mother Goose irony.

> John Pappas didn't go out.
> Posno didn't come in.
> And so it was between them both
> They had much room to sin.
> "Irony," Pappas said with a grin.

"What, Pop?" asked Stavros, cocking his head to one side so he could clearly see his father with his remaining eye.

"Nothing," Pappas said. "Nothing."

Pappas knew too much about Posno. If the police or the State Attorney's Office or Fonesca found Catherine Fonesca's file, Posno would be done; John Pappas would be uncovered. Pappas could not, would not

170

allow that to happen. Pappas had only once killed emotionally. All of the other times, including the stabbing of LeRoy Vincent, had been acts of pride and payment, displays of professionalism. The people who hired John Pappas knew and respected him. Pappas was a legend in the darkened dining rooms of those, like him, who gave little value to the lives of those outside their family.

"We all die," one of his clients, Mitch Dineboldt, had said. "You just make the inevitable happen sooner."

"We're sorry," said Dimitri, playing with powdered sugar between thumb and finger.

"It's all right," said Pappas, reaching over to touch his younger son's cheek and then looking at Stavros. "You?"

Bernice Pappas sat back upright next to her son. Bernice was clean, hair neatly combed, wearing a dark dress and yellow sweater. She had been to church that morning, St. Adolphis Greek Orthodox Church. She had driven herself.

"I think you should kill him," she said.

Her grandsons looked at her. Her son turned away.

Stavros thought his grandmother was telling him and Dimitri to kill their father. Dimitri thought she was telling him to kill his brother. Pappas knew who she really meant.

"Kill them both," she said to her son.

Now the brothers thought their grandmother was telling their father to kill his two sons.

They feared their grandmother as much as they loved her baking. They knew what she had done with a kitchen knife. Dimitri and Stavros Pappas also both knew that she was insane.

"Your grandmother means Fonesca and Posno," Pappas said with a sigh.

"In the pay of others, to protect others, my son didn't hesitate to kill," she said. "Now to protect your family, yourself, you are a Popsicle."

Stavros and Dimitri had not lost their desire to escape, to get away, but it would have to wait. The brothers looked at each other. They both knew, understood, that the threat of Posno and the possibility that Fonesca might find the file were real.

"Posno will die," Pappas said.

"And the nice Italian?" she asked.

"Fonesca," Stavros said.

She nodded.

"We wait till we're sure he has that file or that he won't find it," said Pappas.

"No," she said, shaking her head and moving to the oven.

"We wait," said Pappas.

Neither Dimitri nor Stavros had ever killed anyone, but their father, sitting benignly lost in thought as he drank thick, black coffee, had told them that he had never felt hesitation or guilt when he had "assassinated."

"Tonight," said Beverly, getting up slowly, hand on the table to steady herself. "I'm making my lamb, couscous and peas. Soup will be a surprise."

Pappas wondered what Posno would be having for dinner and where he would be having it.

Andrej Posnitki had a bowl of Vietnamese soup with noodles, vegetables and pieces of fish. He sat at the counter of the little storefront restaurant-grocery on Argyle off of Broadway. His was the only non-Asian face among the twenty-seven customers. He had a Kiran beer, no glass, and ate. The other customers talked quietly and occasionally looked his way.

Posno had tucked a napkin under his collar. He ate seriously. He was more interested in quantity than quality, but he had limits and favorites. Pasta of any kind satisfied him, if there were enough of it. He ate the noodles slowly, carefully, noiselessly, wielding his chopsticks expertly to pluck out noodles, bits of fish and even tiny peas.

Music was playing, generic Asian music, the same rippling strings, the same beat, that he heard in every Thai, Japanese or Chinese restaurant.

He would kill Fonesca. The little wop would find that incriminating file of Catherine Fonesca's and then he would kill him and then deal with Pappas. He and Pappas, the phony Greek, had never been friends, but they had been tenuous partners. And now Pappas wanted to protect himself, to let Posno take the blame for all that they had done. Pappas wanted to destroy him.

It would not happen. It would not happen unless Pappas was willing to go down with him. It would not happen if Fonesca were dead and that file found and destroyed. And that is just what Andrej Posnitki fully intended to do.

7

Inside Toro's Garage, Lew sat behind the wheel of a white 1993 Cutlas. The car had belonged to Ernest Palpabua, a Samoan former left tackle for the Green Bay Packers and later a wrestler. Ernest had plowed the Cutlas into a horse. It turned out to be a stroke of luck for the Samoan, but not for the dead horse or the Cutlas.

The horse belonged to a park policeman. The Cutlas belonged to Ernest Palpabua and Ernest belonged to the media. His encounter with the horse landed him on the front page of the *Sun-Times,* photograph and story. That night the Marigold Stadium, where he was wrestling, was jammed. Ernest, now suddenly known as the Samoan Horse Killer, was popular. He had enough money for a new car. Toro bought the old one and Lew Fonesca now sat in it.

Lew hadn't driven in Chicago for a little

more than four years. He didn't want to do it now.

The car was idling in the shadows in front of the wide entrance to the garage, hiding from the October sun. On the other side of Taylor Street beyond the entrance, he could see the walls of a soot-stained three-story yellow brick apartment building. In front of the entrance to the apartment was a small circle of dirt in the cracked concrete sidewalk. Inside the circle was a lone stunted tree, its few yellow leaves fluttering in the wind.

The leaves were beckoning him to come out of the shadows. Lew didn't trust the leaves.

When he and Franco had gotten back to the house, Angie had been there. Franco, the book tucked under his arm, had eagerly told her what had happened, ending with the confrontation with the four young men and the bullet that hit the truck.

Angie didn't look happy. She didn't even look tolerant.

"Let me get this straight. You were in a black neighborhood," she said. "Four guys confronted you. Someone shot a gun. There's a hole in the truck."

"Well, that's the short tale," Franco said.

"It's the one I prefer," said Angie. "Who

was the shooter trying to kill or was he just having his usual afternoon of street target practice?"

"Ange, you don't know what it was like."

"I had to be there," she said.

"Yeah, you . . . no. I'm glad you weren't there. Listen."

Franco, book still under his arm, retold the story, adding a dance of hand and body movements.

Lew had sat at the dining-room table, hands folded in front of him. Though he had said nothing, his sister's eyes returned to him as Franco savored his tale. Angie spoke to her brother without saying a word and Lew answered silently.

"You should have seen, Ange," said Franco with a shake of his head. "You should have seen. We're gonna grab something to eat and go after the guy in the car that —"

He was going to say, "killed Catherine," but he caught himself. Franco held the book out to Angie. She looked at it.

"I just finished this one," she said.

"I know," said Franco. "Open it."

She did and read the inscription: " 'To Angela, Imagine that we are holding each other's hand and walking together through the forest of the night. Rebecca Strum.' "

She looked at her brother.

"Is this real?"

"Yes," said Lew.

"What's she like?"

"Probably what you'd expect her to be from her books," said Lew.

"You haven't read any of her books, Lewis," Angie said.

"I'm going to."

"Think I could meet her?" asked Angie.

Franco put his arm around her and said, "Sure. We just knock at the door. Right, Lewie?"

"I'm going alone," Lew said in answer.

"What do you mean?" Franco said. "Go where?"

"He means," Angie said gently, "he's going alone to find the man who killed Catherine. Call Toro. Tell him to get a car ready."

"That right, Lewie?"

Lew nodded. It was right.

"Hey," Franco said, "What if . . . ?"

"Lew can deal with 'what if,' " Angie said.

Now, behind the wheel of the Cutlas, window slightly open, Lew could smell the grease of the garage, hear the shush of the wind bending the beckoning tree.

He remembered Rebecca Strum's inscription for Angie. There's a forest of the day too, he thought, and only one hand he wanted to hold. He turned on the radio and pushed the buttons seeking a voice, any voice. What he did not want was music.

He stepped on the pedal and drove into the day.

"The ulcer," said Dr. Royale after he finished his examination of John Pappas.

Donald Royale was John Pappas's physician for one reason: he made house calls and asked no questions about why John didn't come to his office the way the rest of the dysfunctional family did. Dr. Royale did not believe in agoraphobia. Oh, yes, there were half-crazy people like Pappas who didn't or wouldn't leave their houses, apartments, mental hospitals or sewers, but the reasons were all different. Lumping them together and giving them a name was of no help in treatment. Each case had to be dealt with individually. It needed a psychiatrist. Dr. Royale wasn't a psychiatrist. He didn't even want to talk to his patients about their fears of flying, shellfish, small spaces, death, water, tomatoes, Africans and going outside their homes. Such cases he immediately referred to Jacob Crasker, who was a psychiatrist. For Jake Crasker's prescriptions, the borderline crazies would pay mightily. For Jake Crasker's willing ear and tough-love advice, they would pay even more.

There were times when Dr. Royale believed the cost of Jake Crasker's treatment was the price these people deserved to pay for not taking care of the problem that they created. Royale had his own problem, a painful, twisted and inoperable vertebrae. He had lived with it for more than fifty years. He took pain pills, new ones when they came out, and prided himself on not letting the pain ever show. He stood straight, smiled benevolently and catered to the well-to-do. Dr. Royale was corpulent and double-chinned, hair brushed back and flat, the collar of his shirt always a bit sweat-stained under the same blue suit he always wore. Donald Royale was a mess, but John Pappas also knew he was smart and a damned good doctor.

The examination was done in Pappas's den-office and now they sat across from each other, Pappas in his usual seat on the sofa by the low table, Royale in the same place Lew Fonesca had sat the day before.

"So," said Pappas, "I just keep taking that white stuff and that's it?"

Pappas knew what the white stuff was and Dr. Royale knew he knew. Pappas smiled. He lived for games like this.

"That's it," said Royale. "And something new."

"What?" asked Pappas, reaching for an apple in the silver bowl on the table.

"You should get out of this room, this house," Royale said. "It's closing in on you and your ulcer. You didn't call Dr. Crasker for an appointment."

Pappas held the green shiny apple in his hand and looked at the doctor.

"I'll think about it. What else? You were going to say something else."

"Forget it," said Royale, getting up and reaching for his black leather bag.

The bag, which looked exactly like the black leather bag in Norman Rockwell paintings, had cost almost five hundred dollars. Dr. Royale didn't want to risk his retainer, but his obligation to his patient overcame his love of fine new cars, a home in the Bahamas, another in Maywood and an apartment on 57th Street in New York that was a block away from Carnegie Hall. All of them had hot tubs that soothed Royale's spine.

"I think you should see Dr. Crasker."

"Shrink? You want me to get shrink-wrapped?"

He bit into the apple, grinning.

"He would be willing to make a house call. Talk to him once. Then decide," said Royale.

"I told you last time I don't need a thera-pist," said Pappas, taking another bite of apple before he had finished chewing the first bite. His words came out with a gentle spittle that rained on the fruit. "Nothing wrong on that end. Trust me."

"I have a choice?" asked Royale.

"You take care of the body. I'll take care of this." Pappas tapped his head, still chew-ing. He got up, stepped around the table, remnant of apple in his left hand, jaws work-ing. He put his hand on Royale's shoulder and guided him to the door.

"Suit yourself," said Royale.

Pappas dropped his apple core in what looked like a ceramic bowl big enough to hold a bowling ball. The bowl was decorated with white figures of almost-nude men chas-ing one another around the bowl. Dr. Roy-ale had been told it was ancient Greek. Pap-pas was using it as a garbage receptacle.

"Want me to walk you to the door?"

"No," said Royale.

"You know, Doctor, you should get more exercise, work out a little. Forgive me, but you're a little overweight. You're busy, okay, but there's always a little time."

"I'll consider it," Royale said with a smile.

Taking advice from a neurotic patient who wouldn't listen to advice himself was not a likely scenario for Donald Royale.

"Oh, wait, almost forgot," said Pappas, snapping his fingers.

He moved to his desk and picked up a white paper bag. He handed it to Royale who knew from the smell that he was holding a bagful of *loukoumathes,* Greek donuts. Royale had considered trying again to convince Pappas to be seen by a therapist, but the prospect of losing the retainer and the goody bags of homemade Greek pastries was more than Dr. Royale could bear.

Pappas's mother, amazingly healthy, was beyond help. He was sure of that. Bernice Pappas, multiple murderer, made him uneasy. Whenever he treated her, she had looked at him with unblinking eyes as if he were an uncooked pork loin ready for roasting. At least it felt that way. Pappas? Well, there was definitely something wrong inside the head to which his patient had occasionally pointed. Pappas was alternately grandiose, paranoid, given to long ramblings about everything from Mayan Indians to the difficulties of establishing colonies in outer space. Royale couldn't give it a name. Crasker could and, if given the opportunity, would give it a name. Donald Royale really didn't want to know his patient's secrets, certainly didn't want to know the body count for which these people were responsible.

The sons might be salvageable. Probably not, but Royale was the family physician and he took his responsibility seriously.

Dimitri seemed almost normal, in need of his father and grandmother's approval, unwilling to step out of the circle of his family. Stavros, whose eye socket had healed well, was loyal to his father and dedicated to getting the man who had turned him into a cyclops, the man who was his father's enemy, the man whose name Royale had heard whispered. Posno.

When the front door had closed behind Royale, Pappas went down the stairs and to the kitchen where his mother sat drinking coffee and reading her favorite magazine, *Cottage Living.* She looked up over her glasses.

"The ulcer," Pappas said, touching his stomach.

"Stress," she said. "You've got too much stress in your life. Get rid of the stress. Get rid of Posno and then just kill the little Italian."

He nodded. She was right. She was a great cook but more than a little crazy. It ran in the family. His grandfather, Bernice's father, he had been crazy too, killed some people with a shotgun in a fishing village in Greece, had to get out of the country.

"They were looking at me with eyes of the devil," the old man had explained once, a year before he died.

Yes, his mother was nuts, but she was also right.

"The boys are out looking for Posno," he said.

"Good," she said. "It's time for Posno to die."

She kept repeating that. She was right, but she kept saying it and he wanted her to stop.

"It's time," he agreed.

A remnant of forgotten nightmare burst open. The doorbell had been ringing, ringing. Pappas had hurried to open it. When he flung it open, there stood Posno, grinning.

"Is this a bad time?" Posno had asked.

The doorbell had not been ringing. Posno was not there. But even Posno in his fleeting daydream had been right. It was a bad time.

Posno knew that Stavros and Dimitri were trying to find him. He had played with them, dangled hints, whiffs, suggestions through the words of a doorman, a waitress, a drugstore clerk.

Now he looked down at the street as the car parked and the brothers got out. They would go to his apartment. He had already moved out, but he had left hints, clues — a parking stub, a receipt for dry cleaning, a pad of paper with names and phone numbers. All of it was invention, none of it led to him. He enjoyed the moment. He liked the boys, was even sorry that he had shot Stavros. The shot had been a warning to the father. He had not meant to hit the son.

Couldn't be helped now.

While the brothers bumbled on, Posno came down the stairs in the building, went through the alley door and to his car parked a few feet away.

Fonesca. He had to find and kill Fonesca. Posno had decided that Fonesca couldn't be allowed to find Catherine's file. Something might go wrong. He might turn it over to the police before Posno could take it. Fonesca might not even find it, at least not this time, but would he come back? Wherever the file or files were, someone finding them, if anyone ever did, might not know they were important. No, the biggest threat to Posno was Fonesca. If he lived, the little man with the idiotic baseball cap could be the end of Andrej Posnitki.

Posno drove to his new apartment.

As Lew Fonesca pulled out of Toro's Garage on Taylor Street, the killer sat drinking a fresh too-hot cup of coffee. The cup was white ceramic with a quotation from his favorite president, Teddy Roosevelt, printed in red block letters: DON'T HIT AT ALL IF YOU CAN HELP IT; DON'T HIT A MAN IF YOU CAN POSSIBLY AVOID IT; BUT IF YOU DO HIT HIM, PUT HIM TO SLEEP.

He had entered Claude Santoro's office just after the sun had come up and found the lawyer behind his desk. Santoro had looked up with four seconds remaining in his life. Santoro had recognized the man who entered his office and took four steps toward his desk. Santoro couldn't remember the name of the man who now raised a gun and pointed at his face. If he had time, he might have remembered who his killer was, but probably not. If he had time, lots of time, he might think of a reason why someone would want him dead, but he had no time. If he had time, he might have done something to save his life.

The man with the gun had fired. The silencer had worked. He wasn't sure it would. He had never used one before.

He unscrewed the silencer, dropped it in

his pocket, and tucked the gun into the holster under his jacket. Then he had gone around the desk, checked the drawers and the dead man's pockets and stuffed the things he had taken into a jacket pocket. He had left enough to make it appear nothing had been taken. He had flipped through the dead man's appointment book. The killer's name wasn't there. He hadn't expected it to be. As he left, he was careful not to leave any fingerprints. His, if found, would be easy to match.

He had stood up and found himself looking into the dead eyes of Santoro, who had not even had time to register surprise.

He had neither hated nor disliked the lawyer. The two times he had met him briefly he had found Santoro pleasant, even likable. This had not been about hate or retribution. It had been necessity. If Santoro lived, the man who faced him now would go to prison. He would lose everything: his freedom, his home, his family, his self-respect. He had seen no choice. For a few moments just before entering Santoro's office, he had considered shooting himself, but that had passed. He had too many promises to keep. There were too many dark streets to drive down before he could sleep.

And, he recalled, carefully sipping the too-hot coffee, having once killed, it had been easier to kill Bernard Aponte-Cruz. Aponte-Cruz had been in Santoro's apartment when the killer got there to search through the dead man's papers.

Aponte-Cruz had a gun on the table a few feet from where he sat. A heartbeat later, the killer, who had killed no one before that day, was a double murderer.

And then Fonesca. He had followed Fonesca and his brother-in-law to the South Side diner, had parked in the alley, had waited. He saw Little Duke Dupree come out of the Tender. He knew Little Duke. When the detective was out of sight, the four young black men had moved from the sidewalk where they had been laughing, chattering.

He had heard one of the young men say, "Let's have us some fun."

"Pa-thetic," said another young man. "Messin' with couple of scared white civilians. Pa-thetic. That's all we got to do?"

"GG, just lean and be cool, chill, freeze," said another member of the group. "Dry ice."

"Whatever," said GG, leaning against the tow truck and crossing his arms.

And then Fonesca and his brother-in-law had come out and the hassle had begun and

Franco had grabbed one of the young men and then . . . the killer had fired.

He was not a bad shot. He wasn't a great shot. The bullet had pinged into the truck door a few inches from Fonesca's head. It wasn't until he had actually fired that the man who had already killed twice with this same gun realized that he had not meant to kill Fonesca. Had he killed him, the killer could have lived with it. He had been living with his guilt for four years and he had added murder to his shopping cart. But he couldn't kill Lew Fonesca unless he had to. Maybe the other thing he had done to deal with the Fonesca problem would be enough to send the man back to Florida empty-handed. Then again, it might not be enough.

As Lew Fonesca pulled out of Toro's Garage on Taylor Street and passed the thin small tree waving to him, the man who had run down Catherine four years ago and almost killed Rebecca Strum rose from his desk and looked around. The cardboard box he had filled with things from his drawers and on top of his desk sat on the floor near the door. He didn't pick it up. He had sort of planned to take the box, to the extent that he had planned anything.

He walked through the open door and

down the hall past the cubicles on his right where people worked silently and seldom looked up. He had withdrawn all of the money in his bank account. The thick wad of bills was wrapped inside a blue dish towel in the trunk of his car. It wasn't the same car he had been driving when he killed Catherine Fonesca. He had gotten rid of that car, sold it at a loss to Ralph Simcox, the mechanic.

It was early. He would go to the cafeteria and watch the clock. He would finish out his last day. No one would care. They would be happy to see him go. There was no denying that he had been drinking, though he had done his job, but there was also no denying that he brought an aura of gloom and doom when he entered the Mentic Pharmaceuticals building each morning. His expertise would be missed, but he could be replaced. Everyone can be replaced.

He was alone in the cafeteria. The lights weren't on but the sun was still high and the windows were tall and wide. The light on the coffee machine was glowing red but he didn't get a cup. He sat facing the brace of trees across the well-trimmed lawn.

As Lew Fonesca pulled out of Toro's Garage on Taylor Street and passed the thin small

191

tree waving to him from the small circle of dirt in the cracked concrete sidewalk, Dimitri and Stavros Pappas were waiting.

They followed in the car they had rented, Dimitri driving because he had two eyes. Fonesca knew their car, which was why their father had told them to rent this one, a bronze Mazda.

"We're really going to kill him?" asked Dimitri, staying back, being careful, remembering a few days ago when they had been cut off by the tow-truck driver.

They followed as Lew headed for Dan Ryan.

"You've got a gun. I've got a gun," said Stavros, his head and eye turned forward.

Stavros put his hand on the white paper bag between them, reached in and came up with two small, round cheese *tiropeka.* He held out one to his brother who took it and said, "That's not an answer. I like the guy. I feel sorry for him. Why does Pop want us to kill him?"

"To keep him from finding the papers, files, whatever his wife left. There's something in them that could hurt Pop. Hell, Dimi, you know that."

"I thought there was something in the files Pop could use to get Posno off our backs."

"There is," said Stavros.

"Then why did we stop looking for Posno? I could see us shooting *him.*"

"We can't find him. Fonesca is right in front of us."

"I know that," said Dimi.

They drove. Ten minutes. Twenty.

"We've never killed anyone," Dimi finally said, as much to himself as his brother.

"Tell me something I don't know," Stavros said, reaching into the bag for another pastry.

His stomach would surely bother him later. He was lactose intolerant. He had forgotten his pills. His grandmother always made her pastries with cream. It always gave him a stomach problem even when he took the pills, but he couldn't stop himself. No one in the family could resist his grandmother's cooking. Immediate brief comfort won out over common sense. It always did. He pulled out a sticky square of baklava.

"Five of Johann Sebastian Bach's sons became successful composers. You didn't know that."

"No, I didn't," said Stavros. "What's your point?"

"I want to go home and practice on my viola. My chamber group has a concert tomorrow. You remember that?"

"No."

"Well, we do. I want to play music, not kill people."

"We'll put that on your headstone: Dimitri Pappas. He wanted to play music, not kill people."

"Okay, so laugh."

"Hah."

"You want to be somewhere quiet, creating Web pages, inventing computer programs, whatever it is you do. You don't want to kill people either."

"Have a *melomakarona.*"

He handed Dimitri a Greek Christmas cookie. Dimitri popped the whole cookie into his mouth. Ahead of them Fonesca weaved the white Cutlas through traffic into the right lane. They followed. When he exited, they slowed down.

"We lost him," said Dimitri.

"He's right there," said Stavros, pointing at the car ahead of them.

"I don't see him," said Dimitri. "I think we should turn around and tell Pop we lost him. I think we should tell Pop that we're not going to kill anyone. If he wants someone dead, fine. He or Grandma can do it. They've done it before. They've got the experience."

He pulled the car off the road and stopped. Fonesca joined a stream of traffic moving away from them. Stavros turned and looked at his brother.

"We lost him," Stavros agreed, handing his brother the last pastry in the bag. It was another Christmas cookie.

8

His name, KEEN, was in capital black letters on the bronze rectangular badge pinned to his pocket. Keen's gray uniform, a size too large, sagged. He was somewhere in his late sixties, maybe he was seventy. His white hair was done in a buzz cut and his skin was the color of a flamingo.

Lew felt that if he touched the guard-receptionist's cheek, which he did not intend to do, he would leave a permanent white circle in a sea of pink.

Keen had been working on a fifth of Dewar's under the desk for almost an hour. It was the first time he had ever taken a drink while on the job, but today he had his reasons.

"Yes, sir," said Keen, seated behind the curved desk in the lobby of the five-story main building of Mentic Pharmaceuticals.

His voice echoed in the marble-tiled space sparsely filled with chrome-and-black leather chairs. The walls were empty except for one that held dozens of color photographs of smiling men and women.

Lew tucked his Cubs cap deeper into his pocket.

"I'm looking for a man who works here who drives a red sports car."

Lew had looked at the more than one hundred cars parked in the company's parking lot. Eighteen sports cars, two of them convertibles, none of them red. He had checked all of the sports cars to see if they had been repainted and if they were old enough to have been the one that killed Catherine. They were not.

"Why?" asked Keen.

"I'm a process server," Lew said, taking out his wallet and handed him his card.

Keen looked at the forlorn face on the card and at Lew.

"You're from Florida," Keen said. "You can't serve papers outside the state."

"I'm not here to serve him papers. I need some information from him."

An elevator pinged open behind the desk. A man and a woman in their thirties, carrying identical briefcases, both smiling, came out. The man said something. Lew thought it was, "Chestnuts."

Keen nodded to the couple who signed

out in the black leather-bound book on the desk. The couple looked at neither Lew nor Keen. When they had gone, Lew said, "He's Asian, the guy who has the red sports car."

"Asian? Four hundred and seven people work here, about one hundred are Asians. Biologists, microbiologists, immunologists, geneticists. What's he look like?"

"Asian," said Lew.

"Narrows things down," said Keen. "You don't know his name?"

"No."

"Never seen him?"

Lew shook his head no.

"Your lucky day, Fonseca," Keen said, handing the laminated ID card back to Lew.

"Fonesca."

"You got me on my last day," Keen said. "I'm retiring."

"Congratulations."

"Yeah. I'm officially retiring tomorrow, but I won't be coming in. You know why?"

Keen's hands were folded in front of him now, thick knuckles white.

"You don't like goodbyes," Lew said.

"You got it," Keen said. "You get called into the cafeteria. Everybody is standing there. There's a cake. It says: Thirty-four Years, Owen Keen, We'll Miss You."

"That's a lot of words to put on a cake,"

said Lew.

"Yeah. They'll smile at me, be taking peeks at their watches and the wall clock. Avery Nahman will make a little speech, hand me a bronze plaque that I'll stick in a box in my garage. I'll have to say a few words that no one wants to hear. No, I won't be there. Today's my last day. Why am I telling you all this?"

"I'm listening."

"You are that," said Keen. "Go over to that wall, the one with the photographs."

Lew moved to the wall, eight rows across and seven down of seven-by-nine-inch color photographs of people, about half of them Asian. On the bronze plaque above the photographs it read: EMPLOYEES OF THE QUARTER.

"Like Wal-Mart or something if you ask me," said Keen, still seated behind the desk.

"What am I looking at?" asked Lew.

Keen pointed and said, "Third row down, second photograph."

"Victor Lee," Lew read.

"Yeah, when some of them say it, it sounds like Victory. Not Dr. Lee. No accent. Good guy."

"He has a red sports car?" asked Lew, staring at the lean, dark-haired man with glasses and a smile that was something less than a smile.

There was a familiar look of something, maybe sadness in Victor Lee's face.

"Had a red sports car. Alfa Spider. Years ago. Had it and then one day he came in and didn't have it, switched to a Kia SUV, sort of gray."

"Is he here?"

"Signed out half an hour ago. Ask me he looked like a turtle turd, wiped to shit. That picture on the wall was the last high for Victor. Started to stop even faking a smile after that."

"When?"

"Don't remember. Three, four years ago. Funny, when my wife was alive we all the time planned to go south, New Orleans. Now there's no Ophelia. Hell, there's no New Orleans. My wife had a sense of humor. Said her claim to fame was that they had named a hurricane after her."

Keen laughed. Lew smiled.

"Fonesca, I'm retiring in two hours and I don't know what the shit I'm going to do or where I'm going. I'd move in with my brother, but he has a damn cat that . . . hell, I've only known you five minutes and you're my goddamn best friend. Everyone else I knew, family, friends, they're back in Philly or getting skin cancer in Florida. Our only kid, Dennis, got killed skiing when he was twenty-one."

"I'm sorry."

Keen looked up and said, "Yeah, I'll be damned, you really are. She was a good woman. He was a good kid. And I've always been a tough asshole. Now I'm old and I'm just an asshole."

"You have an address for Lee?"

"Hmm?"

"An address. Lee."

Keen nodded, punched open a pop-up address book and came up with an address in Oswego.

"I think I'll find an apartment around here someplace, settle things and then maybe try Florida. Where is it you live?"

"Sarasota," Lew said, writing the address in his pocket notebook.

"That where they have the race track?"

"That's Saratoga. Sarasota has greyhound racing."

"You like greyhound racing?" Keen said with some interest.

"Never went."

Keen nodded and looked down.

"Sarasota," said Keen to himself. "Might try it."

Twelve hundred miles away, in Sarasota,

the phone rang on Lew's desk. There was no answering machine. At the urging of Ann Horowitz, he had installed one for a while, but had dreaded the flashing red light that intruded on his sanctuary and refused to stop blinking.

Now the phone rang six times before Ames McKinney picked it up and said, "Yes."

Ames was making his daily stop at Lew's office-home to pick up the mail, see if anything needed fixing or cleaning up. Ames's scooter was parked in the Dairy Queen lot about thirty feet from the bottom of the concrete stairs and rusting railing of the two-story building. Lew had helped Ames when he had shot an old betraying partner on South Lido Beach. They had been friends since and just two days before Lew had left for Chicago, the two had sat at a table in the Texas Bar and Grille where Ames worked keeping the place clean and where he lived in a small room next to the exit near the kitchen. They had celebrated Ames's seventy-fourth birthday with a beer. No one else had been invited. No one had been told. Lew had given Ames the latest biography of one of Ames's heroes, Zachary Taylor.

"Fonesca?" said the man on the phone.

"No."

"Is he there?"

"No."

"Will he be there soon?"

"Don't know."

"Where is he?"

"Couldn't say for sure."

"Can I reach him? It's important, very important."

"Name and number," said Ames.

"Earl Borg. Tell him dogs and hogs. He'll know."

"Dogs and hogs," Ames wrote on the pad of lined paper he had brought and placed next to the phone.

Lew worked with worn-down pencils, writing on the backs of envelopes and flyers. His notes, including addresses and phone numbers, were stacked neatly in the bottom drawer of the desk.

Borg gave Ames the phone number and address.

"It is extremely urgent. A life is . . . just have him call me."

"You got troubles, maybe I can give you a hand till he gets back."

"You are . . . ?"

"Ames McKinney."

"And you . . . ?"

"Work with Lewis sometimes," said Ames.

A double beat and then Borg hung up.

Ames looked around the room, the outer room. There wasn't much to do. There wasn't much in the room to clean, straighten or fix. Ames had turned the window air conditioner on low when he had arrived. He had swept and straightened the lone painting on the wall, the painting by Stig Dalstrom was of a dark jungle with a hint of a moon blocked by black mountains. The only color was a small yellow-and-red flower. The painting was Lew. No doubt.

He had checked the other room, the small space with a closet that Lew called home. That space, Ames knew, would be neat and clean, everything in place, a cell waiting for inspection.

Lew had left his sister's phone number with Ames, Ann, Flo and Adele. Ames picked up the phone and dialed.

Victor Lee's house was in a three-year-old development called Oak Branch Park, two-story frame and brick family houses on lanes that circled, separating every seven or eight houses into discrete cul-de-sacs.

Three children about seven or eight years old, two girls and a boy, wearing sweaters and giggling, ran in the driveway. Lew parked and walked up the brick path.

One of the girls, a pretty, giggling girl who might be Lee's child, ran in front of him, looked up, shrugged her shoulders, said, "Excuse me," and ran on with the other two children in pursuit.

He pushed the button next to the door and a chime echoed inside. He waited and pushed again. When the door opened, a woman in her late thirties opened it and looked at him.

"Mrs. Lee?"

She was pretty, Chinese, dressed in a business suit and wary of the sad-eyed man wearing a baseball cap.

"Yes."

"Is Mr. Lee home?"

"I don't know. He doesn't live here anymore."

Lew said nothing. Waited.

"He hasn't lived here for almost two years," she said.

"I'm sorry," Lew said.

"So am I," she said. "Who are you?"

"I just came from Mentic Pharmaceuticals. This is Mentic's address for your husband."

"He didn't want anyone to know," she said. "He was, is, ashamed. You are the first one from the company who has ever come here. I can get a message to him if you like."

"Where does he live?"

"He . . . Victor is . . . is this really important?" she asked, still standing in the doorway.

The children screamed behind them.

"Yes."

She stood considering.

"When did you last see him?" Lew asked.

"More than a year, but I know he sometimes goes to our daughter's school and watches her come out and get on the bus. He told me. We talk a little on the phone, not much. Is this something that will cause trouble for Victor?"

"If there's trouble, it happened a long time ago," said Lew.

"Four years?"

"Yes, four years," said Lew.

She nodded and said, "He would never tell me, but one day he came home and he wasn't Victor anymore, not the Victor I knew. For two years he tried, but . . . he sends me almost all the money from his check every month."

Lew nodded.

"Can you give me his address?"

She hesitated and then told him the address and apartment number.

"He called me a few hours ago. He said,

'Goodbye.' That's all he said. Please go there."

Lew nodded.

Mr. Showalter,
  I have moved out. Here is my check for this and next month's rent. You may keep the deposit I put on the apartment when I moved in. I'm sorry for any inconvenience.

Victor Lee

The note and the check were inside an envelope with Mr. Showalter's name neatly written on it. The envelope was tacked to the door of the apartment.

Lee's apartment was on the second floor of a renovated three-story brick walk-up building in Aurora. The hallway smelled like strawberry Kool-Aid. A battle had been waged against determined mildew. The battle was being lost.

"I think that's for me."

A hand reached around Lew and took the note, envelope and check.

The man was about fifty, black, a compact car of a man, wearing a business suit and tie.

"Showalter?"

The man answered, "Umm" and read the note, shaking his head.

"Yes," he said, looking up. "Ving Show-alter. Who are you?"

The man could be thinking only one thing, that Lew, a little man in a jacket wearing a Cubs cap, was here to steal and had almost gotten away with the check Victor Lee had left.

"Lew Fonesca. I'm a process server."

Lew got his card from his wallet and handed it to Showalter who looked at it and handed it back.

"Florida? You've come a long way. What did Lee do in Florida, murder the governor?"

"He didn't do anything in Florida," said Lew.

"You want to show me the papers you are serving on Victor Lee?"

The man who weighed well over two hundred pounds set his legs slightly apart and blocked the way to the staircase.

"I'm not here to serve papers, just ask him a question."

"Yes," said Showalter slowly. "And that question is?"

"Did you kill my wife?"

"Did I . . . ?"

"No, that's my question for Victor Lee: Did you kill my wife?"

"You think Victor Lee killed your wife?"

"Yes."

Showalter shook his head and thought, Stay focused, Ving. Shit happens. You've seen worse and more will come. Just keep your focus on the investment. Clean the apartment, rent it if you can, remember you've got a two-month check in your pocket and you don't have to return the deposit.

"You know anyone looking for an unfurnished efficiency apartment?" Showalter asked.

"Maybe, a security guard at Mentic who's retiring, looking for something small, month to month."

"Really?"

"Yes."

"Okay," said Showalter. "What's his name?"

He had a pocket-sized leather-bound notebook in his hand now.

"Can I take a look at it first?" Lew said, looking at the door.

Showalter tapped the notebook against his leg and said, "Why not."

He opened the door and they walked in. A single wooden-floored room with a small bed against a wall, a desk and chair and a refrigerator and sink. Only one wall had windows, two of them looking down at the street. On the opposite wall was an open door to a small bathroom. The only thing on the walls was a small framed painting of a rainy empty city street at night, office buildings looming like black shadows, the only spot of light coming from a tiny window in one of the shadow buildings.

The room was also clearly and completely clean, sparse and orderly. The room seemed familiar to Lew. He knew why.

"As you can see, the apartment comes furnished," said Showalter, walking to the bathroom. "Including towels. But if the tenant has his or her own furniture, we can clear everything out."

Lew moved to the desk and opened the middle drawer. The only thing in it was an unframed and folded university degree.

"Okay if I take this?" Lew asked, holding up the degree.

"I don't —" Showalter began.

"Owen Keen," Lew cut in. "The man who might be interested in renting. His name is Owen Keen."

"Owen Keen," Showalter said, writing the name in his notebook. "I'll give him a call. Mentic Pharmaceuticals, you said?"

"Yes, can I take the painting too?" Lew asked, tucking the folded sheet of paper carefully into his pocket.

Showalter looked at the dark noir canyon on the wall.

"Sure," he said, moving to the window. "You want to give Mr. Keen a call and tell him?"

"I will," said Lew, moving to the painting and taking it from the wall.

"Is that valuable?" asked Showalter, glancing back at Lew. "If it is . . ."

"In money? No. I don't think so."

"I'll be damned," Showalter said, now looking down at the street. "He's back."

Lew, framed painting tucked under his arm, was at Showalter's side. There were plenty of spaces on the street. The gray Kia SUV was pulling into one of them directly across the street.

"Changed his mind," said Showalter with disappointment.

Victor Lee, lean, shoulders slightly slumped, got out of the car, adjusted his glasses and started across the street.

"No," said Lew. "He forgot to take something with him. He's coming back for it."

"What?" asked Showalter.

"This," said Lew, holding up the painting. "All right if I give it to him?"

"He can have it," Showalter said.

Victor Lee looked up at the apartment window. He stopped. He saw two figures, sun glinting, hiding their faces. His head dropped. He turned and moved back to the SUV. Lew moved quickly past Showalter. As Lew went through the door, Showalter called, "Call Keen, right away, okay?"

9

"Man said it was urgent," said Ames.

He was sitting at Lew's desk, blinds open, sun dancing in dust, sending a yellow band across the floor. Outside beyond the Dairy Queen lot, a sports car whoomed up a few gears and shot away.

"How each of us sees urgency is a matter of perspective," Ann Horowitz said. "What is urgent to this man may not be to Lewis."

She was in her office on Bay Street, a patient sat in the closet-sized waiting room beyond her wooden door. Ann was purposely keeping the patient, Stephen Mullex, waiting beyond his appointed time. Mullex should complain about his hour being cut short. She wanted him to complain, to assert himself. If he didn't complain, she would make that the issue of the session.

"Yes, ma'am," Ames said evenly.

"One man might well say he has an emergency, and mean it and sound like it, screaming, crying, when his car won't start and he will be late for a tuna match."

"Tuna?"

"Tennis," Ann corrected herself, wondering what, if anything, her slip might mean. Age? The ghost of Freud?

"Another man might call the police from his home and calmly announce that his family was being murdered by two men with axes downstairs and add that there was no hurry because everyone was dead."

"Were they?" asked Ames.

"Hypothetical," Ann answered. "How would you react?"

"Find a gun, knife, chair, lamp and go down after the guys with axes," he said. "By the time the police got there, they'd all be dead."

"Unless he killed his family," said Ann.

"Yes, ma'am. That's possible. If Lewis calls you, would you please have him call me at the Texas Bar and Grille. I left a message on his sister's phone, but he hasn't called back."

"I do have another number," she said.

Ames said nothing, waited.

"He asked me not to give it out. It's his brother-in-law's cell phone."

"Ma'am."

She looked at the digital clock on her

214

desk. The numbers were large. The time was ten minutes after the hour. Stephen Mullex had been kept waiting long enough. Ann gave Ames the number of the phone in Franco Massaccio's tow truck.

"I can be disbarred for betraying this confidence," she said.

"You're not a lawyer. You're a psychologist."

"Then getting disbarred won't hurt my career, will it?"

"No ma'am, it won't."

"I was making a joke, Mr. McKinney."

"So was I," said Ames. "Thanks for the number."

"Have Lewis call me."

She hung up. So did Ames. He dialed the number Ann Horowitz had given him, got an answering machine and said: "Lewis, it's Ames. Call me at your office."

Ames McKinney had a bachelor's degree and a master's degree in civil engineering. He had, less than a decade ago, been rich. He had written a book published by the University of New Mexico Press, *Some Things a Man Can't Walk Around: Individual Responsibility in Nineteenth-Century America.* The book had been well-reviewed in journals and even a few newspapers in New Mexico, Texas and Colorado. It had even been nominated for a Chino best nonfiction award. He had never mentioned the book to Lew or anyone else. When Ames's partner had taken all the money in their business and hid in Sarasota, Ames had come here, found him and the two had shot it out on South Lido Beach. The partner died. Ames had spent minimal time in jail because he had a witness, Lewis Fonesca. He owed his sad little Italian friend, but beyond that Ames liked him.

Ames called the Texas Bar & Grille and told Big Ed that he'd be coming back late. The collection of old guns on the wall, the choice of twelve different beers, the thick all-meat nearly raw burgers the size of a pie plate and Ed were the prime attractions of the Texas Bar & Grille. Ed, who grew up in New England, had decided one day to sell his chain-link business, part his hair down the middle, grow a handlebar mustache, buy a shinny vest and go West to become a saloon keeper. He got as far as Sarasota. He was red-faced and happy.

"Do what you gotta," said Ed.

Ed was also fond of saying, "There are some things a man just can't walk around," "Suit yourself," "I said I'd do it and that I full intend to do," "I'm a peaceable man so let's not have any trouble here." He had always avoided "A man's gotta do what a man's gotta do." There are some clichés a man's just gotta walk around.

Two hours later, after finishing the paperback copy of a Larry McMurtry novel, Ames picked up the phone and dialed the number Earl Borg had given him.

Pappas sat on the sofa listening to a CD of Dionysious Savopoulos's *Garden of the Fool.* The singer was one of his favorites, had been since he first heard his voice on on a Greek radio station almost forty years ago in Philadelphia. Philadelphia was home, had been home. It was where the good memories were, at least many good memories plus the ghosts of many friends and enemies. Philadelphia, in Greek, means "City of Brotherly Love." Savopoulos had been a kind of Greek combination of Frank Zappa and Bob Dylan with strong traditional Greek influences.

Pappas wanted to squeeze the coffee cup, but if he did, it would break. One of the reasons for using the delicate cups was that they were so delicate. They reminded him that he should have a soft touch. Sometimes, however, he forgot.

Loose ends. Holes. Sticky fingers. Weak sons. Weak knees. Mother is always right.

Like Hell. If mothers were like Bernice, they were wrong at least half the time and when they were wrong, they were wrong big time. I mean, I'm telling you, big, big time. But a mother is a mother. This one could kill and bake and loved her family.

Enough. Tomorrow he would personally take care of Posnitki. Their relationship was far too dangerous for Pappas and his family. The dead Posno would take to darkness behind the wall of death whatever information he had on Pappas. Posno would also take with him responsibility for all he had done in Pappas's name. He would even take with him responsibility for crimes he didn't commit. The door would be open.

Pappas felt his legs bouncing nervously. He got up, cup still in hand, and began to *sytros,* the traditional dance move that was simply part of him, the dance move popularized in *Zorba The Greek, Never On a Sunday* and *My Big Fat Greek Wedding.* Right foot out, arms up, circle counterclockwise in a shuffle-drag. The music wasn't quite right, but the dance was of the blood and the song in Greek.

It was a celebration now, a wake, a near-ecstasy. He smiled, eyes closed. He didn't hear the door open or close, but he did sense a presence near him. He could smell his mother, sweet of honey, crisp of phyllo. He opened his eyes. She was dancing next to him and smiling.

He imagined Posno next to him, dancing, smiling. Posno, his dark round face, bald head, deep eyes, heavy lips. Posno dressed in black knit shirt, slacks, shoes and jacket. Had they once danced like that? Pappas wasn't certain.

"Tomorrow," Pappas said. "He will die."

"Tomorrow," his mother repeated. "It will be easy."

"Yes," he said, moving his shoulders to the distinct beat, but he knew it would not be easy.

The SUV stayed inside the speed limit and out of the passing lane as it moved south on I-56. Three cars behind, Lew Fonesca knew where Victor Lee was heading. Lew had been down this highway before, before and after it had been widened.

Lew had no change of clothes, no phone, no credit cards. He had three hundred and eighty-two dollars in his wallet, all of what was left of the cash he had brought with him to Chicago. It should be enough. It would have to be.

He would have to call Angie and Franco as soon as he could, but that might not be soon. Victor Lee had stopped only once, at an Exxon station to fill his gas tank and buy something in a paper bag, probably a sandwich and a drink. Lew was parked at a pump four lanes over. He filled his own tank, went in to pay, looked out the window and saw Lee leaning back in his seat, rubbing a finger on the skin above his nose.

Lew took a chance, got a handful of change, moved to a phone against the wall near a window and fed the slot keeping his eyes on Lee, who now sat up and turned on the ignition.

"Massaccio Towing," said Franco.

"Franco, I'm following the guy who killed Catherine."

"Where are — ?"

"Franco, listen. I have to go. I'll try to call tonight, but I won't be back till tomorrow, maybe later."

"Lewie, McKinney is trying to reach you."

"I'll call him when I can."

"Lewis, what are you going to do?"

"I don't know," he said, and hung up.

He hurried out of the Exxon, but he didn't run.

The direction they were going, the diploma, the university degree Lew had taken from Lee's desk, pointed the way. Somewhere Lew had a similar diploma from the same institution. It too had been in a drawer, probably still was in Uncle Tonio's warehouse.

He turned on the radio, pushed buttons, flashing past Chicago FM stations he could still pick up, Spanish, Polish, Japanese, Swedish. Searching for a voice, any voice. He hesitated at a Greek station. Whatever song was playing made him hesitate and think of Pappas. He listened to the plaintive music that somehow felt right and left it on.

On the seat next to him was Lee's painting of the dark mountains of the city with the one spot of light.

In two hours, they would be in Urbana-Champaign.

Lew knew the way to I-56 and south through the corn fields, seed towers, bales of hay, dairy cows who had long ago stopped looking up at passing cars and noisy trucks, turnoffs for small towns, roadside diners with names like Mom's, Eat Da Voo, Minnie & Zane's.

What was it Ames had said once when they were driving across Florida from the Gulf Coast to Miami on the Atlantic Coast? They had passed farms, horses, cows and penned-in hogs.

"Government pays people not to raise hogs, not grow tobacco," Ames had said.

"Some people even buy farms just to not grow or raise something. You don't and I don't raise hogs or grow tobacco. Why doesn't the government give us money? Or better, why don't they stop giving money to people for not raising anything."

It was easy to remember this on-the-road exchange because it was the longest single speech Lew had ever heard from Ames McKinney. Lew hadn't said anything after the speech. He wasn't sure if Ames was or wasn't joking. Lew didn't want to find out. He did wonder what his friend would make of the massive fields on both sides of the highway.

Lew picked up a Springfield FM radio station. An English professor who specialized in the history of the early eighteenth-century British novel at Sangamon State University was taking on the president of the United States, solemnly doing his part to condemn and execute the president for everything from how he liked his eggs prepared to what he was or wasn't doing to stop the three-hundred-year-old battle between two small tribes in Gabon. The professor, with a reedy, excited voice, seemed to have memorized or was reading a list of offenses about which the professor had strong opinions. Lew listened through oil drilling in Alaska (the professor was against it), housing for the homeless (he was for it), saying Jesus in school or Wal-Mart (he was against it), abortion (he thought it was a good idea), intelligent design (he didn't see much evidence for it).

There was a call-in number. If he had a phone, Lew would have called in and asked if the man had any jokes he could share.

Lew turned off the radio when Lee stopped at a gas station to refuel and pick up a cup of coffee and a prepackaged box of half-a-dozen glazed chocolate donuts. Lew hurried to the men's room, past the urinal and into the stall that had a door that closed but didn't lock.

Lew finished and started to get up. The outside door to the men's room opened. Under the partition Lew could see Victor Lee's legs as he moved to the urinal.

"You're driving the white Cutlas?" Lee asked flatly.

"Yes."

"You're following me."

"You?"

"The SUV," Lee said.

"I'm driving down to Urbana," Lew said. "Class reunion. I think I did see you on the road but . . ."

"Forget it. Sorry," said Lee, flushing the urinal.

Lew waited till he heard the door close. Lee was going out the front door with his coffee and donuts when Lew moved to the refrigerator case, pulled out a sandwich wrapped tight in see-through plastic, grabbed a bottle of vanilla Diet Coke and pulled out his wallet to pay the skinny sullen girl behind the bulletproof glass window. Lee was just pulling out of the lot. Lew thought he could see the man holding up a donut.

"No protein," Lew said.

"Fresh out," the girl said, brushing back her stringy straw-colored hair. "Had some last week I think."

"Some . . . ?"

"Protein."

She handed him his change.

"I was talking about the man who just left," Lew said.

"Your friend, the Jap guy?"

"He's not my friend and he's Chinese."

"Same difference," she said, sliding the change to Lew through the two-inch gap at the bottom of the glass plate. "All gonna get our jobs. Indians, Japs, Chinks. We're fuckin' obsolete."

She looked at him, arms folded, waiting

to see if he would agree.

Lew shrugged. Lee's car was out of sight and he was probably two donuts to the wind.

"Got nothing against them," the girl said, brushing her hair back again. "Sister's husband is one of 'em. Good guy. Works in a tire shop in Chester. Oh, shit, almost forgot. Chink guy with the donuts and no protein told me to give you this."

She picked up a small lined sheet that had been torn from a notebook and slid it to him. It had been written quickly, was hard to read: Boneyard Tavern tonight.

There was no signature.

There was no need to hurry.

"You're from Chicago, right?" the girl asked.

"Right."

"Been there," she said, looking over her thin shoulder in the general direction of Chicago. "Too big. Been to St. Louis too. Too big in a different way. Know what I mean?"

"Yes."

Lew looked down at the sandwich. It was tuna salad on white. He unwrapped it.

"How old are you?" he asked.

She turned to face him.

"Young, mostly. Seventeen. You?"

"Forty-two."

"You hitting on me?" the girl said with a smile. "Wouldn't be the first."

"No," Lew said. "The man who left this note . . ."

"The chink," she said.

"Did he say anything?"

"To me? Just 'Give this to the guy in the washroom.' He did say something to himself though, come to think on it. He said, I think he said, " 'No more.' "

Ames McKinney waited for two hours. The sun was going down and a quartet of teens who said fuck a lot were laughing in the DQ parking lot beyond Lew's office window.

He picked up the phone and punched in the number Earl Borg had left. It took Borg one ring to answer.

"Yes."

"Name's McKinney. I work with Lewis Fonesca. He's out of town."

"And you can help me?"

"I can try," said Ames. "Till he gets back."

Silence.

"I have a thirteen-year-old daughter," Borg said. "She's missing."

"Called the police?"

"No. If I told them what happened, they

wouldn't believe me. I have a . . . let's call it reputation and history with the police that make me less than reputable. The problem is that my daughter does not have my name. Neither does her mother. We were never married. I have no evidence, except the word of the girl's mother that she is mine. And I doubt if the girl's mother would vouch for my paternity to the police."

"You think she was kidnapped?"

"I'm certain."

"Know where she might be?"

"Yes, and who took her. There is a reason I can't look for her myself."

"Tell me what I need to know," Ames said.

"Don't do anything till you talk to Fonesca," Borg said.

"Won't."

"Okay," said Borg, who told his story.

When Ames hung up the phone, it began to ring immediately.

Inevitable. He had put it off. He didn't want to do it, but he had, he was sure, very few options. From the alley on the South Side, he had fired a single bullet in the hope that it would get Lew Fonesca to back off, let his wife's memory rest, go back to Florida. It was a hope he had no faith in even when he fired, the shot coming closer to Fones-

227

ca's head than he had planned.

Okay, so he could simply shoot himself, which he had no intention of doing for many reasons. It would cancel any insurance payments. He could kill Lew Fonesca. That he did not want to do. It wasn't that he was against killing. He had done it before, twice in the last two days. No, he truly liked Fonesca. Fonesca, sad as he was, didn't deserve to be murdered.

Fonesca wanted to know who had killed his wife and why. Not unreasonable, but if he kept looking, Fonesca would find out what he had done. It would end the shooter's life, his reputation, his family, his freedom.

Fonesca had to die.

10

The Boneyard Tavern was a little under a mile from the east end of campus. When Lew was an undergraduate, it had been two miles from campus. Eventually, the university would embrace the the Boneyard Tavern, which wasn't yet an institution and wasn't a student or faculty hangout. It was, and had been since it opened in 1934, a neighborhood tavern. University people did come, eat the burgers, have a beer, in a place that didn't blare the walls with music, a place where people could talk to and hear other people. It was a place where the wood-paneled walls were always polished, the light a soothing, isolating amber, and the photographs on the wall were of past and present owners on pier decks solemnly pointing at large puzzle-eyed fish they had caught hanging next to them. It had been Lew's getaway of choice in Urbana when he was an undergraduate.

It was the place where a couple who looked like they had grandchildren and maybe great-grandchildren sat, showing photographs to the tubby bartender who smiled and nodded at each picture. It was the place where three men and a woman sat at one of the six round wooden tables playing cards. All four wore black lined zipper jackets with the words U.S. AIR FORCE printed on the back in red script. It was the place where Victor Lee sat at another table, watching Lew come through the door and head toward him.

In front of Lee was a nearly full glass of dark liquid. Lew sat across from him and handed Lee the painting he had carried in under his arm.

"I was coming back for it," said Lee, looking at the dark cityscape and then gently propping it on the table against the paneled wall. "That was you in my apartment, you and my landlord?"

A long pause, a double beat. One of the card players laughed at something, and the bartender looking at the photographs said, "This is Jason? Got big like his dad."

Lew took Lee's folded B.S. degree and handed it to him.

"Forgot that," Lee said, taking the sheet and placing it alongside the painting.

"You're the husband?" asked Lee, looking down at painting and document.

"Yes."

Lee nodded and went on, "I've been waiting for you for four years."

"You could have found me," said Lew.

The bartender called, "What are you drinking?"

"What he has," said Lew, nodding at Lee's drink.

"It's root beer," said Lee.

"Got you," called the bartender.

"I couldn't . . ." Lee began and trailed off, looking at the city canyon. "I killed her, your wife."

Lee took off his glasses and cleaned them on his shirt.

"I know."

"I'm . . . sorry isn't enough, is it?"

"It's a start."

"It's not enough for me," said Lee, rubbing his eyes and shaking his head. "I thought that when I told you . . . but it doesn't work that way, does it? I killed her."

"Why?" asked Lew.

The bartender placed the glass of root beer in front of Lew, took away the small empty wooden bowl on the table and replaced it with an identical bowl filled with pretzels and beer nuts.

"Hey, Larry, take a look at this one," called the woman at the bar, holding up a photograph. "It's a hoot."

The bartender moved from the table. Victor Lee ate a pretzel, gulped and took a drink.

"Thirsty," Lee said.

Lew nodded. It had come to this, sitting across from a shaken man who needed a haircut, a man who had lost his family, his confidence, his life. There was evil out there, in the canyons and forests of cities and towns and jungles, and sometimes Lew sat across from evil, but more often then not, as it was now, he sat across from someone lost who had committed someone's sense of their own sin.

"What happened?"

"What happened?" Lee repeated.

Victor Lee told his story.

Lee was certain he would be offered the job. The interview over lunch and drinks had gone more than well. Doctor Mitchell Waltrop, Executive Vice-president for Research of Permigo Pharmaceuticals, the third-largest drug manufacturer in the United States, had all but promised him the position of head of Experimental Research. It was more than a step up.

Lee, his wife and baby daughter, would have to move near Permigo corporate headquarters here in Skokie or nearby. No problem.

The only problem was that Victor Lee did not drink, never, but Waltrop had not given him an option, had poured him a full glass of wine over lunch to match his own. Waltrop talked, asked questions, poured a second glass, talked more, listened, another glass of wine.

Lunch had ended with a handshake, the promise of a call as soon as Waltrop had conferred with the CEO and the president of Permigo.

Then the ride back.

There was a better way home, a faster way, but Victor didn't know it. He had seldom left the far-south suburbs, ever expanding with malls, traffic, developments like the one in which he lived. He took the safe way, the way he knew after he had stopped to call his wife, tell her the news.

The ride back.

South on Skokie Boulevard. He remembered that. South. He drove, turned left on Dempster. Had he turned right, in less than ten minutes he would have hit the expressway. What was this street? Did he remember it? Chicago Avenue. Right on Chicago. He was lost. He had laughed. Victor Lee could follow and remember the theoretical variations of a strain of repellent-resistant fleas for seven generations and project it for more than seven thousand more. City streets, however, puzzled him even when he was quite sober, which was always, with the one exception of this day.

Older brick buildings, storefronts, resale shops, television-repair shops, faces on the street black instead of white. Hispanic faces now. IHOP, bars, a bank. Asian faces, restaurants. Vietnamese, Koreans, no Chinese. Didn't matter.

The ride back.

The radio was on. A man with a rapid voice kept saying, "You know what I mean." Change. Change. Change. Lake Michigan on his left. "That's the ticket," said the man on the radio. Hospital, park, apartment buildings. He opened the windows. Cold air. "Hold your horses there," said the radio man.

The sports car had almost been a gift, sold for so little by a Mentic board member. The car had been that of the man's teenage son, who had been given a new one by the boy's widowed grandmother, whose name . . . what was it? What did it matter? Bargain. Still big enough to hold Victor's family till it grew, which was now going to be financially possible. He was frugal. She was frugal. They saved. It had been the way of both of their families forever. Save something, something for the inevitable destruction, the certain disasters. The good risk.

The ride back.

Victor Lee didn't see Catherine Fonesca crossing Lake Shore Drive, lake still on his left, skyline of downtown on the right, couple walking. He didn't see her. There was a traffic light. He didn't know if it was red, yellow, green or polka dot. Then he hit her. Then he saw her, tumbling, rolling away toward the couple he had passed. There was no thought. Stop? And do what? He had been drinking, drinking wine, three glasses. More? With Dr. Mitchell Waltrop. The wine had been red.

Over. Everything. Choice now. No time. He was already thirty or more car lengths ahead of the image in his rearview window. He went faster, passing cars, weaving, knowing that he should slow down, not attract attention.

"You know what I mean, don't you, Gwen?" asked the man on the radio. The radio man cackled.

The ride back.

He hit the other car near the turnoff to

Hyde Park at 51st Street. The University of Chicago ten blocks in. He had been there for conferences twice. He had given a paper, "A Theory of Collision of Sub-Organic Particles in High Density." There had been no questions.

The car he hit bounced away, almost collided with a pickup truck, came to a halt. The car he had hit was now a miniature in the mirror world. He sped. He hit the steering wheel with the heels of his hands till they hurt. He wept.

The ride back ended, the driver a different Victor Lee from the one who had left five hours and twenty-seven minutes earlier. He had arrived home.

He told his wife he wasn't feeling well.

When the job offer came the next day, he turned it down. He told his wife that he had thought about it on his way home, found too many problems.

He held onto his job at Mentic, lived in the penumbra of a dream, bought the painting of the dark canyon of the city with the single apartment of dim light.

Three years and four months later, Victor Lee, who had made his own and the life of his wife and child a misery, left his home and moved into an apartment, taking with him only the framed painting, his University of Illinois degree and a canvas and a slightly dented aluminum Samsonite bag.

He had lost his ability to read for more than half an hour. He lost track of television shows. At first he could lose himself in his work, the numbers, the formulas, the possibilities. Then that too had changed and all that remained was the memory of the day, from morning to night, that he had killed Catherine Fonesca.

Every night when he lay in bed or on the sofa or on the floor with a pillow in his arms, he had repeated in his mind a forty-minute movie of imagination.

And so, Lew realized, there had been no murder.

If Catherine had a secret file, it had nothing to do with her death. Pappas, Posno. The murder of Santoro and Aponte-Cruz. Nothing to do with Catherine's death. But it did have something to do with Catherine. There were loose ends. He wanted to get back to Sarasota, his cell, but he owed it to Catherine, and whatever peace of mind he could hold, not to leave loose ends.

"I'll go back with you," Lee said, sitting up with a sigh.

"Why?"

"I killed her."

"Will turning yourself in bring her back?" asked Lew.

Lee's shoulders dropped forward and his eyes turned to the last bubble of his almost-finished drink.

"No," said Lee.

"Do you want to go to prison?" asked Lew.

"Yes . . . no. I . . ."

"You're going to pay," said Lew.

"Yes."

"I mean for the drinks."

"Yes."

Lew stood. Lee looked up and said,

"I had considered killing you. To protect my family. Hide my shame."

Lew said nothing.

"I couldn't, can't do it," said Lee.

Lew turned and headed toward the door.

The grandparents at the bar had shown their last photograph. The card players were showing their final hands of the night. "And here comes the River," called out one of the players slapping down a card.

Lew had seen a pay phone on the wall at the end of the bar. He decided to find a different one somewhere in a darkened motel room where he could hear traffic, turn on the television, find an old movie, anything in black and white, and try to pretend that he was back in Sarasota.

He knew it wouldn't be easy.

And he was right.

It was dark, starless, the threat of rain had turned into the reality of a cold drizzle. Lew began silently singing "Adeste Fidelus" to the beat of the windshield wipers.

Off of I-56, he found a one-story pink concrete block of rooms. Under the parking lights, the rain reflected the neon of the North Star Motel's office. It wasn't up to the ambiance or quality of the Bates Motel. It looked more like the stone-and-sand jails in Westerns, the kind the good guys or bad guys blow holes in to escape. It would do.

When he entered the office, he could see the television on the other side of the desk and a man sitting in a wooden swivel chair. The man's back was to Lew and his front no more than six feet from a rerun of *Jeopardy!.* The man didn't turn.

"Hi," said Lew.

The man didn't answer. He was absorbed in trying to come up with the question to "It saves nine."

"Jesus," the man said. Then he urged, "Morons, Jesus saves lives. No, a cat has nine of them. That's it. What does a cat have? Nine lives. Right?"

The thin man stood now, still staring at

the screen. He was wearing a wrinkled long-sleeved white shirt that wasn't fully tucked in. On his head was a dish towel.

"Head cold," the man explained, pointing to the towel.

The man's nose was puffy and pink, his eyes wet. He sneezed, possibly to convince what he thought was one who doubted his distress.

Lew said, "A stitch in time."

The thin man turned to face him. Time was running out. The clock was ticking. The clerk held up a finger showing that Lew should wait for one second, minute, turn of a century.

"Gina?" asked Alex Trebek in a rerun from a time when Alex's hair and mustache were black and his dark eyes amused.

"A stitch in time, Alex?" the chunky mother of four or five said.

Lights flashed. Bells rang. The audience applauded. The desk clerk turned off the television and said, "Wrong fucking answer. What can I do you for?"

The man's lean face was weathered. He could be almost any age. He wore a thin green tie loosely under his collar and the word etched on on the shirt pocket was SA-LUKIS.

"A room," said Lew.

"A room?" the man said.

"This is a motel. You have a room?"

"You headin' to or from a place?"

"Does it matter?" asked Lew.

"Sometimes."

He took the towel off of his head, examined it, smelled it and returned it to his head.

"Heading north."

"You got cash or a credit card?"

"Cash."

The man smiled.

"You're in luck. We've got eleven empty rooms. Price for a man of distinction like yourself is twenty-one dollars and I'll put you right next to the Coke machine."

"Is it loud?" asked Lew.

The man wiped his nose with the towel and said, "Silent as the few seconds before a church hymn."

The man reached under the counter and came up with a key. He held the key till Lew handed him a twenty and a single.

Lew filled out the guest information card.

"Don't have all the amenities," said the man. "But the place is quaint. We still use real keys 'stead of those plastic things with black strips and blue arrows and such. Room Six should do it. Clean towels, washed 'em myself, soap still wrapped, sheets clean."

"Can you hear the road from six?"

"Well. Can't tell you a lie, mister. Truth is I can. I know all the rooms down to the names of the roaches and the scratches in the wall behind the night tables. I've got a cultivated memory."

He looked around the small office and added, "But not all that good so's I could make a career out of it. Tried though. Three years of college at Southern Illinois."

He looked up at the bottom of the dangling towel drooping down from his head. "History major, but my job, which I owe to my uncle Willy Hart, is my comfort and my tomb and my real passion now is old license plates. Got 'em from all states and lots of different years. Trade some time with a guy owns a barbecue place outside of Towson Falls, North Carolina."

Lew tried to smile.

"You think that's stupid, don't you?"

"No," said Lew. "Politicians tend to be stupid. License plate collectors tend to be honest."

"You know a lot of politicians?"

"A few."

"License plate collectors?"

"One, you."

"Don't talk much do you, mister?"

"No," said Lew. "Room six is fine."

"Great," said the man. "Hey, take some M&M's out of the bowl. It's okay. They're wrapped six in every bag."

Lew reached into the bowl on the desk and took four packets of M&M's.

"Phone in the room?"

"I can turn it on," said the man. "Local calls free. Outside the county, you're on your own. Credit cards or collect calls."

Lew nodded.

"Oh, yeah, hell, almost forgot, the TV in Six is fritzy. You know picture sort of sizzles. Channel seven is clearest. Sometimes it's bright and clear. Other times it sizzles. If you can't live with that . . ."

"I can live with that," said Lew at the door.

The clerk looked down at the card Lew had filled out and then looked up.

"You're a vagabond from Genesis? What the hell is that? Wait. Now I get it. You're with that rock group Genesis, and you're the bass guitar player, Vagabond."

The clerk looked at Lew and dug into his memory.

"You don't look like a rock musician-type person."

"I need a joke."

"A joke? A rock music joke?"

"Any joke," said Lew.

The clerk had been behind the counter every night and all night for the past eleven years. The sad, mad, scary, touching, religious, famous — if you count Bob Denver's accountant — biking, ugly and beautiful had stopped, usually for no more than one night. They had been too tired, high or low, or lost to go farther. Most were cordial. A few were friendly, but the rest . . . Never before had he seen a vagabond from Genesis. Maybe they all were vagabonds from somewhere.

"Anything else?" the clerk asked, wishing to hell that the sad-faced bald guy at the door would say no and walk back into the night with the key to Room Six in his hand, but he didn't.

"Just the joke."

"Clean, dirty? Know a few about license plates. Heard a lot of good ones sitting in here. Forgot most of them."

"Clean," said Lew.

"Clean," the clerk said, tilting his head to one side and running a hand down his tie. "I'll think about that one."

John Pappas knew exactly where Posno would be, exactly. Posno would be in a car across from the house of Lew Fonesca's sister's. He would wait patiently, for days if he had to, till Fonesca returned. No one would notice. John Pappas knew that no one would see him.

Posno's plan would be to simply shoot the little Italian, drive away and disappear, maybe for years, maybe forever. That would depend on whether Catherine Fonesca's files were ever found.

That would be his plan.

Posno, Pappas was certain, would be composing poetry as he sat. Many nights and days Pappas had sat with Posno in a car, heard the torpedo-shaped killer compose or recite not only Greek poets, modern Greek poets, but his own poems. Posno was most prolific and creative just before he killed. He existed to hurt and kill and when the job was done he disappeared.

One of Posno's poems, unbidden, returned to Pappas. It was not surprising that he remembered it. He had heard Posno reciting it, revising it dozens of times. Besides, it was short:

If we link our arms,
none but a demon can
with all his charms
break the chain of man.

John Pappas took a *frigadelia,* fried and

rolled slices of lamb stomach filled with seasoned strips of calves' liver, from the blue bowl on the window ledge. There were three left. His mother's favorites were pastries. She was an artist in the kitchen with a butcher's block table and a warm oven. But there were some specialties her son loved and *frigadelia* was one of them.

Her son had many things to worry about, but food would never be one of them.

John Pappas ate the first *frigadelia* so quickly that when he plucked up the second one, it was still quite warm to the touch.

After eating the packets of M&M's, Lew turned up the heat in the room, stripped to his shorts, placed his shirt on a wire hanger and his pants on a wooden one, turned on the hot water in the shower and hung his clothes over the curtain rod where the water wouldn't hit them. Then he laid back in the bed, lights out, listening to the running water beyond the bathroom door, hearing the whirr of cars and bumping trucks on the highway a little over a hundred yards away. He was too tired to watch television. It was too late to make any more phone calls but one.

He had called Angie and Franco, told them he was all right, that he was no longer looking for the man who had killed Catherine, and that he would be back late the next morning.

"Lewis, remember Ames McKinney wants you to call him," said Angie. "Says it's important. You have his number?"

"Yes. I'll call tomorrow," he had said, carrying the phone, walking a small, slow circle.

"Lewis," said Angie. "You sound like shit."

"What does shit sound like?"

He could hear the rain thudding harder against the roof of a car pulling into the parking lot of the motel outside his window. Lew pushed back a slat in the faded yellow plastic window blinds and looked out.

"Lewis, where are you?"

"Not sure, but I'm on my way. Tomorrow, Angela. When there's sun. I have to make some stops first."

"Lewis, maybe it's enough. You know? Let it go. If you can't let it go, live with it. Every day spent thinking about the last day is a wasted day."

"Rebecca Strum," he said.

"Paraphrase," said his sister.

By the single light atop the twelve-foot post to his left, he could see the lean, slump-shouldered figure, eyes slightly open, hair pounded forward and dripping.

Victor Lee was speaking to someone who

wasn't there. Lee looked up at Lew's window and their eyes met. Lee's lips moved. Whatever he was saying, he had to know that Lew couldn't hear it. Lewis let the slat drop.

"Lewis?" said Angie. "You hear me?"

"Yes."

"Wherever you are, you should be somewhere else."

"I know."

11

The next morning about an hour before Herman came to work, Uncle Tonio got to fire his carbine for the first time since Korea. He had always thought, and often said, the compact, light rifle was the best weapon ever invented. As a sergeant in the Signal Corps responsible for storing electronic equipment, primarily phones, Tonio had carried a carbine. It didn't shoot as far or quite as straight as an M1, but it wasn't a weight on his back, a constant reminder of where he was and what he was doing.

Tonio had started checking the doors and the windows, as he always did, when he heard the sound in the darkness. He could tell where it was coming from. He knew the echoes and scurries of mice, cats and rats, the creaking of boxes and furniture, the groaning of the floor and walls when weather changed.

Tonio went back to his office, opened his

closet, reached behind his clothes, pulled the carbine out of its leather carrier, loaded it and walked back out into the warehouse.

The sound was definitely coming from one of three mesh-enclosed storage rooms. One of the three was the one in which Lewis and Catherine's furniture, papers, all the remnants of their lives, were stored and protected.

They were back, he decided, as he walked in the shadows outside the reach of the dim overhead nightlights.

Tonio had shot two soldiers in Korea, one Chinese, the other North Korean. They, in turn, had shot him in the thigh. Still hurt. Once, years ago, he wondered if the two men he had shot had lived, were still alive, what it would be like to get together, try to talk about memories that didn't exist in words. Show them, give them his Purple Heart. Maybe they would give him their equivalent of the Purple Heart, if they had one.

No doubt now. He heard it. Tonio was angry. He kicked off his shoes gently, turned the corner to his left and, carbine at the ready, looked down the aisle. The overhead lamp in the storage room had not been turned on. The wavering beam of a flashlight clicked off. Silence.

Tonio moved forward, carbine raised.

"Come out," he called. "Come out you son of a bitch or I shoot."

But Tonio knew he wouldn't shoot at the room, wouldn't risk destroying his nephew's memories of his wife.

There was a shuffling in the darkness. No sound of the door being opened. Was it already open? Had the burglar left it open? Was he, she, they, now in stockinged feet like Tonio, padding toward a door or worse, was he —

The sound was behind him now. Tonio turned, weapon up as he heard the cocking of a gun. Then the sound was gone. Tonio had a choice: fear or anger. He chose a combination of the two, or, rather, they chose him.

It took four or five seconds and then Tonio was after the intruder. Tonio limped. The intruder ran.

Tonio turned down the aisle toward his office. The door to the dock was open. Morning sunlight silhouetted a man's figure. The man was holding something in his right hand.

Tonio, panting heavily, put the rifle to his cheek and tried to aim, fired. Suddenly, a second figure dashed out of the warehouse darkness, pushed past the man in the doorway and turned left.

"Herman?" Tonio called, moving toward the open door.

"Who was that?" asked Herman.

Tonio moved past him and went out on the dock. There was no one in sight. Herman joined him and looked around. The question came simply, logically. The man in the dark had crept behind him. The man was armed. Tonio had a rifle.

"Why didn't he shoot me?"

"Don't know."

"What did he look like?"

"Man, lot younger than you and me, lot older than a college kid," said Herman. "White. Can't say more. You'd best sit down."

Tonio put his arm on Herman's shoulder and the two went into the office and sat. Tonio propped his rifle against the wall, within reach.

"Want to give me the rifle and I'll go after him?" asked Herman, who had been a sniper in both Korea and Vietnam.

"No," said Tonio.

"Suit yourself," said Herman, unzipping his jacket. "This is for you."

He handed Tonio a blue plastic bowl.

"Cake. Celia made it last night. Plastic

spoon's inside the bowl there. We ran out of forks."

Tonio had caught his breath.

"Thanks," he said.

"My birthday," said Herman. "Yesterday."

"Happy birthday," said Tonio.

"We get some people for guard duty tonight?" asked Herman.

"Special people," said Tonio.

The rain had stopped, but the sky was Chicago gray, and thunder rumbled and rippled off of Lake Michigan, drowning out the sound of traffic.

It was morning. Early. Ken Sing, whose real name was Kudlup Singh Parajer, and Debest Williams, whose real name was Debest Williams, were walking their usual route from the one-bedroom apartment they shared to the University of Illinois campus where they were graduate students and assistants in the chemistry department.

The subject was Jochim Bachem, the professor for whom they worked, the professor Ken nearly worshiped and Debest thought was a sham.

"Oh, come on, Kude," Debest said. "How many times I have to tell you to watch him. Nods his head, chews on that damn stained yellow stem pipe, acts like he's thinking.

Then what does he say when someone, anyone, you, me, asks him a question?"

"Sometimes he says, 'What do you think?' "

They were walking past a few half asleep children shuffling in the opposite direction toward the Catholic grade school.

"He always says that," said Debest. "Maybe he had answers once, but not now."

Debest slammed his palm down on the car they were passing. Something inside the car moved. The horn went off. Ken and Debest stopped and looked back.

The head propped over the steering was deep red with blood. Debest and Ken tried to open the car doors. The horn kept wailing. Doors opened in the homes across the street. People stepped out.

Ken looked around and called, "Call 911."

A bulky man in jeans and a black sweatshirt moved across the street to the car. He touched Debest's shoulder to move him out of the way, took a knife from his pocket, pushed the window in far enough to insert the knife against it and down the glass, pushed down on the door handle. The door popped open. The dead man slumped off the steering wheel and the noise stopped.

A small group of kids and residents, all wide-awake now, stood on the sidewalk.

"We're going to have to stay," said Ken.

"Yeah, but that asshole Bachem won't believe our reason."

Franco closed the knife, put it back in his pocket and waited for the police to arrive.

"I have three jokes."

It was the first thing Ann Horowitz heard when she picked up the phone in the morning after two rings. She had her first client in fifteen minutes. Lew knew it. He was sitting in the phone booth of a Shoney's, twenty miles outside of Chicago. He had eaten the breakfast buffet, drunk two cups of fully leaded coffee, and watched the parking lot for signs of Victor Lee's car. There had been none.

Ann had accepted the collect call.

"Three," she said, taking a bite of biscotti as she sat in her office chair. "I am to be thrice-blessed."

"I saw a man on the street when I driving. He was holding up a sign that read WILL WORK FOR MONEY."

"Did you really see this?"

"No, it's a joke."

"Some jokes are taken from life," she said. "The second joke?"

"You go on a picnic and you're having a good time. Then you open your basket of food and the flies start coming. You close the basket. Flies go away. You open it. They come back. Conclusion: Flies time when you're having fun."

"That's a good one," she said. "You make that one up?"

"Yes."

He could hear her crunching the biscotti.

"You said three jokes," Ann went on.

"I'll save it. I only owed you one."

"So, what happened?" she asked.

"I found him," Lew said. "The man who killed her."

"Catherine."

"Catherine," he echoed.

"And what did you say to him, he to you?"

"He's Chinese."

"And that is relevant?"

"No."

"What else?"

"He has a wife, a daughter, a painting of a dark city street. He wasn't trying to kill Catherine. He was drunk."

"And what did you do?"

"Nothing."

"Not possible to do nothing, not for you," she said, finishing the biscotti and licking her fingers. "You've tried it."

"I know. I walked away from him."

"Why?"

"He was sorry."

"And?"

"He was suffering, has been since he killed her. He's lost his job, his family, his future," Lew said.

"Remind you of anyone?"

"Yes."

"When are you coming back?"

She was now drinking coffee she had poured into a cup from her yellow Thermos.

"Tomorrow, I think."

"Good. People are looking for you."

"Tell them I'm coming back tomorrow."

"Lewis, how do you feel?"

"I don't know."

"Let's consider that progress," she said. "I'll let you know how much this call cost when I see you."

"Wait. Rebecca Strum," he said.

"I've read her books, met her twice at conferences," said Ann.

The outer door to her office opened. The next client had arrived.

"I met her," said Lew. "There's something —"

"A good human being, a troubled human being who is brilliant enough to turn her denial into successful philosophy of coping with the vagaries of life," said Ann. "I didn't just make that up. I'm quoting myself from a paper I wrote on her in 1983. You understand?"

"Yes."

"Read one of her books," said Ann, taking another sip of coffee. "They are filled with vivid memories of horror and inhumanity and the determination to endure."

"Just what I need."

"Yes, it is," said Ann, finishing her coffee. "Goodbye."

She hung up. So did Lew.

Franco's friend Manny Lowen was the first officer on the scene. The beefy cop was on the overnight shift, which gave him the opportunity to keep an eye on Franco and Angie's house. He had been on Maxwell Street about to drive back to the station when the call came through.

Normally, he would have let it go to Abel Rodriguez, but not this time. Manny Lowen knew the address. Besides, he was one hundred percent sure that when he got home, his wife would be on him again about taking in her mother. Heather never raised her voice, never got angry. She just stayed with the case, backed away for a while, a short while, and then came back again till she wore him down, nerve by nerve, guilt by guilt.

Franco was standing on the sidewalk in front of four neighbors and two college kids, one black, the other a kind of Indian or something. They were all looking into the window of the car that, Manny noted, was in almost the same parking spot from where he had rousted Santoro and Aponte-Cruz, who were now dead.

"Manny, hey," said Franco. "Curse of Cabrini Street. You park here. Look what happens."

Two old ladies behind them argued while they stared at the dead man half sprawled out of the car, arms out, eyes closed, mouth open.

The old ladies were speaking Italian.

"Anyone here see what happened?" said Manny, turning to face the group.

All the head shakes were negative. Manny knew the routine. If there were a chance the man slumped out of the car was alive, Manny would be working on him, but the deep purple hole in his neck surrounded by slowly drying blood and the open mouth decided it for him. He looked dead. He smelled dead. He was dead. He would wait for the detectives to make it official. Manny would not risk touching something or doing something that might contaminate the scene. Last time he had done that had been eight years ago when he picked up what looked like a silver dollar at a rape scene. The silver dollar was an aluminum foil condom packet. The condom wasn't in it and the person who owned the packet had left fingerprints that were then under those of Patrolman Emanuel Joshua Lowen.

"You okay, Franco?" Manny asked.

"No," Franco answered. "These crazy sons of bitches are turning my street into a graveyard. I'm a simple guy, Manny, a simple guy with a simple new mission in life: to kick the crap out of whoever is killing people in front of my house."

A blue car, revolving light on the roof flashing, pulled up and parked in the middle of the street.

"I'm gonna have to tell them, Franco, about the other night," Manny said as two detectives drove up. Longworth was short, heavy, white and breathing hard, and Trahairn, who was almost as heavy, was three inches taller than his partner, and in possession of a deep purple birthmark on his neck. They got out of the car slowly. They weren't in a hurry.

"I know," said Franco.

The two detectives stepped next to the dead man's car and looked down at him.

What Franco knew was that Manny would

have to tell the detectives, if they didn't already know, that two men who had parked in this same spot were also dead. He would tell them about talking to Angie and Franco. That would lead to Lew and lots of questions about all these dead people and what Lew had to do with them. Longworth and Trahairn told Manny to do what he already knew he was supposed to do, keep the citizens from touching the car.

The detectives put on white plastic gloves, took out flashlights, reached over the dead man and looked into the car. They popped the trunk with the switch on the floor. Without touching anything, they came to the same conclusion, except for the blood, the car was clean, not even a gum wrapper or a bitten-off fingernail. And, except for one of those plastic spare tires, the trunk was even cleaner. For more, they would have to wait till someone from the crime scene division showed up.

"People walk by and don't see a dead man on the street?" Longworth asked the crowd.

"He wasn't on the street," said Franco. "Not till I opened the door."

"You have the key?" asked Traihairn.

"Don't need one," said Franco, looking across the street where Angie, dressed for work, was standing in the doorway with a cup of coffee in her hand.

"Who're you?" asked Trahairn.

"Tow-truck driver."

Lew's second call from the phone booth at Shoney's was a little trickier. He couldn't reverse the charges. He had a pile of quarters piled next to the phone, five dollars in quarters.

"Texas," said Big Ed when he answered the phone at the Texas Bar & Grille in Sarasota.

"Fonesca."

"You back?"

"No."

"Things interesting?"

"Yes."

"You are a payload oil gusher of information, amigo. I'll get Ames."

Lew watched a stringy woman in her sixties paying her bill at the cashier's counter. At her side was a rotund boy about four years old. His hair was thin and the color of corn. His cheeks were pink. His beltless pants were slipping and his principal task was keeping them up. The boy looked at Lew.

"McKinney," came Ames's deep raspy voice. "You okay?"

"I'm okay."

"You find him?"

"Yes."

"Turn him in? Shoot him? You in jail?"

"No to all three questions."

Ames knew where the line was between what he should and should not ask his friend.

"Earl Borg, remember him?" said Ames.

Lew remembered the man, the name, the sight of the dying boar and the snarling pit bill, the happy little girl, the smell of blood, sweat, tobacco. Lew remembered Earl Borg.

"Yes."

"Wants to see you. Says now isn't soon enough and yesterday might even have been too."

"Tell him tomorrow," Lew said.

"Told him that yesterday."

The fat little boy was holding his pants up with both hands and staring at Lew, who stared back. Then the woman took the boy's hand. The untended right side of his pants drooped. As they walked away, the boy smiled over his shoulder at Lew, who did his best to smile back. He held the smile, turned and examined it in the mirror on the wall. He saw the face of regret.

"I'll tell him again," said Ames.

"I'll call him as soon as I get to Sarasota."

There should be more to say, to tell, but

Lew couldn't do it. Ames would listen and somewhere inside him he would judge. His code was simple, right out of John Wayne. There was right. There was wrong. You didn't need a god or a devil to tell you that. Ames would judge in silence and support his friend. The listener who did not judge, Ames knew, was Ann Horowitz.

"Good enough," said Ames.

They hung up.

By the time Lew parked the car back at Toro's and walked to Cabrini Street, the dead man in the car across from Angie and Franco's house had been taken away, and the car towed. The small crowd was gone. Franco and Angie stood in front of their house, coffee mugs in hand.

"Cold?" he asked.

"Fine," she said. "Think it's too early to call Terri?"

"Nah. Let's do it."

They had just hung up when Lew came through the door.

"Lew," Angie said. "You look . . ."

"I need a shower. Franco, are you busy today?"

"I'm as busy as I want to be," said Franco. "If I wanna hustle, there's always plenty of work. You need a ride or something?"

"A ride and something," said Lew, heading for his niece's room.

"Lewis," Angie said. "A man was killed in a car across the street last night."

"Looks like the drawing you've got of that Posno," said Franco. "They've even got ID."

"And the police know about those other two," said Angie. "That they were looking for you before they got killed."

"Santoro and Aponte-Cruz," said Franco. "Manny had to tell the detectives."

"I know," said Lew. "I think I'll take a shower now."

In his office-home in Sarasota, Lew had no bath, no shower, just a sink and a toilet stall that he shared with other tenants in his building and whatever homeless person may have made his or her way there. He did his showering at the YMCA, where he worked out. Teresa's shower, however, had something his building and the Y didn't have: privacy.

He shaved, soaped, rubbed and shampooed, hoping to not lose more hair, and rinsed. He dried himself with the towel Angie had laid out for him, then brushed his teeth, and brushed back his hair. Showers had their own sense of humor. When water pelted, the mirror told Lew that his hairline had decided to beat another hasty retreat.

The battle line was moving back.

He put on fresh clothes, packed, called the airline to change his ticket, put on his Cubs hat and met Angie and Franco in the dining room. There was half a lemon cake on the table. Angie cut a slice for her brother and put it on a plate.

"I'm going back tomorrow," Lew said, accepting the fork his sister handed him.

"And the guy who killed Catherine?" she asked. "You don't have to be here to testify or something?"

"No."

He dug into the cake. The taste and smell brought memories without images.

"Guy's got to be punished, Lewie," said Franco. "Taken down, put away."

"He's punishing himself."

"Something happened here this morning," Angie said, nodding in the general direction of the street. "Before you got here, remember?"

"ID., photo," said Franco. "It was Posniti."

"Posni*tki*," Lew corrected.

"Right," said Franco.

Lew nodded, ate and asked if he could use the phone. Before he could, Angie said, "Someone broke into the locker in Uncle Tonio's warehouse. He didn't see who but he almost shot him."

"Uncle Tonio's okay?"

"He's fine."

"It ends today?" Angie said. "I mean what you came back to do?"

"It ends today."

"Sure?"

"No."

Lew picked up the phone, punched in the numbers and waited two rings.

"Hi," he said. "I found him."

"Good, and —," said Milt Holiger.

"That's all," said Lew.

"That's all? Who is it? Did you kill him? Is there . . . ?"

"No more," said Lew. "If I told you and something happened that led to an investigation —"

"Then all I could say was you told me you found the person who killed her, but you didn't tell me anything about him."

"Or her," Lew added.

"Got it."

"One more thing," said Lew. "Andrej Posnitki was found dead in a car parked across the street from my sister and brother-in-law's house. Can you find out when it happened and what killed him?"

"Not a problem," said Milt. "I'll tell whoever's handling the case that it might be linked to the killings of Santoro and Aponte-Cruz."

"Thanks."

"I'll call you when I have something. You're going back to Florida?"

"Yes. Tomorrow."

"Cup of coffee and a couple of sinful donuts before you go?" asked Holiger.

"Let's see how the day goes," said Lew.

"Call you later."

Lew said, "Goodbye."

12

The man across the desk was James Edward Simms. Lew didn't have to ask him. The name was embossed on his office door and the brass plate on the desk. Simms, slim and smiling, looked like a white-haired doctor in a magazine ad for overcoming erectile dysfunction. He put the printout sheets in an envelope, and handed the envelope to Lew.

"Thank you," said Lew.

"Please call me directly if you have any questions or need anything," said Simms.

It wasn't the right time or place to ask for a joke. Simms probably had some good ones, ones Ann would appreciate. Simms probably had a safety deposit box filled with jokes. Lew didn't ask. He stood up and Simms came around the desk, guided him out of the office and escorted Lew to the front door.

"I'm glad you came by, Mr. Fonesca. Have

a good trip back to Florida. Goodbye."

Franco was parked to his left in a bus stop. When Lew got in the truck, Franco handed him the phone.

"Holiger," he said.

"Lew? I just got off the phone with a guy in the P.D. The body in the car may have had Andrej Posnitki's wallet in his pocket, but he isn't Posno. Traced the fingerprints. Dead guy's name is Terrance Chapel, fifty-five, picked up twice for panhandling using some very aggressive persuasion, two more times for petty theft, meaning grabbing fruit and potato chips from street-vendor carts. No known address. Chapel was homeless. Conclusion: Posno is still out there."

"Maybe," said Lew.

"The dead man isn't Posno, Lew," said Holiger.

"Three o'clock good for you?" asked Lew.

"Three? Fine. Where?"

"Dunkin' Donuts on Jackson," said Lew.

"See you then. Maybe I can come up with something more? Lew?"

"Yes."

"How are you holding up?"

"Just fine," Lew lied. "See you at three."

When he put the phone back on the charger pad, Franco reached past Lew, pushed open the glove compartment and took out two Snickers bars. Lew managed to catch a Milky Way that tried to escape. He put it back in the compartment, and accepted the Snickers bar from Franco.

"Where to now?" asked Franco tearing the wrapper.

"The Dark Tower," answered Lew.

Franco understood.

"Suits me," he said, pulling into traffic.

There were no cars on the street in front of the Pappas house. The sun was bright, air cool. Lew remembered reading about the note left by a Mexican poet who jumped off his apartment balcony twenty years earlier: "The sun is bright. The clouds are beautiful. The air is warm and I am in a good mood. It is the perfect time to die."

The door opened about fifteen seconds after Lew had pushed the button. The smell that met them was a temptation. Bernice Pappas stood in the doorway. She looked at them, wiped her hands on her dress and said, "We're celebrating. Come in."

Lew and Franco followed her inside.

"The door," she said.

Franco closed it. It locked automatically.

The woman started walking to the left.

"I'm still cooking," she said. "John and the boys are upstairs. Tell them lunch is in half an hour."

She took two more strides, put her hand on the kitchen door, turned her head toward them and said, "You're Christians, right?"

"Yeah," said Franco.

"Then you're invited to lunch."

She went through the door. Lew and Franco went up the stairs toward the music. The door to Pappas's sanctuary was closed. Lew knocked.

"Come in. Come in," Pappas called.

Pappas was standing with Stavros and Dimitri in the center of the room. Each held a wineglass. The wine was white. The music was a man singing in Greek.

"We're celebrating," Pappas said, looking at Lew.

"We know," said Franco. "Your mother told us."

The three Pappas men looked somber.

"We're invited for lunch," Franco added. "Because we're Christians. But to tell you the truth . . ."

"Posno," Lew said.

"I heard he's dead," said Pappas, holding up his glass in a toast. "I know. We're celebrating his demise and we're respecting his memory. We were partners, even friends for a long, long time. Well, maybe not friends, but close."

"I know," Lew said.

"I can go outside now," said Pappas, taking a full sip of wine. "Maybe. Maybe I'll try tomorrow. Oh, manners. Stavros, get our guests some wine. Karipidis winery. They still make it like it was made six thousand years ago."

Stavros blinked his good eye at Lew and moved to the bottle and glasses on the desk.

"Can we talk in private?" Lew asked.

"Private? I've got no secrets," said Pappas.

Lew met his eyes.

"All right. My sons, Mr. Fonesca and I will talk in here. Give Mr. . . ."

"Massaccio," said Franco.

"Stavros, give Mr. Massaccio a glass of wine and you two take him to see the garden."

"The garden?" asked Dimitri. "What's there to see in the garden?"

Pappas shrugged and said, "That's what you're supposed to say in situations like this. Go, play pool in the den or something."

"I think I'll stay with Lewis," said Franco, accepting the glass of wine from Stavros whose good eye met both of Franco's.

"It's okay," Lew said. "Go with them."

Franco reluctantly followed the brothers Pappas out of the room, looking back over his shoulder at Lew.

When they were alone and the door was closed, Pappas took another sip of wine and said, "Sure you won't have a little? It's good."

"No, thank you."

"Want to sit?"

"No."

"You don't look happy," said Pappas. "But then, you never look happy. What makes you happy?"

"Safe children laughing," said Lew.

"We should both be happy today, Fonesca. Posno is dead. He killed your wife. He wanted to kill me. He —"

"He didn't kill Catherine," said Lew. "I found the man who killed her."

Pappas looked surprised.

"Good for you," he said, refilling his glass and holding it up in a toast. "So it wasn't Posno? Well, did you kill him, this man who ran down your wife?"

"No."

"Will you?"

"No."

"Well, then, have him arrested," said Pappas. "Or better, tell me who it is and he will be dead in forty-eight hours, as God is my witness."

"The man the police found dead with Posno's identification wasn't Posno," said Lew.

Pappas paused, glass almost to his mouth. Then he took a long drink.

"Posno is dead," Pappas said, pointing a finger at Lew. "I know it. I feel it. He did not get away. Somewhere he is dead."

"The way most people would look at it, he can't be dead."

Pappas reached for a remote control on the desk, pushed a button, and stopped the music.

"Why not?" asked Pappas.

"Posno never existed except in your imagination," said Lew. "You made him up to take the fall for everything you did, everyone you killed. It wasn't Posno who was afraid of what Catherine had in her files. It was you."

"You're a crazy person, Fonesca. Maybe that's why I like you. Crazy people are interesting as long as they're harmless."

Pappas poured himself more wine and sat down, legs crossed, trousers straightened smooth.

"Posno exists," he said. "Believe me."

"There are no authenticated photographs of him," said Lew. "No fingerprints on record. He was never arrested. No one but you has ever seen him."

"My son Stavros —"

Lew shook his head no.

275

"Posno tried to kill him, took his eye."

"You told your son that Posno was after you. You were the one doing the shooting. My guess is you were keeping Posno alive. You wanted to come close, but you accidentally almost killed your son."

Pappas finished the wine in his glass, put it on the table in front of him, tapped Lew's knee and said, "Door's closed. Just you and me. You've got an imagination. Okay, I've got one too. It's the poet in me. I think the police are going to find that the man with Posno's identification was dead before he was shot. Heart attack, stroke, who knows. Died in a doorway on Roosevelt Road. Who knows? Then someone shot him and drove him to your sister's house. Just a guess, but . . ."

"Who knows," Lew repeated.

"Stavros set up that Posno Web site?" asked Lew. "Never mind. I'll ask him."

"Hey," said Pappas, standing suddenly. "I killed nobody this time around. Not your wife. Not the homeless guy who, by the way, was the work of an idiot. You get what you pay for. And for the record, whatever that means, I did not kill or have killed those two others."

"Santoro and Aponte-Cruz," Lew supplied.

"Yeah, them. I didn't kill them, didn't have them killed."

"You're clean?"

"Clean?" Pappas said with a smile and a shake of his head. "Hell no. I just didn't kill those two guys, but between you, me and the floor, I've killed people, all but one of them men. No regrets. I've got it worked out with God. I only killed people who deserved it. On that I'm clean. But, between you and me and Bobby McGee, I've got an inoperable brain aneurism. That's not clean. I know it's there. Can pop anytime. Could kill me just like that."

He slapped his hand down on the table.

"Worse," he went on, "it could leave me living the life of a pickled artichoke. So, *clean* is not the word I'd think of for me."

"Pain?"

"Not really," said Pappas.

"I'm sorry."

"You know what? I believe you."

"I believe you're in pain," said Lew. "I don't know about the aneurism."

"My doctor —"

"I'd get a second opinion," said Lew. "Unless you're just making up the aneurism and the doctor telling you about it and the myth of Posno."

Pappas was shaking his head no and smiling tolerantly.

"Why would I lie about an aneurism?"

"To get your family to do anything you wanted them to do," said Lew. "Mind if I talk to your doctor?"

"Yes," said Pappas, looking passively at the drink in his hand. "Doctor and patient . . . you know."

"I know you have no palsy," said Lew. "Your pupils aren't dilated. You don't show any signs of double vision or pain above your eye or localized headache. No signs of nausea or vomiting, or stiff neck or —"

"You're a doctor and a process server," said Pappas. "Interesting combination."

"I know a bail bondsman in Sarasota who also sells pizzas," said Lew. "My father died of brain aneurism. I watched it happen. I can find out about you. It's what I do."

"I wish you would not tell any of this to my family," said Pappas.

"Or you'll kill me?"

Pappas looked at Lew and shook his head.

"No, it would be too awkward in my own house and it was clear when I first met you that you had no fear. Fonesca, why do you think my mother keeps baking rooms full of pastries? Why do you think my sons do whatever I tell them to even though they don't agree with any of it? Because they're scared shitless they'll be on their own. And maybe, just maybe, they love me. What do you think?"

"I think you need a second opinion," Lew said.

"Now, what are you doing here, Fonesca?"

"I don't think Catherine's file on you is in that locker at my uncle's warehouse, or in the State Attorney's office. Too many people have looked. If there is a file, it'll turn up and there you'll be."

"If there is a file," said Pappas. "And if it turns up. I'm not worried."

Lew looked directly at Pappas's face and said, "No. I guess you're not."

"Simonides was Posno's favorite poet. Sixth-century. Doesn't translate well into English. You'll stay for lunch?"

Lew looked at the clock on the wall. There was plenty of time before his next appointment.

"Yes."

"Good," said Pappas, moving next to Lew and putting an arm around his shoulder. "Perhaps we'll set an empty place for Posno. What do you say?"

Pappas escorted Lew to the dining room where Dimitri, Stavros and Franco were already seated. On top of a sun-orange tablecloth were six place settings, each with a blue-rimmed plate, a knife, fork, spoon, napkin and wineglass. Pappas took his place at the head of the table and Lew sat at his right. In front of Pappas was a large dark bottle of wine. Pappas picked up his napkin, revealing a black metal handgun. The only sounds in the room were Franco chewing on a macadamia nut and a bustling of metal-on-metal, dish-on-dish from the kitchen.

No one mentioned the gun.

Pappas reached for the wine, noticed that the cork had been pulled and rested in the mouth of the bottle. He removed and examined the cork, looked around the table and nodded his approval.

No one mentioned the gun but everyone at the table looked at it.

"Dimi opened this bottle," Pappas said, leaning toward Lew with a smile. "Impatient. Look at the cork. Bruised. Small bruises, yes, but in wine you need to strive for perfection."

Bernice Pappas bustled into the dining room carrying a large tray with platters piled with food and hot bread.

She did not see the gun next to her son's plate.

"Smells like nearly forgotten memories," said Pappas.

"LAZARIDI AMENTYSTOS," said Pappas, pouring a full glass of wine for Lew, doing the same for himself and then handing the bottle around as his mother hovered between her grandsons.

When the food was laid out, Bernice Pappas sat across from her son and saw the gun. Her eyes went from the weapon to her son's reassuring face.

Pappas smiled and said, "*Lam Paldakai,* thin slices of lamb with my mother's own sauce. Begin, please."

And the family began, silently taking small servings of lamb, peas, black olives, salad saturated in olive oil. Bernice Pappas put nothing on her plate.

Franco broke the silence.

"And that?" he asked, nodding at the gun on the table near Pappas's hand.

Pappas stopped chewing and looked at the gun as if he had just noticed it.

"Ah, that. It's just desert. An acquired taste. Most people I've known taste it but once."

Pappas looked past Lew at Franco and kept smiling, raising his glass in a toast to his mother.

"Johnny."

It was Bernice Pappas. John Pappas seemed to be frozen in his smile at Franco, who met his eyes but didn't smile.

"Johnny," she repeated.

"Pop," said Stavros. "Please."

"I always try to please," said Pappas, holding out his arms. "Let's talk about the Bears, bird flu, the oil crisis, global warming, if Shakespeare was Shakespeare and if Homer was really four different writers. Pick a subject, Mr. Fonesca. Not what we talked about a little while ago. There's time for you to talk about that with Stavros and Dimi and my mother after we finish, if you must."

Franco dug into his food, eyes up and darting from face to face in this family he couldn't quite figure out.

"The Bears are going to have a great season," said Franco.

"I don't think there are any Greeks on the team," said Pappas.

A game was being played between Pappas and Lew with Pappas conducting it, Franco in the middle, and Lew quietly eating his peas.

Dish after dish, subject after subject was consumed and disappeared from the table and from memory.

Gone were the salad bowls; Dimitri helping his grandmother clear the table.

"The Bears are doomed forever to be up

and down. Cycles," said Franco. "Professional football is about cycles."

All about cycles. Pappas nodded his approval.

"There isn't going to be any bird flu," said Stavros nervously, his good eye fixed on his father, his glass eye staring at something interesting on the wall. "It's all Chicken Little. The sky isn't falling."

The sky is falling, thought Lew.

"Global warming?" asked Dimitri of no one. "People didn't cause it. It's natural. Turn off your engines and walk eighteen miles to work. Besides, a warmer earth means longer summers, more music. You still want to blame someone, blame God. It's all his idea."

"God is oil," said Bernice Pappas, head down, thin darkly veined hands slowly, shakily spearing a piece of lamb and guiding it to her mouth. "Oil is a miracle. How many goddamn dinosaurs you think died and left their oil. King Kong would have been up to his ass in dinosaurs and that still wouldn't have come close to accounting for the oil we've sucked out of the ground. Now they're finding it in the dirt in Canada, billions of gallons," she rambled.

"Oil, that's the real X-File. Did my husband Alex see that? Hell no. Did he say anything, hear anything I ever said to him?"

She stood across the table, steak knife in hand.

"Did he? Shit, look at all of you. You're not listening either."

"Momma, please sit down," said Pappas gently.

"Then put that goddamn thing away," she said, pointing at the gun, knife still in hand.

"Momma, please sit," Pappas said firmly.

She sat, defeated.

"I'm sorry," Pappas went on. "My mother . . ."

"She gets very intense," Stavros explained.

Bernice went back to silently eating.

Franco was working on his second glass of wine, Pappas his third, Bernice her third, Stavros and Dimi their first. Lew had only sipped the wine. Now he looked up at his host.

"Well, I think it's time for dessert," said Pappas with a grin. "It's a beautiful fall day. The grass is green, the leaves a cascade of color, the clouds a fine cotton white, the sun bright and I am together with my family and some new friends. It won't get better than this."

"Don't," said Lew, looking up at Pappas, who met his eyes.

The others at the table, except for Bernice, looked puzzled. She kept up her eating pace.

"Will there ever be a better day to die?" asked Pappas, picking up the gun.

Franco was on his feet, chair kicked back, dish in his hand. Olive oil was dripping from the plate. Stavros and Dimi rose together and said, "Pop."

Pappas nodded at Stavros, smiled at Dimitri, looked at his mother who continued to look down, a glass in her hand. He winked at Lew who quietly repeated, "Don't. I know you didn't —"

"But," interupted Pappas. "There is trial, prison. Secrets exposed. Shame."

"Pop," said Stavros. "Please."

"I choose Greek tragedy, not courtroom farce," answered Pappas, turning the gun and firing into his own left eye.

No one screamed. No one jumped up. The only voice was Franco's saying, "Holy shit." For an instant, the only movement was Franco's, who crossed himself.

Then Lew got up, leaned over the blood-covered face. The two sons knocked over their chairs and went to kneel and weep in their father's blood. Franco stood behind them. At the far end of the table, Bernice Pappas said, "I didn't make any dessert."

"She knew," said Dimitri. "She knew he

was going to do this. Why the hell did he do this?"

He looked at his dead father, then at his brother and finally at Lew.

"What did you say to him? What did he say to you?" asked Stavros.

"The sky is falling," said Lew.

Stavros stood up and said, "Dimitri, get Grandma to her room, give her one of her sleeping pills. No, give her two." Dimitri rose, looked back at his father's torn face and hurried to his grandmother.

"You two," Stavros said. "You don't have to be part of this. Go."

Franco placed a hand on Pappas's neck to be sure he was dead and then stood.

"He shot himself in the same eye as me," said Stavros quietly while his brother coaxed his grandmother from her chair at the other end of the table. "Why don't I feel any-thing?"

Lew knew, but he didn't say. Stavros would have to make his own deal with his father's ghost.

13

At five minutes to three, Franco dropped Lew in front of Dunkin' Donuts and went to park the truck. The sky grumbled an introduction to a promise or threat of rain. At a newsstand four doors away, two men stood arguing. Lew stopped. He recognized one of the men. The one he didn't recognize had a round belly, blue sweatshirt, rolled-up sleeves and arms moving to the beat of his anger. The angry man pointed a threatening thick finger at the sidewalk as he said, "Right here. Right now. You got a brother could help you. Fine. Get him here fast so I can lay him on his ass and get back to work."

The man he was talking to was about the same height as the angry man but from another world. His belly was still under control. He wore a dark suit with a tightly knit, loosely wrapped purple tie. The tie had little spots of sunlike orange. His hands were folded against his chest and he neither turned his head nor lashed out at the raving man who was in his face.

People flowed around them. No one had yet struck a blow, no one had addressed the passing crowd.

"What's it about?" a slouching man in a well-worn khaki Army surplus topcoat asked Lew.

The man was black, in need of a shave or a good beard trim. He pulled and shifted from leg to leg as if he were cold and tugged at his dirty red watch cap. At the side of the watch cap was an orange T.

"So waddya gonna do about it?" the hairy man said.

"You from Tennessee?" Lew asked the man next to him.

"Been there, been there," the man in cap said sagely, "but born right here in Detroit."

"We're in Chicago," said Lew.

The man in the cap looked around at the buildings, the street signs, the people and said, "Chicago? I need to wake up and call Leanne. Leanne, that's my daughter. She lives here in . . ."

"Chicago."

"Yes. You see I've been a little under the weather since the war."

"Which war?" Lew asked as the hairy man began to poke the well-dressed man in the chest with a finger.

"Pick two, your choice," said the man with the cap, hunching up his shoulders, hands in his pockets, moving from foot to foot. "World War Two, Korea, Vietnam, Grenada, Kosovo, Afghanistan, good old Iraq, some secret places I couldn't even pronounce when I was there and a couple I never knew the name of. Pick two and I'll jab them in your eyes like Moe in the Three Stooges."

The hairy man was inches from the well-dressed man now. The hairy man was now shouting, insisting, "Cash, now, all of it."

"I didn't take your newspaper," the well-dressed man said calmly.

People were pausing now. Something was about to happen. It had to. The hairy man became aware of the gatherers and tried to up the language ante.

"You have taken that which is rightfully mine," he said, face turning red. He slapped his open fist against his chest, making a thumping sound like that of King Kong.

"This paper is mine," the well-dressed man said calmly, wearily. "Brought it from home this morning."

"I saw you take it, you lying son of a bitch."

The hairy man's spittle sprayed the other

289

man, but the other man showed no emotion.

"You're wrong," said the well-dressed
man.

The hairy man swung a brick-sized right
fist at the other man's head. The well-
dressed man stepped to his right and the
hairy man's momentum took him into the
unwelcoming arms of a couple from Duluth
celebrating their fifty-ninth anniversary.

"Just like on the television," said the man
in the red cap. "Someone ought to help that
fella."

Lew wasn't sure which "fella" he was supposed to help.

The hairy man, fists clenched, making
growling sounds, was striding toward the
man in the suit. The man in the suit didn't
move.

"Which one?" asked Lew.

"Which one? Donald Trump with a good
haircut, that's who? I'd bet you a buck
against him if I had a buck."

"You'd be picking a loser," said Lew.

"You know somethin' I don' know, right?"

"Right," said Lew.

"Well, I know other stuff you don't know."

"I'm sure," said Lew as the hairy man
moved in.

"Just this A.M., over by the drain over

there at Navy Pier, a guy named H. Lee zwooped a knife right into the arm of another guy name of Crazy Proof, on account he carries an old shit-up piece of paper says he's crazy. How's your day, man?"

The hairy man was moving slowly now, determined to end the show, satisfy the onlookers.

"I had a nice lunch and watched a guy shoot himself in the head," said Lew.

The man in the cap nodded knowingly and said, "I seen stuff like that too. Guy named Willie, Silly Willie they called him, jumped off a roof. Splatter, you wouldn't believe 'less you saw it. Your guy? Lots of blood?"

"Lots of blood."

The hairy guy feinted with his body, shouted, "Newspaper!" and threw his weight into a decent right cross. The well-dressed man grabbed the lunger's sleeve as he punched and helped his momentum carry the man through a space made by the crowd.

The hairy man landed on his face, tried to get to his knees, groaned and looked around. He had temporarily lost track of time and space. The fight was over without a punch landing. The crowd clearly felt cheated. The man in the red knit cap said, "Well, least we didn't pay for a ticket."

"Small blessings," said Lew.

"Amen, brother. You think you might . . ."

Lew fished a handful of change from his pocket and handed it to the man.

The crowd was almost gone. The well-dressed man was helping the dazed gladiator to his feet, being careful not to cover himself in blood.

"Thank you," said the red-capped man.

"What were you before?" Lew asked.

"Before what? Oh, first a soldier and then I was a very bad preacher of bootlegged and distorted meanderings randomly recalled from the Holy Bible."

The man in the suit was steadying the bleeding man with one hand and speaking to him softly. The bleeding man nodded in understanding as he stained Jackson Street.

"Whomsoever will take my hand," the man in the cap suddenly bellowed. "So shall he walk with me through the valley of monsters and devils and emerge on the path to a bright eternity. And that is no shit."

People were not attracted by his call to salvation.

"I still got it," the man said, smiling. "Haven't done that in years. Feels good.

Come on. Get down. Feels good. Feels good."

"It doesn't feel good," said Lew.

"Give it half a shot."

"It's not in me."

The man in the knit cap plunged his hands into his coat pockets, backed away and looked at Lew saying, "I see that now."

He turned his back and swooped through the crowd.

"Do I have any blood on me, Lew?" came a question from Lew's left.

Lew turned to face the well-dressed man. There was no visible blood on Milt Holiger.

The bloody man, the crowd and the preacher had drifted away. A new line of hurrying pedestrians and grinding cars took over.

"His newspaper," said Holiger, looking at Lew. "I once had a guy, little guy, mean face, lips pushed out like this."

Holiger jutted his chin out and opened his eyes wide.

"Little guy says I'm wearing his pants. Won't give up. Stays in my face. He was too pathetic to hit. I told him where the Good-will store was on Madison and gave him a buck. He, can you believe it, struts away mumbling about my stealing his pants. Guy had maybe a twenty-four waist, tops. The pants were thirty-eights."

There weren't many people inside the Dunkin' Donuts and there was no line. Milt Holiger ordered a black coffee and a sourdough donut. Lew ordered a coffee with cream and double sugar and a corn muffin. Franco came in. He nodded at Holiger, looked over the counter at the trays of donuts, muffins and pastries.

"Hard to decide," Franco said. "Okay, a chocolate chip muffin, a chocolate-frosted donut, not the fluffy one, the cake kind, and a coffee straight."

Lew paid for all three orders and headed for a small table for two in the back near the restrooms.

"It's okay. I'll sit over there," said Franco, nodding at an empty table across the room.

"Gracie got accepted at Vanderbilt," Holiger said, pulling his chair up to the table.

"And your son?"

"Alan's still straight A at Northwestern," Holiger said, tearing his donut in half and dipping one of the halves into his coffee with his right hand. The left he used to keep his tie from dipping into the coffee. "So you want to tell me more about the person or persons who killed Catherine?"

Lew looked at his muffin and coffee but didn't reach for them.

"His name is Victor Lee."

"And you haven't turned him in? You want me to do it?"

"No."

"He's alive, right? Wait. Maybe I don't want to know," Holiger said, working on his coffee and muffin.

"He's alive. I talked to him."

"What did he say?"

"He's suffering."

"He said he was suffering?"

"I could see he was suffering," said Lew, touching his coffee cup but still not lifting it.

"Where is he now?" asked Holiger, starting on the second half of his donut.

"Lost," said Lew, looking over at Franco who had finished both his muffin and donut. "Pappas is dead."

Holiger paused, soggy wedge of donut halfway from the table to his mouth. Then he leaned forward, but it was too late to stop the end of the donut from dropping into the coffee.

"Killed himself right after lunch," Lew continued.

"Today? How do you know?"

Holiger checked himself to be sure no drops of coffee had splashed on him.

"I was there," said Lew. "Catherine, Pap-

295

pas, Posno, Santoro, Aponte-Cruz, all dead."

"Posno, dead?" said Holiger.

A very fat young man with a well-trimmed beard had replaced the two who had left the next table. The fat man was wearing a Chicago Bears jacket and cap. He glanced at Lew and went to work on some large iced drink covered with whipped cream.

"And another hundred people just got off of the train," Lew said. He thought he had said it to himself but Milt Holiger said, "Train?"

"Nothing," said Lew, breaking off a corner of the muffin.

"Lew, you all right?"

Their eyes met. Holiger's concern was sincere.

"Making a dollar a minute," said Lew.

"You're losing me here, Lewis."

"Catherine's missing files don't have anything to do with Pappas, Posno or Victor Lee," said Lew.

"They don't?"

"No," said Lew.

Franco had finished eating. He stood and looked at Lew, who motioned him back down. Franco sat.

"Okay, but what about Santoro and Aponte-Cruz?" said Holiger. "Did Pappas own up to killing them before he died? Did — what's his name — Lee kill them?"

"Pappas didn't kill them. Neither did Lee."

"You know who did?"

Lew took the folded bank statement and the bullet he had taken from the door of Franco's truck out of his pocket and placed them on the table in front of Holiger.

"You did, Milt," Lew said.

A woman, trying to keep her bulky flower-patterned bone-handled purse from falling from under her arm, held her white paper bag in front of her, scanning for an open table. There was none. She sighed and headed for the door.

"I think Catherine's missing file is the one with bank statements in it," said Lew.

"Lew," Holiger said with a sigh.

"You're holding the one I picked up from the bank this morning," Lew said. "You told me you went to the bank, talked to someone. You didn't. They log in every visitor. They've also got video surveillance. You're not going to be on that tape are you, Milt?"

Milt Holiger looked down at the statement and the bullet that rested on top of it. He touched neither.

"No."

"I saw the computer file," said Lew. "The

file shows individual checks, front and back."

"You know I can . . ."

"That bullet's going to match your gun, isn't it?"

Holiger looked away and played with a crumb on his plate.

"It's also going to match the bullets in Santoro and Aponte-Cruz," Lew went on.

"I could have changed guns," Holiger said.

"Why? No one suspected you."

"You're right," said Holiger, readjusting himself in the chair.

"You've been taking our mail, our bank statements, forging checks," said Lew. "You've got real identification. You really are a State's Attorney investigator. You had the mail rerouted. I can find out where."

Holiger looked around the room. Smiling faces. Sad faces. A fat young man with a well-trimmed beard holding a donut in one hand, coffee in the other. Franco in a stare down with a thin woman holding a coffee cup who wanted his table. The two young women, one black, one clearly Latina, behind the counter in trim uniforms serving, scurrying.

"A post office box," said Holiger. "The mail goes to a post office box in White Plains. In your name. Lew, I didn't start writing the checks till almost a year after you were gone. You left no address. You could have been dead."

"When I left there was less than a hundred dollars in the account," Lew went on. "Then, all of a sudden, four hundred thousand dollars. Now there's a hundred thousand."

Holiger shook his head, reached up to tighten his tie, changed his mind.

"You want to be exact? Four hundred and twenty-two thousand, Catherine's life insurance. I had it deposited in your account. There's one hundred and nine thousand dollars and forty-seven cents in there now."

"And no one at the bank or the insurance company asked any questions?"

"Why should they? I had it directly deposited into your joint account. Lew, I was in the hole. One kid in college, another about to go. Ruthie's diabetes is, well, it's bad."

"You killed two men, Milt."

"No, I . . ."

"Santoro was working for the bank," said Lew. "He came to you to see if he could find a lead to me. So, you killed him, him and Aponte-Cruz."

"I could say I'll find a way to pay you back the the rest of the money," Holiger said, leaning over the table, whispering.

"How are you going to get three hundred thousand dollars, Milt?"

"I don't know. Overtime?"

Holiger smiled. Lew did not.

"You murdered two people, Milt."

"You're going to turn me in. That guy Lee, he murdered Catherine and you didn't turn him in."

"He killed Catherine. He didn't murder her."

Franco had lost the stare down contest with the waiting woman. He was up now and heading toward the table where Lew and Milt Holiger sat.

"Lew, Ruthie, the kids, what are you going to do?" asked Holiger, sitting back, eyes closed, rubbing his forehead with his fingers.

"What are you going to do?" asked Lew.

He hadn't touched his coffee or the muffin. Franco was standing next to the table now.

"I don't know," said Holiger. "I'm not going to shoot myself or jump off the Sears Tower if that's what you're hinting at. There are too many people dead in the last few days. You know why, Lewis?"

"Yes, because I came back to town."

"Okay, I'll turn myself in, plead . . . I don't know what."

"Not going to eat that, Lewis?" Franco said.

Lew shook his head no. Franco picked up the muffin.

Lew stood up. Franco saw the bullet on top of the unfolded bank statement.

"I'll call Dupree tomorrow," said Holiger. "I want to tell Ruthie first."

Franco looked puzzled.

"What?" he asked. "What's goin' on?"

Holiger looked up at Franco and then at Lew and said, "Watch the ten o'clock news tomorrow."

Lew walked past tables toward the door, Franco at his side. Franco bumped into the table where two black men wearing identical blue long-sleeved turtle-necked sweaters swept up their coffee cups before they spilled. Franco excused himself. Lew looked back at Milt Holiger, who was staring down at the bullet.

"Mind telling me what that was all about?" Franco said.

"I'm going home," said Lew.

And after the family dinner that night, he did.

14

To Lew's right on the Southwest Airlines flight to Tampa, a woman in her thirties, large, heavy, was trying to untie a knot around a package wrapped in blue paper. She kept pushing her slipping glasses back on her nose and mumbling to herself as she struggled.

Lew was on the aisle, eyes closed, seeing dead people.

On the other side of the mumbling woman was a young man in an orange T-shirt. The young man's arms were folded, his green baseball cap pulled down over his closed eyes.

"I don't want to tear it. I don't want to tear it. I'm not going to tear it," the woman mumbled.

Lew opened his eyes. Through the window past the three people across the aisle, he could see a forever of darkness pricked with tiny white pulsing stars.

"Oh, God," said the woman, leaning back and placing the package on her lap while she reenergized to continue her battle with the string. "What's inside? What's inside? What's inside?"

"A book," said Lew.

He regretted his two words before he had even finished getting them out. The woman had turned her head and was tight-lipped.

"It's supposed to be a surprise," she said. "He said it was a surprise. Now you've god-damn spoiled it."

"I do that sometimes," Lew said.

"Trying to be funny? That it? Stand-up comedian wannabe?"

"No," said Lew.

"Okay, do something useful, George Carlin. Untie the knot."

She handed him the package.

A flight attendant, the sleeves of her white blouse rolled up, came quickly down the aisle, smiling as she passed. Lew thought she looked tired. Wary? Terrorists? Crazy people? Drunks? Turbulence? Rockets from the ground? Every flight brought down the odds for her. But then, Lew thought, every day brings down the odds for all of us.

"Can you untie it or not?" the woman said.

Then she suddenly brightened, a smile on

her face.

"Hey, can you untie it or knot? Get it? Not like with a *k* in front not *n-o-t.*"

"Yes," said Lew, working on the string.

The young man in the orange T-shirt and green cap shifted and turned his back on the woman and Lew.

Lew untied the string and handed the package back.

"My fingers," she said. "Too short, too stubby, for which I blame my mother who has them too."

"It could be something worse," said Lew.

"Could be?" said the woman, carefully pulling back the paper. "It is worse."

She folded the paper carefully, placed it in the pouch on the back of the seat in front of her and looked down at a paperback copy of *Heart of Darkness.* She put her right hand on the book and sobbed.

"That sun-diddly son of a bitch." She looked at Lew. "He remembered. We had to read this back when we were in second year of high school. I hated the damn thing. But he liked it. You know what?"

"No."

"I'm gonna keep this book, and the paper in my handbag," she said. "Carry around something from someone you love and you hope-to-hell loves you even if he's not there

304

for you and never will be. You know what I mean?"

Lew's hand was in his pocket, touching Catherine's wedding band on his key chain.

"Yes," he said.

The woman leaned forward and looked out the window past the sleeping or pretending-to-sleep young man.

"Almost there," she said. "That's Tampa."

"Almost there," Lew agreed. He closed his eyes and thought about a conversation only hours old.

Angie had wanted to have the family over. Lew could leave the next day. Franco had agreed. Angie had looked at her brother's face and understood.

"Okay," she had said, taking his right hand in both of hers.

"What's okay?" asked Franco. "Uncle Tonio's gonna be here, Maria and the kids, Jamie . . ."

"Next time," Angie had said.

"Next time," Lew had agreed.

It was close to midnight when Lew pulled the rental car into a space at the rear of the DQ on 301. He would ask Dave if he could leave it there for a while. If Lew didn't think of someone to give it to in the next few days, he would call a charity that takes vehicles and have it hauled away. There were advantages to having the Saturn, but he could think of only one, ready transportation. There were lots of negatives, including responsibility for keeping it running, feeding it gas, getting a vehicle tag. There would be the resistible temptation to drive when he should walk or use his bike. There would also be the resistible temptation to keep the vehicle clean.

Tonight was sleep. Tonight was doors locked and darkness.

When he opened the door and flicked on the light, he was aware, probably for the first time, of how bare the space was. Three folding chairs, small desk with ping dents and one empty lone wire box on it for letters, and on the wall, the painting. Tonight was sleep.

He went to the painting, stood in front of it. Not long, a few seconds, enough to refresh his memory. Darkness shrouded mountains and the lone spot of color. Stopping to look at the painting had become not a compulsion but a ritual. For the first time, he realized that. Don't think about it. Tonight was sleep.

He turned off the light, made his way to the small room off of the office, clicked on the floor lamp and looked at the cell in which he lived. Cot. Television. VHS player.

His few clothes on hangers in the closet and in the low unpainted three-drawer dresser against the wall. Everything was neat. Order. Keep one small space clean. Order. He put down his bag, put his dirty clothes in the small wicker basket in the closet, placed the book Angie and Franco had given him on the wooden chair next to his bed alongside the black traveling clock with the relentless red numbers. He took off his clothes, folded them neatly on the waist-high closet shelf Ames had built and pulled on his oversize Shell T-shirt. Then he turned out the light and got into bed, but not under the thin khaki blanket. Tonight was sleep.

But he did not sleep. They weren't ghosts. They weren't vivid memories. They were part of him. Everything that happens, every moment spent became, he felt certain, part of him. Dreams, movies, imagination, distorted and real memories. All took up bits of the real time of his life, were as much a part of him as a chocolate cherry Blizzard. He let the dreams and thoughts come, beginning and ending with Catherine.

And then he slept.

There was light and the faint rustle of someone in the next room. Lew blinked at the window. He had forgotten to close the blinds. The morning sun, rising above the shops on the other side of 301, cut through the spaces between the plastic slats.

Lew sat, bare feet on the floor. Then as he rose, he reached for his faded leather pouch with his soap, razor, toothbrush and toothpaste. He took a fresh blue towel from his closet, draped it over his shoulder and went through the door into his office.

Ames McKinney leaned back against the wall across from the door a few feet from the Stig Dalstrom painting. Ames wore his usual naturally faded jeans, a long-sleeved blue flannel shirt under a blue denim jacket. His gray-white hair was cut trim and his face cleanly shaved. He was reading a paperback book, but looked up when Lew entered the room.

"You look sartorial," said Lew.

"I'm a trendsetter," Ames said, putting the book in his jacket pocket. "How did it go?"

"Found the man who killed Catherine. Watched a man shoot himself. Talked to a man who had killed a lawyer and a bodyguard and stolen Catherine's and my savings."

Ames didn't ask for further explanation.

"Busy few days," said Ames, pushing away

from the wall. "Got a busy one for you today."

"What are you reading?"

Ames touched the pocket of his jacket into which he had slipped the book and said, "*Ivanhoe,* Scott. Wanna put your pants on, chief?"

"I'll be right back."

Lew opened the door, stepped into the cool morning facing the fully risen sun. Twenty steps to his right was the washroom. It was the only washroom for the six offices in the two-story building.

No one was inside when he entered. Sometimes a vagabond from Genesis, a tattered soul cast out of Eden by a vengeful God, would make the cracked tile floor his home for the night. The two toilet stalls had doors that wouldn't stay closed and a sink with a perpetual slow drip that had left a dark stain leading to the drain. The room had two pinging overhead fluorescent lights. At the moment, they both worked.

Lew looked in the mirror and saw his mother's face. It was impossible to avoid the resemblance, the pouting lower lip, the dark, sad face, brown eyes. He took off his shirt, hung it over the top of a toilet stall, washed, shaved, brushed, combed back his hair. It was the best he could do. It was all he wanted to do. While he liked to keep himself, his living space, his clothes clean and neat, he wasn't obsessive. The world was chaotic. He wanted his part of it to be reasonably free of that chaos.

When he got back in the office, Ames said, "Borg."

Lew moved into the other room and raised his voice. "You saw him?"

"Talked to him on the phone. Don't know what his problem is but he won't go to the police with it."

When Lew dressed in jeans, a white dress shirt and his Cubs baseball cap, he said, "I've got a hundred and nine thousand dollars."

Ames looked at him.

"Catherine's insurance," Lew said. "About a quarter of it. The other three-quarters was stolen."

"Way you live that could stretch you for four or five years," said Ames.

"It could," Lew agreed. "I'll think about it."

They drove to Long Boat Key and straight up Gulf of Mexico Drive to the entrance of Conquistador Del Palmas. The uniformed guard at the gate was old, with perfect false teeth and a smile. Lew's name had been left at the gate and he and Ames were waved in.

Earl Borg's condo was in an eight-story building. Borg was on the sixth floor. He buzzed them in and they crossed the highly polished azure tile lobby to the elevator, which took them silently to the sixth floor. The door to 604 was closed. Lew knocked.

"Come in. It's open."

The apartment wasn't large. A dining-room table and four chairs sat to the left in front of an open kitchen. Another door was open to Lew's left. Beyond the door was a fully made double bed, ebony end tables and a matching dresser. To the right of the living room in which they were standing was an office-den. The leather smell of the den furniture dominated the apartment. On the small balcony across from Lew and Ames sat a man facing the Gulf of Mexico.

Something didn't look right, feel right about the place or the man. Lew looked at Ames and knew that he sensed it too.

"Drink?" Borg asked. "I've got sangria out here. Ice. Glasses."

Ames and Lew went out on the small balcony. There were two white canvas-backed director's chairs.

"No, thanks," said Lew.

"I'll take one."

"Mr. McKinney," said Borg, without looking up. "I recognize your voice. Distinctive."

"Montana mostly."

And then Lew realized what was wrong with the apartment and the man. There was no television set, no computer, no paintings on the walls. There was no reason to put them there. Earl Borg was blind.

Lew and Ames sat, their backs to the Gulf.

"You figured it out," said Borg, reaching slowly for the pitcher. "I've learned to read pauses, silences, inflections, hesitations over the past two years. I do have a television in the den and a computer that likes to talk."

He found the pitcher and a glass and carefully and accurately poured till the glass was more than half full.

"Mr. McKinney?" he said, holding up the glass.

"Thanks," said Ames, taking it.

"You wanted to see me?" asked Lew.

"Very much, but since I'm blind, that won't be possible. I'll settle for straight talking. I'm diabetic, knew it would take my sight someday. Took my father's too and I'm pretty sure my grandfather's. Happen to remember the little girl back at the hog-dog?"

"I remember."

"That little girl is my daughter. She's thirteen now. She has also been kidnapped. I want you to find her and take her back to her mother."

"The police," Lew said.

"Officially, I'm not the child's father and I'm certainly not nor ever was Denise's husband. Denise wants me to pay the money. She won't tell the police. She's afraid of what might happen to Lilla. They've had her three days. Denise is now convinced they might kill her."

"Are you convinced?" Lew asked.

"Oh, yes," Borg said, taking a long sip of his drink. "I know them, know what they're capable of."

"You know who they are?" Lew asked.

"Yes, you met them at the hog-dog. They're my sons, Chet and Matt. Different mother than Lilla. Mr. Fonesca, Mr. McKinney, I have many regrets, those two boys being high on the list, but that girl is the lone glow in my life of darkness. I live simple, but there's not much meaning to it without that one pinpoint of light whose name is Lilla." He paused and then said, "I laid it on a little too heavy-handed, didn't I?"

"A little," Lew said.

"Are they in Kane?" Lew asked.

"I don't know, but I'm confident you can find them. You found me four years ago. I've asked some people who know people who owe people and I know you're good at situations like this. They know about you."

"They?" Lew asked.

Borg kept staring toward the horizon. Lew resisted looking at whatever it was Borg seemed to see out there.

"In my often wicked business, I meet and use and am used by people who have connections below the line of legality," said Borg.

Lew looked at Ames, whose nod of yes was almost imperceptible.

"I need some information," Lew said to Borg.

"Whatever you want," said Borg. "Want to talk money first?"

"How much is she worth to you?" Lew asked.

"My fortunes have diminished a bit since you last saw me, but I'm far from impoverished. So, I'll pay, at the far end of reasonable, whatever you ask if you bring her to me or her mother safely and get those two whelps the hell out of Florida forever."

Lew looked at Ames, who met his eyes. Across the table Earl Borg stared between them.

"Gas, car rental, expenses, reimbursement for any information I have to buy."

"That's it?" asked Borg.

"There's a children and family services fund in the county," Lew said. "Give them a donation."

"Four thousand?"

"Four thousand," Lew agreed.

"Best deal I've ever made if you don't count the time I got four acres of downtown Sarasota from a half-wit named Tarton Sparks," said Borg. "Ask your questions. Take your time."

Three hours up I-75 through heavy snowbird and normal traffic they passed a jack-knifed truck that lay dead on its side. The truck's hood was open like a *King Kong* dinosaur. After the gapers' block, traffic moved faster, but not much. Early in the afternoon, Lew pulled into the same gas station and general store he had gone to the last time he had come to Kane. The boiled peanuts sign was still there, now peeled away so that it read: B ST OILED PEA TS IN THE SOUT.

Another change from the last time Lew had come to Kane was that Ames McKinney was with him and armed with an impressive long-bareled revolver in the pocket of his yellow slicker. The revolver was there courtesy of Big Ed and the Texas Bar & Grille. Big Ed told people that the gun, which usually rested in a glass-covered display case on the wall behind the bar, had belonged to John Wesley Hardin. Ames doubted the legend, but admired the weapon. Ames's job, among his others at the Texas, was to keep the display guns clean and in working order.

Lew filled the tank with gas.

The overweight woman behind the counter was the same one who had been there the last time. It even seemed to Lew as if she were wearing the same dress. She looked at Ames and then at Lew and back at Ames. Her hands were facedown on the glass countertop.

Lew handed her a twenty-dollar bill.

"Sixteen-twelve out of twenty," she said as if making the transaction were a burden.

She opened the cash register with a soft grunt, deposited the twenty, counted out change, closed the register and faced Lew and Ames with a gun in her right hand.

"Why the gun?" asked Lew.

"Everyone in this town has a gun," she said. "When a couple of new folks come to town and one is carrying a gun under his slicker, you consider if you might be on the wrong end of a holdup."

"Makes sense," said Ames. "But it's not so."

"I've been in here before," said Lew.

"Don't remember you," she said, gun steady.

"Guess not. You know a girl named Lilla Fair, a woman named Denise Fair?" asked Lew.

The gun was steady in her hand. Her expression didn't change.

"I know everybody in and around Kane," she said. "All four hundred and eighty-two of them."

"How many are named Lilla Fair?" Lew asked.

The woman's eyes moved back and forth from Lew to Ames.

"Why?"

"She's missing," Lew said.

"No," said the woman, shaking her head. "She's with the Manteen boys. Left two days ago, stopped for gas. Ask me, I'd say Denise is some kind of fool to let Lilla go anywhere with Chester and Matthew. Lilla's not a baby girl anymore, if you know what I mean."

"I know," said Lew. "Would you mind putting the gun down?"

"You related to Denise?"

"No," said Lew. "Lilla's father wants to be sure she's safe."

"Well, he will not soon have his wish," she

said. "Long as that girl is with those nut-crackers, he will not have reason to be sure she's safe."

She put the gun back under the counter and handed Lew his change.

Denise Fair stood on the wooden stoop of her two-bedroom, one-story box of a house. The house was about a two-minute drive from the gas station. From the look on her face, both Lew and Ames concluded that the overweight woman had called to announce that they were coming.

She wore tan slacks and an extra-large orange University of Florida sweatshirt. Her arms were folded against her chest. She looked like a college student, hair tied back in a ponytail, skin clear, pretty.

"My name is Lewis Fonesca. This is my friend Ames McKinney. Earl Borg has asked us to find your daughter."

She looked at the two of them and was clearly not impressed.

"Tell Earl," she said evenly, "that I am still begging him to pay what they want. They wouldn't hurt Lilla. They've known her all her life. They may be stupid, but they're not going to molest or hurt their own half sister, especially if Earl gives them the goddamn few hundred dollars. Problem is that Lilla is diabetic. Her medication is gone. She took it when they . . . I think she has enough for . . .'' — she shook her head and went on — "I don't know. I know Matt and Chet. Lilla likes them, but they're not . . . no, they wouldn't hurt her."

Both Ames and Lew knew she was trying to convince herself and was failing.

"Any idea where they might take her?" Lew asked.

"Earl's still in Sarasota?"

"Yes," said Lew.

"They don't have much in the way of imagination," she said. "They'd go where they could be close to the money they hoped to get from Earl."

"Sarasota," said Ames.

"Sarasota," Denise Fair confirmed.

"Chet and Matt's mother," said Lew. "Is she in town?"

"Alma Manteen died last week," she said. "May account for why they're doing what they're doing."

"You have a photograph of Lilla we could borrow?" Lew asked. "A recent one."

"Yes," she said. "I'll get it for you. You don't have to return it. Give it to Earl. Yes, I know, he can't see it, but he can hold it. Give it to him and tell him to pay them. He's stubborn, but the Lord knows Earl loves Lilla. If he won't pay, then I pray the Lord guide you to her."

"We'll find her," said Ames.

"Lilla's all I've got," she said. "I lost my son in Iraq."

"Fred," said Lew.

She looked at him.

"I was there when Lilla named the hog," Lew said.

Denise Fair, arms still folded, went back into her house to find a photograph of her daughter.

15

If the photograph of the girl was close to her reality, then Lilla Fair was not destined for beauty. She was thin, long dark hair over a smiling face, showing large teeth, round surprised eyes, and a night sky full of freckles. She looked more like Borg than she looked like her mother, but she really didn't look that much like him either.

The bonus in the photograph was that a group of people in the background were standing with beer bottles in hand. Except for one, they weren't paying attention to Lilla. The one looking at her was either Chet or Matt. The other twin was next to him in profile. He was hoisting a blur of a beer bottle toward his mouth.

The first thing Lew and Ames did when they got back to Sarasota was to make ten wallet-size machine copies of the photograph at Office Max on Bee Ridge. The second thing they did was walk to the end of the mall and have dinner at the no-frills home cooking restaurant that featured mini-burgers.

"Dinner's on Borg," Lew said when they were seated across from each other at a small booth.

Lew had three mini-burgers with cheese. Ames had a steak, salad and mushroom soup.

When they finished, Lew gave Ames five of the copies of the photo and made a list of places and the people they should give the photographs to. Ames looked at the list and then at Lew.

"Let's do it," he said.

The list consisted of people whose names Ames recognized.

"Let's do it," Lew agreed. "I'll take you back to the Texas. Then we split up. Take the ones I marked."

"Sure you want it that way?"

"I'm sure," said Lew.

"Suit yourself," said Ames.

"I'm glum."

Matt Manteen made the pronouncement from the bed in Room Six of the Blue Gulf Motel on Tamiami Road. His cap was perched on his head, his hands folded over a pillow on his stomach. He had always slept or taken a nap with a pillow on his stomach. He didn't know why, and no one had ever asked, so he didn't have to think about it. Matt had heard someone say, in a movie or something, "I don't think about what I don't think about." It was his protective motto when asked to give an opinion on almost anything.

Matt had lots of opinions, all of them donated willingly by his dead mother and his brother. He would have welcomed a few more from his father, but he had given up on that. His father, when he had seen him, mostly at the hog-dog, had given orders, not opinions. Now he and Chet were giving their father orders.

Couldn't help it though. Matt was glum.

The shower was running behind the door about ten feet from the foot of the bed. A television on a table against the wall was on but mute. On the screen, an old man with big white teeth and toupee that didn't match the color of what little hair he had left was holding up a white plastic thing like it was first-place prize in the county fair. He was looking right at Matt, talking, saying nothing.

"I'll call him back in an hour," said Chet, sitting in a chair, his feet propped up on the bed he would share with Matt again that night if they were still in Sarasota. Lilla, if she were still alive, would sleep on the couch again, which was fine with her. Matt kept looking at the old man on the television screen. To Chet, the old man seemed happy as shit.

Behind the closed door, Lilla wasn't singing.

"What are we gonna do about Lilla's medicine?" asked Matt.

"She's got enough of the stuff for a couple of days."

The pause was long.

"What if he won't pay?" asked Matt.

Chet was the longer-term thinker of the Manteen brothers, which was not a fact that merited pride. Life for him was a checkers game he could handle only one move at a time. Matt couldn't even play the game. It had nothing to do with intelligence. It was about concentration. When they were in grade school, every other day, as they had been ordered by their mother, they had taken the pills Dr. Winenholt had given her. Hadn't helped. They were put in a "special" class. That didn't help. They were as smart as some of the other kids who didn't go special. The Manteen brothers just couldn't think ahead. Same thing in high school. "Jumpy," that's what their mother had told the teachers and principals. "My boys are jumpy."

"Remember, if he won't pay, we kill her," said Chet. "It's what we said we'd do and we've got nothing much in the world but our word."

Matt shook his head, clutched the pillow more tightly to his stomach and said, "Killing Lilla won't get us the money to make it to Montana. What it'll get us is we're murderers with no money instead of being not murderers with no money."

"What are you talking about?" Chet asked, sitting up.

"I don't know," said Matt.

The shower thundered on. Chet glanced at the bathroom. A thin fog of steam lazily wisped under door.

"We are murderers," said Chet.

"No," said Matt, sitting up and pointing a finger at his brother, pillow still on his lap. "We killed two people. We did not murder them. We did not."

"You shot the guy from Williston," Chet said with weary exasperation. "The guy who won the money at the hog-dog, remember?"

"That," said Matt emphatically, "was not murder. That was a necessity. We were broke. When good old Papa Borg closed the show, we were broke. I'm telling you something you already know here."

"And Miss Theodora in the toilet at the All-Naked Girls Live?" asked Chet. "You shot her."

"I'm not saying I didn't. I did it right there in front of you and I'm saying I killed her, but it was not murder. It was a survival necessity. The difference seems to be a little too subtle for you," Matt said. "Checkmate. That's what they say in chess when you know you've got the game won and I've got this argument won. We are not murderers."

"You don't know how to play chess," said Chet. "You can't even play checkers."

"I can," Matt insisted. "I just don't play it very good."

They had agreed on one thing this time. They hadn't really kidnapped Lilla. They had known her all her life, liked her. Damn, they shared the same father. The problem, Chet thought, was that there hadn't been a plan here. Matt counted on Chet and Chet counted on their mother and their mother was dead. They had left Kane for good, a few things in the car trunk. They had stopped at Lilla's house, asked if she wanted to go for a ride and a frozen Snickers or boiled peanuts. Lilla had said "sure" and climbed in the backseat. Lilla's mom hadn't objected.

When they had stopped at the gas station at the edge of town to put in ten dollars of gas, Lilla, singing, had gone into the bathroom. That was when Chet told him that they were going to hold Lilla for ransom. It was only right. Two years ago, Papa Earl Borg had just padlocked the hog-dog show and walked away, didn't give them a three-dollar thank you.

Where Earl Borg had always made money on the dogs and looked like he was having fun, Chet and Matt had lost what little they had, including the three dogs and two hogs. They didn't even have enough to pay what they owed Ralph Derby for patching up the animals.

Chet figured Earl Borg owed them severance pay or an inheritance or something.

"So," Matt said with resignation. "He doesn't pay and we kill her."

"That's the way of it, brother," answered Chet. "That's what I said. We've got nothing left but each other and our good word. We said we would kill her and that we full intend to do."

The old man on the TV was suddenly replaced by a blond woman who had her own smile and her own plastic thing to sell. The shower stopped.

"That's the way of it, brother," Chet

repeated, reaching for the almost empty bag of Doritos on the bed.

The door of Flo Zink's house on the bay was opened by Adele. She smiled at Ames. In her arms was her baby, Catherine, who squiggled and made bubbles with her mouth. Catherine had been given the name of Lew's wife for two reasons. Lew Fonesca had twice saved Adele's life, and Adele really liked the name Catherine. Now she loved it.

Adele stepped back to let Ames in. The open living-room area had a playpen near the window and the familiar, clean, unstylish Wild West wood and leather furniture. The stereo, which was wired to speakers all through the house, was on low. Slim Whitman was singing "Since You're Gone."

"Flo here?" Ames asked.

"Shopping," said Adele, putting the baby gently on her stomach on the white rug.

Catherine began making the arm and leg movements that would soon lead to crawling.

To Ames, Adele didn't look much different from the way she had cleaned up after she came to live with Flo almost two years ago. Adele was blond, had a full woman's body, and was, Ames knew from experience, one damn smart young lady. She had gone from a life of physical abuse and teenage prostitution to being a mother, albeit un-wed. She was also now a high school student applying to colleges, particularly to New College and the Ringling School of Art, where she could go and still be in this house with Catherine and Flo.

Ames handed her the photographs and said, "You see any of these people, call me or Lewis."

Adele looked at the photograph and then at Ames, a question in her eyes.

"The twins in the picture kidnapped the girl."

"She reminds me of someone," Adele said, still holding the photograph. "Me. Can I get you a coffee, Pepsi?"

There was no alcohol in Flo Zink's house. Temptation had been cast out for almost two years.

"No, thank you. Got to deliver more pic-tures."

"Did he find out who killed his wife?"

"He did."

"And?" she asked, looking at Catherine who looked as if she were about to lurch forward.

"Best he tell you when he's ready."

In the next hour and a half, Ames gave

copies of the photograph to several of the neighborhood's bartenders and also to the clerks at 7-11, Circle K, Burger King, Mc-Donald's, Wendy's and Kentucky Fried Chicken, and asked them to call him if they saw the twins or the girl. He told each of the people he talked to simply, "They may mean the girl harm. Her mother and father are worried for her." Everyone he talked to had listened. On the back of each picture, Ames had printed his name, Texas Bar & Grille, and the phone number of the Texas.

Ames didn't get back to the Texas on his motor scooter till after one in the morning. The Texas was closed and dark except for the nightlights. He let himself in the back door, put the gun back in the case behind the bar, and went to his room where he showered, shaved, put on his khaki pajamas. Then Ames got his reading glasses from the case on the table and read *The Marble Faun.* He finished the book a little before three in the morning and turned out the lights.

He would have four-and-a-half hours until he had to get up and start his chores. He needed no more. As he grew older, he found that he needed and was satisfied with less sleep.

■ ■ ■ ■

Lew had given the photograph to the red-haired girl at the DQ window and shown it to the bartender at the Crisp Dollar Bill across the street from his office.

Then he went back to his office. It was too late to call Sally Porovsky, tell her what had happened in Chicago, ask if she could go out for a pizza after work tomorrow. He decided he wasn't ready to tell her what had happened and was happening. He knew that once he started to talk about Chicago, about Victor Lee, about Earl Borg and the missing girl named Lilla, he would discover things he wasn't ready to deal with. It was all tied together, knotted together inside him, but he didn't know how.

There was someone else he would have to talk to before he could face Sally.

He looked at Dalstrom's painting alone on the wall, the dark jungle with the spot of light and then he looked down at the photograph of the twins and Lilla.

The phone rang. It was two in the morning.

"Fonesca," Earl Borg said calmly. "My idiot sons called. Ironic. For the first time in their lives, they think for themselves and their first decision is to kidnap their sister and demand money from their father. They want the money, in cash, forty thousand, or they'll kill her. I told them I'd do it. But I won't. You know why? Because, though my voice does not show it, I am fucking mad. In addition to which, those morons might just kill Lilla even if I pay them. Or they might take her with them wherever they plan to go even if I pay them and rape her or . . . who knows what."

"Where are you supposed to pay and when?"

"They'll call at nine in the morning, let me talk to Lilla," said Borg. "And then I have half an hour."

"They know you're . . ."

"Blind, yes. I told them I'd send someone. Can't be you. They're not bright, but they don't have Alzheimer's. They might recognize you from the hog-dog business and you might not be able to get close enough to them. Your lanky friend will do quite nicely."

"Pay them," Lew said.

"I will not," said Borg. "I told you once and I told you why. It needs no further elaboration. Goodbye, Mr. Fonesca."

Borg hung up. Lew did too and went to the window.

Lew moved to the office window, lifted

the blinds and gazed at the traffic beyond the DQ parking lot. Traffic was almost nonexistent at two in the morning, but the few cars that did go by sent out a soft whistle of wind as they passed, leaving a lull Lew found comforting.

Then the headache came. Lew knew it would, expected it, almost welcomed it. He went into his room, closed the door, closed the blinds tightly, unfolded a blanket he took from his closet and draped it over the window.

Lew's family had a history of headaches. His mother, Angela, Uncle Tonio, the others, all got headaches, all the same, always on the right side of the head. When it got bad, the only thing that helped was darkness and moaning. Moaning was essential.

When the headaches were really bad, Angie heard music that wasn't there. Uncle Tonio saw flashing colored lights. Lew sometimes smelled gardenias or barbecue sauce. This time he smelled, heard and saw nothing.

He turned off the light, rolled himself in a ball on the cot and welcomed the darkness and the pain. When he lived in Chicago with Catherine, when the headaches came, he would strip to his undershorts and curl in darkness on the cool tiles of the bathroom, his head on a bath towel.

Catherine understood. She asked no questions, offered no help because there was none to give.

Lew slipped into a deep sleep.

When he woke up, the headache was gone. He tried to go back to sleep but fleeting images snapped by like photographs on a home projector: Pappas smiling with his gun to his head; Santoro slumped over his desk; Milt Holiger's pleading and defeated eyes; Victor Lee sitting in a tavern in Urbana and blankly looking at nothing to do and nowhere to go; and then Catherine being hit by the car, a series of flying shots, ending with a close-up of Catherine at the instant of impact, surprise and pain. Lew had not been there when it happened, but it was the most vivid of his images.

He sat up, got a towel from the closet, dried himself, deposited the towel in his small hamper and put on a short-sleeved gray garage sale pullover with a collar and the words TOP SAIL embossed on the pocket.

He took the blanket from the window, letting in the sun. He looked at his watch. It was a few minutes after seven in the morning. Lew went into his office, picked up the phone and punched in the number of the

Texas Bar & Grille.

Half an hour later, Ames came up the cracked concrete steps. He didn't use the rust-tinged railing for balance. He was straight-backed and moving slowly. When he got to the top step, he looked at the window and his eyes met Lew's. Both men knew that the other had made no progress in finding Lilla and the Manteen brothers.

Ames opened the door and stepped into the office closing the door behind him. Lew turned away from the window.

"Borg wants you to make the payoff and get the girl back," Lew said.

"Suits me," said Ames.

"There won't be any money in the payoff bag."

"Didn't think there would be."

"I don't want them killed," Lew said, moving to his desk and sitting. "I think Borg does."

"How about some serious wounding?" asked Ames.

"If you have to," said Lew.

The phone rang a few minutes later.

Ames picked it up, said "McKinney," listened and hung up.

"Ten this morning," said Ames. "I drop the bag in the trash can near the playground in Wilkerson Park. Then I'm supposed to walk over to the fence around the softball fields and watch for them to let the girl go. I'm guessing it'll be a long walk for her and a quick run to the trash for the money. When they see the bag's empty, they'll have the girl in easy gunshot distance."

Lew rubbed his right hand across his balding head.

"Anyplace to hide in the park?" Lew asked.

"They picked a good spot."

"Okay," said Lew. "We do it, but why are they doing the exchange in the daylight instead of tonight? Why stay here longer than they have to? They know Borg. They know he must be trying to find them."

"Don't know," said Ames.

Lilla still had no idea that she had been kidnapped and certainly no idea that her half brothers were seriously considering killing her, that is to the extent that they could be serious about anything.

Lilla had no illusions about her own intelligence. She was no genius, except maybe compared to Matt and Chet, but she was smart enough.

She wanted to go out.

The brothers were staring at the television screen on which a big-bellied man in a red flannel shirt was shooting at clay pigeons being released a few hundred feet away.

"Pow," said Chet as a piece of clay in the television sky exploded.

"Sitting in a hotel room," she had said, "is not my idea of fun."

"This is good stuff," said Matt, eyes still on the fat man with the shotgun.

Lilla was thin, short for her age, long, straight brown hair down her back, eyes blue and wide. She looked younger than her thirteen years.

"We can watch TV in Kane," she said. "Let's go."

"We've got business in a little while," said Chet.

"Business," she said. "What kind of business?"

"Good business," said Chet. "Right?"

"Right," Matt agreed.

"We got you a pizza last night," said Chet. "Later today we take you to Disney."

"Disney World? You've got to be kidding," she said.

"No shit, true," said Matt.

"On the way we get another pizza," she insisted. "And after Disney we go to another movie. Pizza, Disney and a movie in that order or just take me back home. I don't have a good time there but I don't have a bad one either, and when my mom tells me something's gonna happen, it happens."

"We are going to Disney World," said Chet. "Like the guys on Super Bowl say. We are going to Disney World."

"Pizza with olives, black olives, and those little anchovy fish," she said.

Both Matt and Chet hated both black olives and anchovies, but this was most likely the girl's last day on earth and since she was not going to live long enough to have it, they could promise her not only the damned pizza, Disney World and the movie, but a guaranteed spot on *American Idol.*

16

Someone was knocking at the door.

Knock. Loud. And a voice.

"You in there Phone-es-ca?"

Lew and Ames both recognized the voice.

Lew opened the door and there, hands now in the pockets of his oversized blue sweatshirt, stood Darrell Caton.

"You look like shit," said Darrell, stepping in.

"Thanks," said Lew. "Is this better?"

He picked his Cubs cap up from the desk and put it on his head. Darrell made a face indicating that Lew was beyond grooming. He looked over at Ames and smiled.

"You packin' today, old man?"

"Respect," said Ames.

"I ain't disrespectin' you," said Darrell. "You are the man."

"And stop talking like that," Ames ordered.

"Hard not to," said Darrell. "I'm right on

time. It's Saturday, remember, Fonesca? What we got goin' today?"

Darrell was thirteen, thin, black, curious and often angry. He had been given a choice. Shape up or go into the system, juvenile detention, maybe a series of foster homes. His mother was twenty-nine and had been ready to give up on him. Sally Porovsky had conned Lew into being Darrell's Big Brother. It was difficult to tell if the idea had appealed less to Darrell than to Lew. Their lack of enthusiasm for the experiment had been the one bond they had between them.

Over their first three Saturdays together things had changed, primarily because Lew had been involved with cases and had to take Darrell along. Now it was clear that Darrell Caton looked forward to Saturdays with Lew.

"So," said Darrell, bouncing to the desk and sitting behind it, "what've we got going? Missing mom? Murder?"

Darrell was looking over the things on Lew's desk.

"Something like that," said Lew.

"Shit," said Darrell with a smile. "Then let's get to it, man."

Darrell picked up the photograph of Chet, Matt and Lilla.

"Saw these two last night," Darrell said. "Twins, right? Saw the girl too. Skinny kid."

He put the photograph back on the desk and looked up.

"What?" asked Darrell.

"You saw them?"

"Yeah, pizza place over on the Trail. My mom took me there last night. You know, family bonding, that kind of shit. She really just wants to keep an eye on me Friday and Saturday nights. Goes down with me. I get to keep an eye on her. She's a long time crack free."

"You saw them?" Lew repeated.

"Yeah, man. I told you," Darrell said with irritation. "Place on the Trail, right where all those motels are, used to be ho heaven. Now it's full of Canadians and Germans and whatever."

"Hand of God," said Ames.

"Coincidence," said Lew. "Sarasota's not all that big."

"Whatever it is," said Ames, "let's do it before they head for the park."

Darrell bounced out of the chair, smiling.

They went in Lew's rental car. The first stop was the Texas Bar & Grille where Ames went in and came out again in less than three minutes wearing his slicker. The second stop was DeAngelo's Pizza and Subs on Tamiami Trail. DeAngelo's didn't open till five on Saturday.

There were motels on both sides of Tamiami Trail.

It was twenty minutes after nine.

"Split up?" asked Ames.

"Right," said Lew.

"I'll go across," said Ames.

"I'll go with you," said Darrell.

"You stay with me," said Lew.

"Cowboy's got the gun under that coat," said Darrell. "He's the action."

"Come on," said Lew.

"Whatever," said Darrell.

Traffic was Saturday morning light, but it was still the Trail, which stretched north for a few dozen miles and south for a few hundred miles right into Miami.

Lew and Darrell tried their third motel clerk, showing the photograph and Lew coming up with another ten-dollar bill, which he fully intended to get reimbursed for from Earl Borg.

As they had come out of the motel, Lew looked across the four lanes of the Trail. Between the traffic he saw Ames in front of the Blue Gulf Motel, his right hand up. He had found them.

It was time to go.

Lilla was dressed in jeans and the clean Abercrombie green shirt they had bought yesterday at Goodwill for fifty cents. Her hair was tied back.

Matt and Chet said they were going to Disney World this morning, and then back home. She didn't believe them. They were terrible liars and sometimes like on television they walked across the room from her and talked, thinking she couldn't hear them.

What she did know was that she had more than enough of the two of them, thank you. She wanted to go home. She also knew they were nervous. They had kept smiling at her all through pizza the night before. They had the same smiles today. They had a real one that was lopsided, all on one side of the face. She hadn't seen that one for a long time. Then they had the one they had used last night and this morning, when they remembered it, straight across, cheeks up, line of teeth screaming out for a dentist.

She knew that they were going to meet someone in a park. She knew Chet and Matt were both carrying guns in their pockets. The guns weren't unusual for them. Far as Lilla knew, they hadn't shot anyone with them. But maybe she was wrong. What they did do in and around Kane were very odd jobs and beating people up for the

Wikiup Men's Club, where girls from as far as Gainesville, college girls, came to wiggle nude for truckers and old guys.

"Let's go," said Chet.

Chet was wearing jeans, a white T-shirt and a dirty white cowboy hat. Matt was wearing jeans, a blue T-shirt and a dirty blue cowboy hat. Both of them wore boots. They were in their hog-dog costumes. There hadn't been a hog-dog or a dog-dog for a long time, at least a year and it had been a lot longer since the man, Earl Borg, had stopped coming. The brothers had run the fights by themselves, but people didn't like them and they didn't take care of the animals. Dogs and hogs died. Dogs and hogs cost money.

Lilla took the handles of her bag, which had also been purchased at Goodwill for two dollars, and stood up.

"Simple," Chet in white whispered to Matt in blue, "We check the parked cars. We know there's no place in the park to hide, but you stay in the car with Lilla. I go to the trash can. Somebody'll be there. If he pulls a gun, you put your gun to Lilla's head."

"I know, Chet," Matt said wearily.

"Does it hurt to go over it again?"

"A little."

"Well then, just you suffer for a while," said Chet. "Everything goes right, I get the bag with the money and wave to you. You let her get out of the car. Whoever's there will look at her. That's when I shoot him. You see him go down, you shoot Lilla."

"I'd rather not kill Lilla, Chet."

Chet sighed.

"Lilla and whoever's gonna be there never did us harm," Matt went on.

"They will if we don't shoot 'em."

"What're you two talkin' about?" Lilla asked.

"Business," said Chet. "Let's go."

Matt opened the door and walked out, Lilla behind him, Chet behind her. When Chet closed the door, Ames stood up, shotgun in hand, behind the blue Kia parked in front of their door.

"Hands where I can see 'em," Ames said calmly.

"What's this?" asked Lilla, shaking her head, getting angry. "This the gunfight at the all right corral or something? You, Wyatt Earp. We got no money."

"About twenty bucks," said Chet. "It's all yours."

He started to reach down.

"Hands where I can see them," Ames repeated. "This isn't about the money in your pocket. Child, come over here and get behind me."

"No," said Lilla.

Then she saw a man get out of a car parked in a space behind the yellow-slickered gunfighter. The man with a baseball cap pulled down on his head came slowly. Through the rear window of his car she could see the face of a black boy about her age. He was smiling.

"What you want?" asked Matt.

"Two things," said the man with the cap. "Lilla comes with us."

"No," she said.

"Young lady," said Ames. "These two plan to kill you."

"No. Why would they . . . ?"

"Money," said Lew.

"My father wants me dead?"

"No," said Lew. "These two want him to pay forty thousand dollars to get you back alive."

"Back? I've never been with him in the first place," she said. Then she looked from Matt to Chet and said, "Forty thousand dollars. You told me about this, we could have asked for a hundred thousand and you wouldn't have to be thinking about killing me. I give up on you two."

"Someone's going to see us," said Lew.

"Lilla, walk over to my car now and get in."

"I don't —"

"My friend will shoot," said Lew.

Ames nodded and aimed the gun at Chet's head.

Lilla sighed and bag in hand brushed between Lew and Ames. Ames's arm moved and Matt started to reach back.

"Don't," warned Ames.

Matt didn't.

"Get in your car," said Lew very calmly. "And drive up I-75 as far north as you can go with the gas you can buy. Do not stop in Kane. Do not return to Sarasota. Do not return to Florida. We will find you and my friend here will blow your heads off. Now, the guns. Slowly put them on the ground and get into your car."

They did as they were told. Lew picked up the guns. Lew had already searched the Manteen brothers' car. No guns, no drugs, no alcohol.

Matt was in the passenger seat, Chet in the driver's seat, his arm resting on the open window. Ames, gun at his side now, stood next to the car looking down at Chet who had tilted his hat back.

"If we come back, you old fart, you'll be long dead of old age," said Chet.

"Be best if your brother drives," Ames

answered.

"Why?" asked Chet.

Ames lifted the shotgun high and brought it down hard in one move.

"Your arm is broken."

Chet screamed in pain.

"Move over and drive your brother to a hospital," said Ames to Matt. "Maybe up in Tampa. Atlanta if he can make it."

Chet, moaning, rolled into the passenger seat as his brother came around and got behind the wheel.

"You break my arm too and who's gonna drive us out of town?" Matt asked, voice quivering.

"Just you drive away," said Ames.

"If you stop at an emergency room —" Lew began.

"In Atlanta," added Ames.

"— your brother broke his arm in a baseball game," said Lew.

"We don't play baseball," said Matt.

"And it doesn't look like your brother's gonna take it up now," said Ames. "Drive."

Matt drove. Chet moaned. The car pulled out of the motel driveway and made a screeching left turn, just missing a red truck.

"Should have killed them," said Ames at Lew's side. "They were going to kill the girl."

"I've seen enough dead people," said Lew. "So have we all," said Ames.

Earl Borg answered the phone on the third ring. He could have answered the sound at the first ring. He had it on the small table next to his almost silent treadmill in his office-den. He had been running and listening to Bach's violin concerti. Blindness had gradually turned him into a lover of classical music. Before his loss of sight he had no interest in music of any kind. Now, he had speakers in every room and his stereo system had access to almost three dozen commercial-free classical music stations in addition to the huge collection he had accumulated.

Blindness had also made Earl Borg acutely aware of texture. All the furniture in his apartment was chosen not by color but by how it felt and smelled. He had a decorator, who kept him from forgetting that other people were only barely aware of what he felt and smelled.

Pebble stone and mosaic tabletops, leather chairs, fine shelf-sized marble and wood sculpture were always within reach.

It was good, he frequently thought, to be able to afford everything he wanted. All it took was good investments and years of barely legal and quite illegal business deals.

At the first ring, Borg had pressed the cool-down button on the treadmill. On the second ring, he had muted his sound system. On the third ring, he picked up the phone.

"Yes?" he said.

"She's safe," said Lew.

"Did they — ?"

"No, they didn't touch her."

"Good. Are they dead?"

"No."

"I would have preferred them dead," said Borg. "I thought I made that clear."

"You gave me wiggle room. I wiggled," said Lew. "We did break Chet's arm."

"That's some satisfaction."

"They're on their way to the Georgia border and when they cross it, they won't be back."

"No, they won't. I'll get someone else to find them and complete the job."

"You want to see your daughter?"

"No," he said. "Take her to her mother. There'll be two blank checks signed by me at your office by five o'clock, one for you, one for that charity."

"I don't need money," said Lew.

"You're rich?"

"Financially comfortable," said Lew.

"Financially but not otherwise?"

Lew said nothing.

"The checks are drawn on a new account that has exactly forty thousand dollars in it, the amount those two idiot spawn of mine wanted. Divide it between the two checks any way you like. Goodbye."

Borg hung up.

Lew looked across his desk at Lilla. Ames was standing behind him, Darrell Caton at his side.

"I got it," Lilla said, hugging herself. "He doesn't want to see me."

"You're better off," said Darrell.

"He can't see you and he doesn't want you to see him," Lew said.

Lilla looked young, younger than thirteen, only a little older than the kid in the hog-dog circle, the kid who had lost a brother named Fred. Earl Borg was certain Fred was not his son.

"Your father's a blind man," said Ames.

"Blind?"

"Doesn't want you to see him like that," said Ames.

"Yeah," said Darrell, "like he's Jesus Christ on wheels."

"He's a mean bastard," she said.

"That too," Darrell agreed.

"You don't even know him," she said,

351

turning to face Darrell.

"No, do you?" Darrell shot back.

"Take me home please," she said.

"Never saw my father either," said Darrell. "Don't think I missed much."

Darrell smiled at her.

"Great," Lilla said, sitting back in the corner. "Now I'm bringing a black boyfriend home to Kane."

Darrell laughed and said, "Fonesca, this girl is funny. What you say we stop at Denny's or something before we take her home?"

And they did.

17

Lew and Ames had driven Lilla back to Kane and dropped Darrell at home.

When Lew opened his door, the almost-full moon was balanced on the tops of the low storefront and office buildings across 301.

Behind him, as he closed the door he could hear Ames's motor scooter chug out of the DQ parking lot.

Lew undressed, put on clean, blue jockey shorts and an "I LOVE SCHNAUZERS" T-shirt that he had picked up at the Women's Exchange. Lying in bed, pillow upright against the wall, he opened MOUNTAINS OF THE MOON, THE REBECCA STRUM BOOK HIS SISTER HAD HANDED HIM WHEN SHE AND FRANCO HAD DROPPED LEW AT MIDWAY AIRPORT. BOTH HIS SISTER AND FRANCO HAD HUGGED HIM. FRANCO HAD KISSED HIS CHEEK. ANGELA HAD TOUCHED HIS FACE.

Lew looked at the neat pile of VHS tapes next to the television set. Joan Crawford, Bette Davis, Marlon Brando, Al Jolson, John Garfield, Kirk Douglas, Jane Greer, called out to Lew to join them, step out of his chaotic world into their well-ordered one. Later, maybe later or tomorrow. Tonight was Rebecca Strum.

He opened the book. It wasn't thick, less than two hundred pages.

He read:

There's comfort in the darkness, a non-judgmental stillness that banishes time. And that darkness can be found simply in the closing of one's eyes.

But when she opened her eyes, Beck, his eyes bright, glowing yellow like a black cat on a starless night, stood at the foot of Ruth's bed.

In his hand was something glinting from a light that had no source. The thing in his hand was a knife. But this was impossible because there was no way to hide a knife in the Dachau camp, no way for men to get into the women's compound, and no way for Beck to be there because Beck was dead.

Lewis read half of the book and then

placed it on the chair next to his bed. He pulled up his blanket, turned to his left as close to the wall as he could get. Behind the wall he could hear the strum of distant traffic and a pair of voices arguing on the street or in the DQ parking lot. He slept.

In the morning, Lew pulled on his pants, picked up his zippered morning case, used the bathroom and shaved, and went back to bed. At two in the afternoon he put on his jeans and an oversized black T-shirt with the words I WANT TO BELIEVE in white letters on the back. He had watched from his window until there was no one in line. He got a double cheeseburger and a chocolate cherry Blizzard.

Dave, face a copper-crinkled permanent tan, took his order. Dave owned the place but spent little time here. Whenever he could be, Dave was out on his boat, deep in the embrace of sun worship and salt air. Occasionally, Dave even fished.

"Make it to go," said Lew.

"Will do. So how'd you do? Chicago, I mean."

"Fine."

"Fine," Dave repeated, running the Blizzard machine. "So you found him?"

"Yes."

"Short of help today," said Dave.

Silence except for the traffic behind him and the sizzle of meat ahead of him in the dark. Then Dave appeared with a white paper bag.

"I threw in a small fry."

"Thanks."

"You don't want to talk now, do you?"

"Not today," said Lew.

When Lew finished the meal at his desk, he wrapped the remnants, went back to bed, ignored the ringing of the telephone and finished reading the Rebecca Strum book.

It didn't tell him anything he didn't know. It did tell him how he might express it. He fell asleep.

And that was Sunday.

On Monday morning, Lew sat across from Ann in her small office near the Bay. He had brought coffee and biscotti from Sarasota News & Books a block away and now she sipped and said, "So you saw the dead and walking wounded in Chicago," she said.

"I did."

"And you survive."

"I survive," he said, looking at the Cubs cap in his lap.

She dipped her biscotti in the coffee and leaned forward to take a bite and keep from dripping on her dress.

"I enjoy and am comforted by biscotti with almonds, the sight of long-necked water birds, the bright flowers, the night sky, the waves, all the clichés that always turn out to be truths once you are initiated."

"How do you get initiated?" asked Lew.

The colorful, bangled, triple-rowed stone bracelet on her hand clacked as she lifted her cup.

"You don't," she said. "You become or, if they've caught you early enough, you pretend. Did you pretend?"

"About being an Episcopalian?"

"About accepting. Think about it. Or, better yet, don't think about it. You're giving thirty-five thousand dollars to Sally for her children's education."

It was a statement, not a question.

"Yes."

"Will she take it?"

"I don't know. I'll find out tonight. I'm bringing Chinese to her and the kids for dinner."

"And you are afraid that if she accepts, she will take the money with thanks but your relationship will change too," said Ann. "No matter what you tell her she will feel that she owes you."

Ann dunked the last piece of her biscotti

and popped it into her mouth.

"She doesn't owe me. I owe her."

"But you are afraid she'll feel that way, just as you . . . didn't you say you had a backup biscotti in the bag?"

He held up the bag and she took the biscotti.

"What was I saying? Oh, yes, she'll feel that way just as you feel that way about Earl Borg. Drink your coffee. Eat your biscotti. Millions of children in Third World countries would fight for that crunchy pastry. Think of them."

"When I do, I can't eat," said Lew.

"I just upped my biscotti quota to three a week. It's almost time, Lewis."

He looked at the clock on the wall over Ann's desk. On the desk were framed photographs of Ann's children and grandchildren, all smiling, all bearing some resemblance to Ann.

"When I look in the mirror, I see my mother's face," he said.

Ann had started to rise, but sat back down.

"You look like your mother?"

"Yes, and I talk like her, laugh like her."

"And that distresses you?"

"Yes."

"We've never talked about your mother," Ann said. "Is she dead?"

"No."

"Is she in Chicago?"

"Skokie."

"Did you see her when you were in Chicago?"

"No."

Ann sat silently, hands in her lap.

"She's in a facility," he said.

"A facility? The hour is over, Lewis. Take down the wall and speak."

"She is in a mental facility," he said. "She's been a depressive all her life. Four stays in hospitals. This time she's in complete dementia. She doesn't recognize anyone, but —"

"Yes, but . . ." Ann prompted.

"She's happy for the first time in her life."

"And you're afraid you'll become like your mother?"

"Yes."

"Interesting," said Ann. "We'll talk about it next time. Now, you owe me —"

"A joke," Lew said, putting on his cap.

"No, twenty dollars," she said. "Now that you have money, the price goes up. Now that you've told me about your mother, you have a choice. Either tell me a joke or tell me something else about you that I don't know."

Lew was standing, head down in front of

her. He reached into his pocket, pulled out his wallet, handed her a twenty-dollar bill and something small and flat and neatly folded over with thin white tissue paper. She carefully unfolded the paper and looked at what was inside.

"Catherine?" she said.

"Catherine," Lew said.

"She was lovely."

"Yes," said Lew as Ann carefully re-wrapped the photograph with tissue and handed it to Lew, who put it back in the sleeve of his wallet. "She was lovely and I got her killed."

"Abstract guilt, Lewis."

"No," he said. "Real responsibility."

"Sit," she said gently.

"You've got someone . . ." Lew said, looking at the door.

"The person sitting out there can wait," said Ann. "She is too docile. That's part of her problem. If I have her wait, she may get angry, which would accomplish more than fifty minutes of talk."

Lew was sitting again, cap on his knee, looking at Ann's desk, seeing nothing.

"Why do you think you are responsible for the death of your wife?"

"The night before she died we had an argument."

"About what?" Ann prompted.

"I don't think I'm ready to talk about this," he said.

"Not ready? You drop a small bomb of guilt. You sit down. You wait for me to become gluttonous in my search for information and then you say you're not ready? You are ready."

Lew looked around the room for something to distract himself, an uneven pile of mail on the desk, a slightly crooked small print of a seascape, a beam of light through the single high window, a bookcase filled with psychology and history books.

"We had an argument about ambition," he said. "I was happy where we were, where I was. Catherine was ambitious. She was good and she was getting recognized. She wanted to consider some offers from outside Chicago."

"Political?"

"Some. I was willing but not enthusiastic. She wanted and needed enthusiasm from me. She deserved to have it, but I'm not good at lying."

"You lie to yourself like a professional," Ann said.

"There was no shouting, crying. There were no threats. Nothing was resolved when we went to bed. In the morning we didn't say a word till after we had coffee and buttered toast at the window.

"We went to work, didn't see each other much," he went on. "We had lunch together at a deli on Monroe. She told me a District Attorney in Tennessee was pressing her for an answer to his offer. Catherine was admitted to the bar in six states and working to get admitted in others. Tennessee was one of the first states after Illinois that had —"

"Lewis, are you going to start chewing your hat now?"

"No," he said. "She needed enthusiasm from me. I wasn't enthusiastic about moving to Tennessee. Chicago was . . . all I knew or wanted. She packed up her work for the day and told the secretary she shared with Michael Hawes that she was going home to work. She didn't tell me."

Ann said nothing. She looked at him, waiting. He knew what she was waiting for.

"I've been telling you I didn't know why Catherine was going home at three o'clock that afternoon. Catherine left work early that day because of the argument. She left early and was killed by a drunk driver."

"You are a wonderful hysteric," said Ann with what sounded like sincere admiration. "You have, until the last five minutes, displayed an ability over the past two years we have been talking to block out reality. It's a challenge. Maybe I'll write an article for the *Florida Journal of Psychopathology*. I would focus on your depressive hysteria. With your permission of course."

"Permission granted."

"Do you have any idea of why you have given me all these secrets, this cornucopia of bitter fruit at the very end of our time together today?"

"I just wanted to tell you. I don't want to talk about them. Not today."

"Congratulations," she said. "We've made a significant move. We've added guilt to your depression. What we need now is a long session and a reasonable supply of biscotti without hazelnuts. My confession. I really don't like hazelnuts. I've got you down for next Monday. Can you make it this Wednesday too?"

"Yes."

Lew got up and put his cap on his head.

The phone wasn't ringing when Lew got back to his office. There was no new mail under his door. He had no papers to serve for the Sarasota law firms that he regularly worked for. He needed something to keep him from climbing back in bed. He decided it was time for Joan Crawford. He had selected *A Woman's Face* and *Daisy Kenyon* from his stack of tapes.

Someone softly knocked at the door. Lew considered not answering. Another soft knock.

Lew opened the door.

The man looked tired. He needed a shave and a haircut and a clean shirt. His right hand tightly gripped the handle of a duffel bag. Under his left arm was a painting of the jungle of a city night.

Lew stepped back and Victor Lee stepped in.

ABOUT THE AUTHOR

Stuart M. Kaminsky is the author of more than fifty novels, an Edgar Award winner who has been given the coveted Grand Master Award by the Mystery Writers of America. He is the creator of the critically acclaimed Inspector Rostnikov, Toby Peters, and Abe Lieberman mystery series, and in recognition of his Lew Fonesca series, the Sarasota Convention and Vistors Bureau has officially recognized Stuart Kaminsky as "The Voice of Sarasota." He lives with his family, naturally enough, in Florida.

The employees of Thorndike Press hope you have enjoyed this Large Print book. All our Thorndike and Wheeler Large Print titles are designed for easy reading, and all our books are made to last. Other Thorndike Press Large Print books are available at your library, through selected bookstores, or directly from us.

For information about titles, please call:
(800) 223-1244

or visit our Web site at:
www.gale.com/thorndike
www.gale.com/wheeler

To share your comments, please write:
Publisher
Thorndike Press
295 Kennedy Memorial Drive
Waterville, ME 04901